MW01123963

GRINDHOUSE

WWW.CROWDEDQUARANTINE.CO.UK

First Published in the UK 2012

This edition published 2012

The Moral right of the authors has been asserted.

All characters and events in this publication are fictitious, and any resemblance to real persons, living or dead, is purely coincidental.

ISBN 978-0-9571033-8-2

© Crowded Quarantine Publications 2012

www.crowdedquarantine.co.uk

Grindhouse (plural **grindhouses**)

1. An often shabby movie theatre having continuous showings, especially of violent or pornographic films.

READ ORDER

74 (9)	100	7	111
64	167 (12)	49	208
147	22	132	240
157 (10)	36	179	
	194 (14)	83	

CONTENTS

A GATHERING OF MOURNERS

JASON RADAK

The first thing to come to Edward's mind after he read the email with the subject "bad news" was that he was going to get a 4-day weekend. He had been sitting in his cubicle on a sunny Tuesday afternoon in May when he checked his inbox and found the letter from Kaden, an old friend of his. Edward had gone to Camp Fern & Moss when he was 11, 12 and 13 years old, and Kaden had been in his cabin each of those summers. They had communicated sporadically after finding each other on the internet a few years ago, but Edward hadn't thought of Kaden in months when he saw the email in his inbox.

It said that Rob Morris, who had been in their cabin all those years ago, died Saturday night. The funeral was scheduled for Thursday in Port Jervis, NY.

*

When Edward first reconnected with Kaden through Facebook, he described how he had gone to college, got married, got a job with a major company in Manhattan, moved to Jersey City, and got divorced. He never had children. Now he lived in an apartment in a big building, which was much better suited to his lifestyle than a house.

He learned that Kaden had gone back to school recently to get a master's in Art History, got married, and actually put his degree to work by getting a job with Art Critters, an organization in Tampa devoted to bringing art into the lives of impoverished children. Kaden had asked Edward if he

7

remembered Rob, Kaden's cousin, who had come to Camp Fern and Moss with him for a few years. Rob was living in San Francisco and performing in an improv cabaret.

Although Edward had never been great friends with Rob, he responded that that was really cool. He had never cared for the way Rob was able to speak so easily to girls, or how the counselors let him hang out with them. He never contacted Rob.

*

Edward pulled into the parking lot of the funeral home at 6:30 on Thursday evening, about half an hour before the scheduled start of the evening visitation. The parking lot was an asphalt U attached at the top to the highway, with the entrance on one end and the exit on the other. He parked by the weeping-willow that grew inside the asphalt loop. The White-Jackson Funeral Home was inside a tall gray Victorian mansion at the base of the U, surrounded by a green field. About fifty yards to the right was a stone church; to the left was an old mill with a wheel slowly turning in a stream. The mill looked well-maintained, although it couldn't possibly have still produced anything. It probably housed a candle store, Edward thought, or the Port Jervis historical society.

He got his navy blazer off the hook in the backseat of his Corolla, put it on, adjusted his tie and walked up to the funeral home. There were two clusters of mourners standing on the porch. The adults in the group on the left had tattoos and face piercings. Rob's friends from San Francisco. The people on the right looked...*rustic*, Edward thought. Friends and family from that backwater town Kaden and Rob came from in New York. Edward passed through the languid mass of people and went in through the front door, into the noisy, crowded hallway. The guest-book lay on a pedestal to the right of the entrance.

8

Edward was grateful to have an activity that would occupy a minute of his time before he was forced to mix with the crowd of strangers. He saw a couple of names he recognized:

Kaden Murdock
Victoria Murdock

So, Kaden and his mother had made it. Edward had thought that maybe Kaden would be too poor to make it up to New York, what with his nonprofit job and kid to support, but Rob's funeral was too important to miss. Edward signed his name in the guest-book, slid through the gaps between chatting mourners and went into the viewing room.

Three women stood before the casket, which floated in cumulus clouds of flower arrangements. Ed found a chair set against a wall where he would have a good view of the body when there was no one standing in front of it, and sat down. He leaned forward, his elbows on his knees, and cast his eyes downward.

A couple of minutes later a woman approached him. She was middle-aged, and clutched a wad of Kleenex in her hands. Her hair was cut short. Although he had only seen her once or twice twenty years ago, and back then she had worn jeans and a t-shirt, Edward realized that this was Rob's mother. A skinny man with bad skin stood alongside her, his hand lightly touching her elbow. He had long hair pulled back in a pony tail, and a wispy beard.

"Did you know Robby?" Rob's mother asked dreamily, her eyes glistening. She was probably on Valium.

Edward stood. "Yeah, I went to camp with Rob," he said. He knew the woman as Mrs. Hagen, but was pretty sure the man with her wasn't Rob's dad. *That* guy hadn't looked like a bumpkin; he wore aviator sunglasses and black clothes when he showed up on visiting day. "We were in the same cabin for a few years."

She smiled. "Oh, Camp Fern and Moss," she recalled. "I'm Molly, do you remember me? I came on the first day of camp and made Robby's bed for him."

"I *do* remember," Edward said slowly. "A lot of parents made their kids' beds when they got there. That was the only time for the whole summer their beds were nice. But Rob always made his really neat. Once in a while I'd look at his bed with envy and try to get mine just as crisp and flat as his, but there would always be wrinkles. The corners were the hardest." Edward was pleased that the anecdote had jumped into his head.

"Robbie was so neat," his mother agreed. "It was Denny's idea to send him to summer camp." *Denny* – that was Rob's dad, the guy with the aviator glasses. "He wanted Robby to get more experiences than what he'd get in Stone Haven. It was too insular and parochial there is what he always said. It would be a sin to keep a boy with as much talent and charisma as Robby trapped in little Stone Haven. He wanted Robbie to be a jazz musician like him."

"Rob was very talented," Edward said. "He used to be the star of the camp talent show. Everyone loved his skits."

"I never wanted him to be a performer…" she said, and her shoulders started heaving, to Edward's horror. The thin man with the pony-tail put his arm around her.

"I'm Charlie," he told Edward.

"Nice to meet you," Edward said, noticing that Charlie was missing some teeth.

"Denny was god-damn happy that Rob was becoming an artist-type, following in his daddy's footsteps," the man said. "I hope he's happy now."

Edward nodded solemnly. Charlie told Molly that they should get some air. He said goodbye to Edward, and led Molly toward the exit.

10

Edward sat back down and looked around the room. He was envious of the large crowd the event had attracted.

Then the people who had been standing by the casket stepped away, and Edward could see Rob lying there. His head was tilted slightly to his right, toward the room. Edward was surprised to see that Rob's face was a little rounder than he remembered. Not that he was one to judge. Ed had been overweight since he was a kid, and now since the divorce, when there was little reason not to drink five or six beers every night, he had gotten fatter and dumpier. Rob didn't look bad at all for a 33 year old fatal-heart-attack victim.

*

Edward's contemplation of Rob's physical condition was interrupted when he heard his name spoken. He looked up to see Kaden approaching him from across the room. He was taller than Edward remembered, and still thin. They briefly exchanged solemn salutations, and Kaden asked Edward if he wanted to go out for a cigarette. "Yeah, I'll have a smoke," he said.

Standing on the porch, they talked about how neither of them had aged much, how they had managed to get to Port Jervis on such short notice, and where they were going to sleep that night. The clouds of tobacco smoke drifted slowly in the still warm air, hanging in the vast space between the funeral home and the giant willow tree. Edward was relieved that Kaden was much less morose than he expected him to be.

An attractive woman in her thirties approached Kaden. She had no tattoos, no face piercings – she must have been from the Stone Haven contingent. "Hey Becky," Kaden said, and introduced her and Edward to each other. "Becky was a good friend of Rob's from way back."

"Rob mentioned you," she said to Edward. "You went to

11

Fern and Moss." Her eyes and nose were red.

"I hadn't seen him in twenty years," Edward said just to say something.

Becky exhaled loudly. "I didn't see him too much after he left the Haven either," she said. "He came back once in a while, but it was just to visit his parents. Rob and Kaden were the ones that broke out. Most of us stayed on. Denny wanted his son to get out and experience the world."

"Molly was worried about Rob going out on his own," Kaden said, "so she paid for me to go to Fern & Moss with him. My mother couldn't afford to pay the fee, so Molly paid for me too."

"You make Fern & Moss sound like New York City," Edward said.

"It might as well have been," Becky said, "from where we were coming from."

"A lot of the kids at camp were from Brooklyn," Kaden said. "A lot of Jews."

"So, I guess Stone Haven is…xenophobic?" Edward ventured, cautiously.

"Yeah," Becky said.

"I would call it *traditional*," Kaden said.

"Your mom and Molly both went to college and married outsiders," Becky said. "That's why you and Rob were different."

"You call people who aren't from Stone Haven *outsiders*?" Edward asked.

"The families in Stone Haven have long lineages," Kaden said. "We are some *serious* hillbillies." Becky laughed a little. "Our mothers' father was a real liberal by Haven standards. He thought his daughters should experience the outside world before they settled down, so they wouldn't spend all their lives wondering what it was like out there. And maybe a little *learnin'* would be good for them and the village."

"Your grandfather didn't think that maybe they'd get married while they were out there, and bring their husbands back home," Becky said.

"That's what was fucked up," Kaden said. "Once they got married, they should have just stayed away. If they wanted to go back, they could have just brought me and Rob with them, and let our fathers stay on the outside."

"They brought a couple of trouble-making husbands right into our little village. Then they had a couple of free-thinking sons," Becky said, and they both laughed a little.

Kaden sighed and said, "That's what happens when Haveners mix up with outsiders."

*

While Becky and Kaden reminisced, Edward, his mind wandering, noticed a man sitting on a bench under the swaying branches of the weeping willow. He was drinking from a small bottle. Edward realized that it was Denny Hagen, jazz saxophonist and father to the deceased. He pointed this out to Kaden and Becky.

"He's an alkie," Kaden said. "He's getting away to have a nip. I hear his drinking took over his life after he got divorced from Molly. His sisters showed up for a few minutes at the afternoon visitation. They didn't bring their husbands or kids. Denny and my dad's families weren't made to feel real welcome in Stone Haven. Neither of us got to know our paternal relatives very well." Kaden lit another cigarette. "The Haven is old. It was founded with a purpose, something deeper than just being a bunch of inbred hillbillies rejecting modern ways. Everyone had lost sight of that, and Grandpa thought he could shake us out of our malaise, get Haveners to focus on the big picture again like they had in the old days. He hoped they would take some pride in themselves and their heritage. But he just fucked things up."

"What was the 'big picture'?" Edward asked.

There was a loud thump inside the funeral home, followed by a low, doleful wail. Becky and Kaden looked at each other. The group of hipsters on the porch fell silent, standing there awkwardly.

"Why don't you see how things are going in there?" Kaden told Becky. She went inside and closed the door behind her. "Haven funerals can get a little wild. Molly is in pretty bad shape," Kaden announced, and everyone on the porch nodded. "Let's go for a walk," he said to Edward. "It's a beautiful evening."

Edward agreed, even though he thought the night was too warm. The dusky air was humid, and there was no breeze at all. Not to mention the mosquitoes. Still, Edward was flattered that Kaden was paying so much attention to him, with all these other people around.

They walked over toward the stream that ran by the funeral home. The ground was springy. Kaden said, "You know how they always say that funerals aren't for the dead? That they're to give people a chance to say goodbye?"

"People need closure," Edward said. "You need to address your feelings about the deceased."

"Do you believe that?" Kaden asked.

"I guess," Edward said, and shrugged his shoulders. "Do you think that funerals do something for the dead?"

"No. They're for the living. But I'm not sure about the pop-psychology interpretation. It struck me today: here I am with all my family and neighbors. I haven't seen a lot of these people for a long time. It occurred to me: funerals may act as a social occasion to bring friends and family together, especially at a time when the community has suffered a terrible loss. Bonds are strengthened. Alliances are renewed. *You're* smart, what do *you* think of that theory?"

"Sounds reasonable," Ed replied. "Does seeing everyone here make you appreciate your roots more?"

"It does," Kaden replied. "Listen to those frogs. It's like we're at Moss & Fern again."

"Thanks for letting me know about Rob," Edward said. "I'm glad I found out about it. And I'm glad we finally got a chance to see each other again, in spite of the circumstances."

"When I got in touch with you I really had no idea how things were going to go here. I thought I'd reminisce a little with the Haven Hillbillies, then go back to Tampa. And I was real worried about what would happen when all the tattoo people from San Francisco showed up. But I think things are going okay in there. Better than I could have hoped."

"Are you going to move back to Stone Haven?" Edward asked.

"Yes. I realize that that's where my heart is now. I think Rob would've realized it too, if he lived."

"Then some good came out of his death," Edward said.

"Mmm," Kaden agreed. They reached the mossy bank of the stream, opposite the old mill, and stood there. "I think it's good for everyone. Over the generations, Haveners have forgotten their Burden. The Stone Haven Charter was written several thousand years ago and it's hard to stay enthusiastic about anything for that long. I think Rob's death has reminded us what we were put on Earth to do."

Edward thought Kaden must have been exaggerating when he said *thousands* of years, but didn't correct him. "What's Stone Haven's 'Burden'? To be *pious*?" he asked, mostly sincerely.

"When the Charter was drawn up, it wasn't in English of course. Translation is tricky, especially with *this* document. *Pious*. That's not how I would put it, but that is an interesting interpretation."

"I'm just saying, religion was so important back then,"

Edward said, afraid that his question was insulting. You never know with religious people.

"Very important," Kaden agreed. "I think you could say that Stone Haven's Purpose is to be *pious*. But I always thought of it as: *To strangle humanity.*"

"*To what?*" Edward said, but something in the periphery of his vision caught his eye. There was a body floating face up in the stream. "Oh my God, that's a person." The body was snagged on a branch in the water. Edward kneeled and strained to see in the fading light. "Oh fuck. It's Rob's dad…"

Edward stood and pulled his cell phone out of his pocket. "I'll call nine-one-one." But Kaden slapped the phone out his hand. It flew into the stream. Edward looked at him incredulously. "Fuck! Why did you do that?"

"Cell phones don't work here. Why don't you call from the funeral home?"

Kaden must have been unnerved from the sight of his uncle's body. "Okay, I'll go call," Edward said. "*You* pull his body out of there before it floats away," he commanded.

"Okay," Kaden said calmly. Edward turned and marched up the grassy incline to the funeral home. He had beads of perspiration on his face, and he got winded, even though he wasn't going that fast. He went up the steps, strode across the empty porch, and pushed the door inward. He walked down the empty corridor, and turned at the door to the visitation room. Then, he stopped, frozen in the doorway.

The smell of shit hit him like a blast from a furnace. Blood was splashed onto the furniture and walls. In some places, where the carpet could not soak up any more, there were puddles. Body parts were strewn about the room – limbs, organs, heads. Intestines were draped over chairs.

The crowd of mourners looked at Edward. A man stood 3 feet away, cradling a gnawed-upon arm in his arms. A woman and two toddlers knelt beside an eviscerated body, their arms

16

elbow deep in the abdominal cavity. The feasters wore bloody flannel shirts, corduroy jackets, work boots. They had no tattoos.

They were Haveners.

It was Rob's San Francisco friends who had been ripped apart, who were now crimson gelatinous splotches.

Rob was sitting in a chair against the wall.

Edward could tell Rob was looking at him even though his eyes were closed and his sockets stuffed with cotton. There was a strained, crooked grin on his face. His arms were propped on the backs of the chairs on both sides of him, and his legs were open wide giving the impression he was at ease despite the stiffness of his body. Molly sat to his left, gazing at her son, her hand on his shoulder. Becky sat on the floor between his feet, playing with his leathery penis, which hung lifelessly from his unzipped pants. The red smears on the embalmed organ were the same shade as Becky's lipstick.

"He's not really alive," Kaden's voice said from just behind Edward. Edward jumped. "We've amplified some residual energy that was left in his tissues. A tiny little fraction of him is still in there, but Rob is dead and gone. We're having one last party with him."

Edward turned to face Kaden. He stepped on something not quite solid that went *squish*. His shaking legs gave out and he fell on the carpet with a wet thud. He grimaced and started to sob and plead for his life at the same time. All that came out was incoherent squeaking.

"You're in worse shape than *Rob*," Kaden said, and the Haveners chortled and clapped. More of them had drifted into the room since Ed arrived, curious about what was going on. "This stuff is just an amusement: Juicing up the recently dead. Trying to give a corpse a hard-on. Eating a bunch of outsider freaks. This is just Haveners having a good time. We're getting warmed up. Oh, Becky," he said, distracting her from Rob's flaccid penis. "Give it up. It's not going to happen."

He extended his hand to Edward, who was now wheezing and crying. "Come on. You don't have asthma do you? Calm down. Let me help you up." Edward took Kaden's hand and felt himself hoisted up, all 240 pounds of him. His body was wracked with tremors, his clothes imprinted with blood from the carpet. "We really appreciate you coming Eddie, *don't* we Molly?"

"Oh yes," she replied, still gazing at her son. Other mourners were crowding around Edward and Kaden. Edward gave a startled yelp when a bloody hand pawed at him.

"But you gotta *go*, right? You're not like *these* guys," Kaden said, looking at the messy remains on the floor. "You don't have to go all the way back to California. You plan to be back in Jersey City tonight?"

Edward was only vaguely aware of what Kaden was saying to him. Then his nose twitched. He became aware of an odor that was so strong it pushed out the smell of blood and shit that hung heavily in the room. The new smell was formaldehyde. Edward turned his head to see Rob's face, eyes shut, only inches from his own. Rob's mouth no longer produced saliva, so someone had lubricated his mouth and vocal cords with blood. "Go...home?" he croaked, spraying flecks of blood in Edward's face.

Edward felt wet fingers in his mouth, on his face, down the front of his trousers. The Haveners were hungry, and they had run out of San Francisco performance artists.

"Come on," Kaden said to the mob, "you're making Edward nervous. We've made a mess of the place. Let's go outside." The bloody mob giggled and grunted their approval. In a conspiratorial tone Kaden said to Edward, "Let's see if I can get you out of here. They've had *enough* fun."

Kaden pulled Edward from the room and out of the clutches of the Haveners. Edward had trouble walking, but Kaden kept him from falling, and led him out of the house, toward the parking lot. The night air was hot and still, yet the drooping branches of the willow tree swayed. As they approached his car Edward felt a spark of hope in his chest.

"I want you to tell people what you saw here today," Kaden told him. "Even if you say it as a story. I want you to plant a seed in people's minds. We *thrive* on that. The more people who wonder about the Haven, the stronger we become. Can you *do* that?"

"Yeah," Edward replied.

"We'll know if you don't."

"Let's eat him," a woman said. The mob had followed them out into the lot. They were having trouble keeping themselves from pouncing on him, getting more agitated every second.

"Don't let him go yet," a man said. "He can go later, right?"

Several people shouted *Yeah!* and *Right on!*

"This is going to be tricky," Kaden said to Edward. "Please tell me you have your keys."

Edward reached into his pocket just as someone grabbed him from behind. One arm hooked over his shoulder, another under his arm. It was Becky. She pulled her body tight against his back and spoke into his ear. "Why don't you just stay a little longer? Look, Rob's coming!" Edward saw that Rob had just managed to get down the porch steps on his stiff legs, and was gamely hobbling toward the dark parking lot.

Kaden pried Becky's clawing hands off Edward. When she let go Edward went stumbling toward his car. "It's better if we let one of them go," Kaden told the mob.

Edward bumped into his car and steadied himself. Hands caressed him and grabbed at his flabby body. He reached into his pocket and felt the keys. Before he could pull them out something wrapped around his leg. It tightened and pulled it out from under him. He fell hard on the asphalt and grunted. As he gasped for breath he felt other things slithering around his

19

body, pulling him away from the car.

Toward the willow tree.

He looked to Kaden as he was dragged across the asphalt, onto the grass. "Sorry, man!" Kaden shouted.

Edward screamed as tentacles erupted from the earth and bound his arms to his torso. They were red and shiny, like engorged worms. Edward screamed in terror as he was pulled closer to the writhing tree. He felt a cold wet tendril encircle his neck. He struggled helplessly, taking quick gulps of air when he could.

Kaden and the other Haveners were just a few yards away, shouting and laughing.

The Earth opened beneath him. He was not in free-fall, but he was not on solid ground either. Dirt pelted him in his face. He continued screaming even as soil filled his mouth and throat.

*

He awoke in the morning, lying in a field of dirt, where grass had been the day before. The fresh dirt was teeming with beetles and earthworms. The branches of the weeping willow were above. A breeze rustled the leaves.

His heart rate flared as he remembered last night. He sat up with a gasp.

The grass and the asphalt of the parking lot were torn up, but the wormy roots of the tree had gone back underground. His car, and several others, still sat in their spaces. The rental cars of Rob's hipster friends, no doubt. The pick-up trucks and rusty Novas of the Haveners were gone.

Edward's eyes, ears, nose, and ass crack were full of dank soil. His skin was raw where the roots had grasped him. Wincing, he stood, and made some perfunctory motions to brush the dirt from himself. He pulled his pockets inside out to empty the dirt and slugs from them, and found his keys. On any other day he would have been horrified to find snails in his pockets. Today he didn't care.

He checked if he had everything from his jacket pockets, then left the garment on the ground. He had brought a change of clothes with him. He decided to go to the Best Western in Matamoros to clean up and spend the night. He wasn't quite ready to go home. He didn't want to bring all of this *dirt* into his apartment. He wanted to scrub it from his body before going back to his regular life.

He would return on Monday.

But today he'd shower in the hotel, turn up the air conditioner, and watch some TV. Then in the evening he'd go down to the bar, and see how his new story would go over with the hotel guests he met.

THE COLLEGE BOY CRAP-OUT

AFRIKA SNEVE

Keys rattled in a lock, followed by two young men shuffling through the doorway of apartment B-205. Yellow bars of light spilling in from the hallway beyond outlined a shadowy, narrow strip of kitchen to the young men's right. Ahead, a short entry hall yawned into a tight living room space, where late-night shadows folded themselves into amorphous grey contours. The blue digital numbers on the countertop microwave glowed 4:16 a.m.

The guy in the lead, Kyle, flipped a light switch next to the door, tossed his keys on the counter, and slid open a pair of entryway closet doors on a creaky metal track. "Here, just toss your stuff in the closet. Should be some spare hangers in there, too," he said, busily untying his Vans.

"Cool, thanks man," said the second guy, Andy. "I really appreciate your letting me crash here tonight. There's no way I'd be able to stagger all the way down to 15th and University without landing in the cop shop."

"No problem. Any buddy of Jenkins' is a buddy of mine," said Kyle (who had not, in fact, been the most eligible candidate for designated driverhood himself, but since his apartment was only a few blocks away from the party, he rationalized, he was cool to make the drive). He plunked his baseball cap down on the counter next to the keys and turned to his companion.

Andy smiled and nodded. He plopped a canvas satchel down in the closet next to his shoes, then slid the closet doors shut. "I gotta say, that party tonight was *epic*. How many kegs did the Pi guys have, like four?"

"Six."

Andy shook his head, grinning. "*Man*, can those Epsilon Pi guys throw down." He stood in the entryway, thumbs in his pockets, and watched Kyle rifle around in the fridge. He glanced at the cluster-fuck of magnets on the freezer, and zoomed in on a big one holding up a utility bill: "Beer: Helping Ugly People Get Laid Since 1862," it said.

Classic, he thought, and sneered for all the ugly people in the world who weren't him. He licked his lips, his tongue roughing over a slight smattering of acne around the corners of his mouth. He thought of the stuck-up, delusional sorority chick who had had the gall to describe him as *average* at homecoming last year, and scowled.

Average, my ass, he thought. He ran a hand through his short brown hair, oblivious of the dandruff flaking down upon his plaid button-up shirt.

Kyle's voice brought him back to earth. "Yeah they can," Kyle replied. "My frat's been known to throw some pretty killer shindigs ourselves." He pulled out a package of beef jerky from the crisper, and held it out to Andy.

"Want some?"

"Sure."

Kyle dipped his fingers into the bag of salty, shriveled goodness and handed Andy a strip. Their fingers touched briefly. They looked away.

"Andy Lawrence, right? That your name?" asked Kyle, clearing his throat.

"Right," replied Andy. "And you're Kyle Matthews?"

"Right." He popped a strip of jerky into his mouth and leaned against the counter, chewing and nodding thoughtfully. "I can't believe you've been tight with Jenkins and his crew for the whole semester, and I've never met you before tonight. Crazy."

23

"Well, I usually party on the West bank, so I guess I'm not surprised." Andy rocked back on his heels, his thumbs still jammed in his pockets. His head was aswim with the pint of Jack Daniels he had powered through during the evening's festivities. He hoped this Kyle guy had a decent couch, though he was pretty sure he'd soon be out so cold, he wouldn't know the difference between bed nor bedrock.

"So what brought you to the East bank?" asked Kyle, sucking jerky-flavor off his fingers.

"Ass."

Kyle stared at him for a moment, stupefied by his new acquaintance's bluntness, and then both men burst out laughing.

"Hey, I'm not gonna lie," said Andy, shrugging and spreading his hands in laughter. "Joe Evenson told me there was s'posed to be some fine pieces of ass at this party, a bunch of hot little Delta Gammas from our World Lit class. Needless to say, I didn't want to miss out on the action."

"And here you are. Better luck next time, dude," said Kyle, still grinning.

Andy smiled, and shrugged again. *Smug-ass.* Damn right he would score next time—with his lucky AC/DC shirt and a few dabs of Brut, he'd have every hot little coed in the pocket of his Levis in no time, no question. Shit, he might even score two— *at once!* He ran a hand through his dull brown hair, prompting a fresh fall of dandruff to flutter down onto the plaid shoulders of his button-up.

"World Lit? You an English major?" asked Kyle.

"No, art," replied Andy offhandedly.

"What's your medium?"

"Oh, you know…mixed, uh, media stuff." He drummed his fingertips on the counter. "A little of this, a little of that." Suddenly, he tottered on his feet and gripped the countertop for balance. "Dude, I'm fadin' fast. F-n bombed, man."

Kyle strode into the living room and waved for Andy to follow. Andy did, and with a few short steps found himself in the living room next to Kyle, who tugged a pull-string on a nearby lamp. Andy shielded his eyes against the ensuing 100 watts of stark florescence that flooded the room. He closed his eyes and rubbed his temples, wishing to God he had had the sense to stop after a few shots.

"Here, I'm gonna go grab you a blanket," said Kyle. "Make yourself comfortable. The couch is yours."

"Thanks, man," said Andy. "I'm about ready to pass out. Hey, didn't you say you had a roommate?"

"Yeah, he's sleeping at his girlfriend's tonight," answered Kyle distractedly. He was already on his way to the hall closet to dig out the threadbare but still-soft canary-yellow blanket that had served him so well throughout high school and his freshman year in college. Its once-smooth silk trim was now torn and ragged, and it had suffered its share of cigarette burns, but it would do for a wayward stranger about to succumb to the hinterlands of Jack Daniels-induced unconsciousness.

Secretly, Kyle hoped Andy wouldn't stain it with a rank case of way-lingering beer farts, but hey, it was nothing a little Tide couldn't fix.

In the living room, Andy settled onto the scuffed wood-paneled couch. The room was spinning, his head felt way too hot, and all he wanted to do was pass out. He looked disinterestedly around the room, taking in a couple of papasan chairs, a dilapidated entertainment center showcasing a flat-screen tv, a video game console, and a minefield of pizza boxes and empty Mt. Dew cans.

Suddenly, he felt a rumble deep within his bowels. He clutched his stomach; the pint of whiskey he had imbibed was beginning to hit him hard. *Uh-oh,* he thought. *Better hit the crapper before the crap hits me.*

"Hey Kyle?" he said, turning his head to call to Kyle over

25

his shoulder, "Can I use your bathroom?"

"Sure, straight down the hall to your left," replied the voice floating in from the hallway.

"Cool, I'll be right back."

Room spinning, bowels a-clench, Andy staggered down the hallway toward the porcelain haven with which his colon so desperately demanded communion.

*

Kyle was spreading some blankets over the couch when he heard a tremendous crash erupt behind the closed bathroom door, closely followed by a scream. He dropped the blankets and hightailed it to the bathroom.

He pounded on the door, rattling the object flimsily in its frame.

"Andy! Dude, what's going on in there? Are you OK?"

A groan floated up to him from the space under the door. "Andy!" Kyle repeated, and knocked again. "What happened? Do you need help?"

"It's open. Just come in," said Andy in a cracking, querulous voice.

Kyle opened the door. He froze in the doorway and gasped.

There Andy lay in a knobby-limbed pile on the floor next to the toilet. He had a nasty-looking cut on his forehead that seemed to plead for stitches. The towel rack was lying, dismembered from the wall, on the floor next to him. The toilet seat had been jerked off one of its hinges. Worst of all, there Andy lay with his pants and underwear clumped around his ankles, lying in a seeping pool of what could only be—judging by the color and the sulphurous odor—gallons upon gallons of diarrhea.

"What the *fuck*?" exclaimed Kyle. He considered himself a pretty laid-back guy, but when some stranger comes in, breaks

26

your stuff, and craps all over your bathroom, how the hell are you *supposed* to react? What the hell was this jackass going to do next, beat off into one of his tube socks as a way of showing his thanks for the crash pad?!!

Kyle's jaw-dropped, wide-eyed gaze flashed over the bathroom: not only was there shit all over the floor, there were shitty fingerprints on the toilet's porcelain base, and sprays of it all over the wall. It was like someone had stuffed an armload of turds in a blender and finished them off with a pipe bomb. He tried not to look at the other guy's junk, but couldn't help noticing the brown liquefaction smeared on the guy's skinny white thighs like a two-year-old's first fingerpainting endeavor.

Kyle shook his head violently, his frantic hands raking through his formerly neat blond hair.

"Seriously, what the *fuck*???"

Andy was lying on the floor on his back with his legs spread apart and his ankles shackled together by his pants, forming a spindly 'v'. He had an utterly dazed look on face. With revulsion, Kyle noticed that the back of his head was resting against the plunger. It was pathetic. A part of him felt truly bad for the guy, but another part of him, an irrational, vicious part that he was ashamed of, thought, "*You are disgusting.*"

Andy groaned. "I--I had an accident," he said in a small voice. "I think I drank too much."

"You *think*?" Kyle closed his eyes and sighed, running an exasperated hand through his hair. He tried to focus on breathing and speaking out of his mouth, as the thick brown stench was about to make him vomit. "Look. Can you take care of this?"

Andy looked up at him helplessly. "I don't think so. I think I hurt myself. Can you...help me?"

Kyle looked angrily down at the guy on his bathroom floor. The dude reminded him of a grotesque, oversized baby on a changing table. *Look at that guy,* pathetic, *lying there amongst the dust bunnies and pubes.*

Slowly, disgust gave way to pity, and Kyle knew he was going to help--damn his parents and their solid North Dakota values, always telling him to do the right thing!

He sighed.

"Uh, sure, I guess so. Just let me get some towels." He went to the linen closet and returned with a handful of towels.

"You owe me some new towels, man."

"No problem. Just help me get out of this mess."

Kyle nodded and took a step toward Andy. He had never been in this particular situation before (thank God!), so he wasn't quite sure how to handle it. He flipped on the bathroom fan, set the towels down on the sink, and then stripped off his t-shirt, followed by the gray long-sleeved tee underneath. He didn't mind losing some old towels, but no *way* was he going to foul up his new clothes.

He doffed his jeans and tossed them onto his shirts in the hallway. "I'm trying not to get any of your crap on my clothes," he explained. Andy "yeah sure-ed" him, and then Kyle approached in nothing but red lip-print boxers and socks, his lithe athlete's body taut with anxiety over the ensuing task.

Kyle gathered the towels and spread them over the floor. He put his hands on his hips and surveyed the damage: he would need a *lot* of disinfectant, and he could fix the toilet seat and towel rack tomorrow, but first, he needed to tend to his guest.

"Alright, dude," he said, sighing. "Let's get you cleaned up."

Andy gave him a heartbreaking smile from his bow-legged sprawl amidst the pool of poo. "Great. Thanks Kyle," he said, his eyes shining with gratitude.

"Don't mention it." Kyle knelt down and yanked Andy's pants and underwear off, then slid Andy's button-up over his head and tossed it in a corner. Andy held his arms up passively, almost sweetly, while Kyle did it.

Kyle hefted Andy up by the armpits and steadied him into a

standing position. "Into the tub. Ready?" Andy was. "Let's go!"

With that, Kyle hoisted Andy over the lip of the tub and into the basin. Andy settled onto his back. He took a deep breath and looked up at the ceiling, which was still spinning. His pale, naked body glistened like a skinned chicken breast on its way to the oven. Shit streaks criss-crossed his torso and caked his ass and thighs. A pebble of hardening doop hovered like a black booger on his upper lip.

The smell was horrendous.

Kyle gagged. He didn't think he would ever be able to eat his mother's famous triple-chocolate mousse again.

Andy's dolorous voice broke into his ruminations. "I'm sorry, Kyle. I didn't mean to be any trouble."

He gave Kyle another of his disarming, almost heartbreaking smiles, then drew his knees up to his chin and wrapped his arms tightly around them.

"Wipe me," he said. What would have been a command came across as sweetly imploring in his soft, dulcet tone.

Kyle responded. On his knees beside the bathtub, he turned the water on, withdrew the shower head on its long silver snake, and warmed the water. He looked down at Andy, who was smiling innocently up at him with his knees drawn up to his chest. His nutsack, surprisingly large and ruddy, draped over his butthole like an old leather pouch that had wizened upon a rock in the Mojave through countless desert suns. His penis, small compared to the bulbous complex upon which it was affixed, slouched over his balzac like a boneless, defeated pinkie that would never again stand proud in the two-fingered metal salute.

"Wipe me," he repeated, and uttered a lilting laugh. His sphincter dilated and contracted for emphasis. Kyle thought he heard a subtle hiss of air, and blushed.

"Ah—uh—OK." Kyle directed the shower head at Andy's

bony shanks; the low-pressured jet of water peeled the sticky brownness away in wave after warm, cleansing wave.

Kyle caught Andy's eye as he washed, and noticed that Andy was staring raptly into his face, *gazing*, as if Kyle were his savior, and there was no one else in the world but the two of them in that tiny apartment bathroom. Kyle forgot all about the showerhead pumping away in his hand; he felt himself swirling down Andy's dilated pupils the way the yellow-brown water was swirling down the bathtub drain.

He needs me, Kyle thought. A wave of tenderness he had never before felt in his life washed over him. With his free hand, he reached down and caressed Andy's cheek.

Andy's smile grew ever wider, ever sweeter. His penis began to stir, and his three inches hardened into a turret of five.

"Break me," he said. There was no dulcet imploring in this phrase, only a breathy, no-bullshit command.

Kyle did not need to be told twice. He whipped his lip-print boxers off and plunged into the bathtub in nothing but socks and a boner. He had never been this horny or this hard in his entire life.

Strangely enough (circumstances considered), this would be his first homosexual experience. Never in his twenty-two years had he expressed any serious homophobia ("as long as they don't hit on me, I could care less,") and never once did he question his sexuality. He had a stack of Playboys under the bathroom sink, a steady girlfriend in high school, and a few casual encounters afterward—but there was no accounting for the way he felt now. He wanted that ass, wanted it as badly as he knew Andy needed him right now, and he was going to ride the endorphin superhighway all the way to Orgasmo.

He grabbed Andy's shoulders and yanked him up. "Hands on the toilet," he ordered.

"Yessssssir," purred Andy. He splayed his hairy legs to give Kyle a wider berth of entry.

30

Both men were now covered in diarrheal bathwater. It dribbled in runny, almost translucent yellowish sheets down their bodies, clotting darkly on dry patches of skin. Kyle braced his strong athlete's legs, grabbed a palmful of chunky gastrointestinal leavings, and rubbed it all over Andy's palpitating rectum. Andy moaned.

With one powerful thrust, Kyle jammed his cock into the wet pink sun of Andy's private anal universe. He wanted *in*to that sweet-hole, *in*to that salmon vortex where he could lose his mind in the euphoric nether regions of Andy's slippery-hot poop-tube.

Kyle's glutes clenched and released, clenched and released with each hip-shattering thrust. This was the most primal sex either had ever had; they were as one, a complex set of sweating human machinery toiling like clockwork toward a common mechanistic goal.

"Dick me! DICK MEEEEEE!!!!!!!!" screamed Andy in a guttural yowl...

...and dick him Kyle did. He pumped Andy's well with all of his might and fury, gnashing his teeth and tossing his head and shoulders from side to side like a wild animal. He bit and clawed at Andy's zit-spackled back, spitting on the shower walls and grunting like a lunatic. In a fit of ecstasy, he balled his fists up and smacked them down with a hollow rain of *thumps!* on Andy's back.

As the two men balled, they gibbered in a carnal language known only to those particular men at that particular moment:

"Guh!"

"Yes, yes, yes...AYUH!"

"SaKOW!"

"Uh...uh...Gagagaguuuhhh!"

Kyle's deep mid-paced pumps began to jackrabbit, faster and faster, into a frantic frenzy of ecstasy. Tendons corded out on his neck as he sweated and moaned his way to the ultimate moment of release. As he came, he threw back his head and ripped a bellowing yell off the tiled bathroom walls.

Sparkling chandeliers of multicolored fireworks exploded in the pleasure centers in his nerves, mushrooming up into space before bursting into a million dazzling fragments. His dick was a firehose spewing torrents of white molten lava. He was so overcome by the spectacular intensity of release, he did not notice Andy reaching over the bathtub to pull something out of his crumpled jeans.

After Kyle felt like he had excreted every last drop of moisture in his body, he opened his eyes and became conscious of the shower head lying forgotten and spewing away in the bathtub, and of the repulsive mess—now fully dried—that had been sprayed all over the bathroom. The overhead fan whirring away suddenly seemed very loud.

"Well." He became heatedly conscious of his hands on Andy's zitty shanks, and yanked them up as if he had touched a red-hot stove burner. Andy craned his neck around from where he knelt on his hands and knees, red-faced and grinning like a fool. The guys had been rinsed mostly clean, except for the clumps of hardened diarrhea on their torsos where the water had not reached.

"Well, I s'pose we should, ah, get out and clean this up," said Kyle. He could not meet Andy's eyes. He cleared his throat. "What do you say—"

Suddenly, he noticed that his member was still lodged in Andy's ass—more like *locked* inside, from the feel of it. He backed his butt up in an attempt to dislodge it.

It held.

"What the…can you, um, unclench or something?" he asked. "I think I'm stuck."

Andy winked. "I thought you liked me!" he leered in a high-pitched, mocking voice. "You're not trying to *back out* on me, are you?"

Kyle bucked a little harder, trying to free his schmekel of the wrinkled ring of muscle from which he had just minutes earlier derived so much pleasure. When his attempts to yank his penis out failed as he tried first his left hand, then his right, he began to panic, bucking wildly and beating on Andy's ass and back. His shouts bounced like basketballs over the reflective surfaces of the bathroom.

Andy just watched him, bearing his lover's blows with a sweaty, beet-red grin, his laughter intermingling with Kyle's expletives. His evilly grinning visage would have been right at home with any phallic villain's on any Lifetime movie-of-the-week.

To Kyle, Andy's unrelenting sphincter felt like a six-foot python choking the life out of his ramrod. No matter how hard he pummeled or how hard he jerked, the ridiculous asshole held tight. The harder Kyle fought, the tighter the sphincter squeezed until it felt like his cock might just rip off—

...and that is exactly…

What...

It.

Did.

Right before Kyle's eyes, the base of his penis separated, ever so slowly, every so agonizingly, from the smooth, tight pelvis that had heretofore served as a rock-solid base. With bulging eyes, he watched in horrified disbelief as Andy's asshole squeezed his cock clean off. The insane pressure increased until, shred by shred, nothing remained of his manhood but a gristly stump spewing freshets of jewel-red blood. The dismemberment occurred in a matter of seconds.

Kyle's eyes darted frantically back and forth between the ragged stump and the severed dick that dangled out of Andy's asshole like a dead rat in the jaws of a dog. Kyle, his coffee-milk tan now parchment white, unleashed a series of screams in a register that would have made opera great Yma Sumac proud.

*

After Andy had showered and dressed, he made his way to the kitchen and helped himself to some juice and a package of Kyle's strawberry pop tarts.

"Breakfast the morning after," he spoke into the silent kitchen. "Don't mind if I do." He strode over to the entryway closet to put his shoes on. He creaked the closet door open and stood over his canvas satchel.

Smiling slyly, he reached into his pocket and produced a cell phone.

He flipped it open and clicked his way through the album. There, onscreen, popped a close-up of Kyle in a crescendo of ecstasy: eyes closed, sweaty hair awry in short, crazy blond stalks, perspiration a-gleam on his face, lips drawn back in a pleasure-pain grimace, mouth wide open, his tongue poking crazily out the side—this was Kyle in the moment before he realized his cock was about to assume a completely separate existence from his body.

Andy scrolled to another picture, this one of Kyle lying dead and dickless on the bathroom floor. *Ah, the duality of pleasure and pain, light and dark.* To the enlightened mind, extremes were merely gradations on the very same spectrum, and Andy was excited to document this in a stunning work of art that would gain him a standing among history's greatest.

"These'll make some gorgeous prints," he muttered. He tilted his head to the side and looked tenderly at the image. "Beautiful."

He snapped the phone shut and slid it back into his pocket, then dipped into his satchel and pulled out a small corkboard photo collage plastered with a myriad of intimate, up-close face shots of men like Andy enjoying their last orgasmic moments.

34

A collage of cumfaces—beautiful.

Andy flushed warmly at his own brilliance. He tucked the collage carefully back into the satchel and proceeded to lace his shoes up for the ten-block trek home. When he was finished, he turned to face the direction Kyle's bloodless, penis-deficient corpse lay upon the shit-soaked bathroom floor.

"Pop quiz, Kyle! What's my medium?"

He threw his head back and laughed, wishing he could be there to see the roommate's face when the poor bastard got home. This little adventure would undoubtedly blow his cover —fingerprints everywhere, pubes, and hair--but so what? People were bound to discover the bodies eventually (as there were many), and few men were a match for modern forensics. Besides, he thought a change of scenery would revitalize him. He could see himself carrying on his work in a prison environment. Yes, plenty of fascinating subjects there and, best of all, they wouldn't be able to run very far.

"Later, Homes," Andy called into the silent bathroom, and waved.

With that, he peeked through the peephole to make sure the hallway was clear, and marched out into the seeping dawn.

INSANITY

REBECCA BESSER

Brian peeked around the doorjamb and watched his mother finish getting dressed in her uniform for work. He knew she would be leaving in a few minutes and they would again have a babysitter...something he hated.

His ten-year-old brother – Roy – on the other hand, loved to have babysitters.

"Brian," his mother said, spotting him in the doorway. "What's wrong, sweetie? Do you need something?"

He shook his head no and stepped into her bedroom.

She frowned, sat on the edge of her bed, and beckoned for him to come closer.

He tentatively took a couple steps across the hardwood floor toward her, stopping when he was standing directly in front of her.

"Tell me what you're thinking," she said gently, wrapping him in her arms and pulling him close.

He sighed and let his body relax against hers.

"I don't want you to go..." he whispered, and teared up. "I don't want to have a babysitter again."

Her body stiffened and she nodded.

"It won't be like last time – I promise," she assured him, rubbing his back.

"How do you know?" he asked, pulling back to look at her face as tears spilled from his eyes to run down his cheeks.

She sighed and brushed them off his round cheeks with her thumbs.

"Remember what we talked about?" she asked, rubbing her nose against his. "Things are...different now, and it shouldn't happen again."

He smiled slightly at the affection, but frowned again when she said 'shouldn't'.

"But what if it does?" he asked, his voice quivering.

"Let's pray it doesn't," she said, glancing at the clock on her nights stand. "I have to go to work soon and need to finish getting ready." She kissed his forehead as she stood and headed out of the bedroom.

Brian stayed where he was for a few moments, trying to get his fear under control. He knew there was nothing he could do about the situation – everything had been messed up since his father had died. The babysitter would come, Mom would go to work, and the evening would progress; it was that progression that scared him.

"What are you doing?" Roy asked as he passed their mother's room, heading down the hall. "Why are you crying?"

Brian quickly wiped the last of the tears from his face and shrugged.

"I don't want Mom to go..." he whimpered. "I don't want to have a babysitter."

Roy stepped into the room and looked intently at his little brother.

"Don't worry," he said, and smirked. "I'll look after you. I always do, don't I?"

Brian nodded.

"Then stop being such a baby," Roy said, and laughed.

The doorbell rang.

"Babysitter's here!" Roy said, grinned, spun around, and charged out of the room to run down the hall.

Brian followed at a more sedate pace.

When he arrived in the living room, he saw the old woman who lived in the apartment down the hall talking to his mother.

She looked sweet and nice, but he knew Roy would find something about her that he didn't like. He had the urge to scream, to release his fears in a loud outburst, but he didn't...he couldn't. If he did, his family would be torn apart; he'd already lost his father, and he wouldn't risk losing his mom or brother.

He stood in the corner, just watching everything. His mother was smiling and telling the old woman what she would need to know – emergency contact information – and Roy was sitting in the recliner across from him, flipping through a comic book like he didn't have a care in the world.

"Okay," Mom said loudly, looking at her sons. "I think that's everything. I'm off! Come give me hugs."

Roy tossed his comic book aside and threw himself into his mother's outstretched arms; she hugged him close and kissed the top of his head, smiling.

Brian walked over and filled her arms again when she let go of Roy.

"It'll be okay," she whispered as she pulled him close. "I love you."

"I love you, too," he muttered as he was released.

She smiled down at him for a moment before turning away, gathering her things, and heading out the door.

"We're going to have a good time," the old woman said. "You can call me Mrs. Granger – your names are Roy and Brian, right?"

"Yes!" Roy said excitedly.

Brian nodded and eyed his brother; things seemed to be going good so far.

"Have you had supper yet?" Mrs. Granger asked.

"No," Roy said.

Brian shook his head.

"I'll make you something then," Mrs. Granger said, heading toward the small kitchen, just off to the right of the living room.

She passed through the archway and started to look through the cabinets to see what they had, so she could make them something to eat.

Roy plopped back down in the recliner, smiled at Brian, and picked up his comic book again.

Brian breathed a sigh of relief, expelling the breath he hadn't known he was holding. He wanted to go to his room, shut and lock his door, and go to sleep so he wouldn't know about anything that went one throughout the evening, but at the same time he was scared to do it. He didn't want to not know if something got out of hand...or if there was a fire. There had been a fire once, and knowing about it had saved his life...and Roy's.

"Is there anything you won't eat?" Mrs. Granger hollered from the kitchen.

Roy's hands tightened on the comic book for a moment, and then returned to normal.

"No!" he yelled. "We'll eat anything that's out there!"

Brian watched his brother for a couple moments and then walked over to the couch. He sat down, picked the remote up from off the coffee table, and used it to turned on the TV.

He glanced at Roy, who was still looking at his comic book.

Brian sighed, shook his head, and relaxed back into the couch cushions as he flipped through the channels to see if anything was on that he would like to watch. He settled on something and the next half hour went by really smooth with Roy reading his comic book and Mrs. Granger cooking. But when the food was ready, things started to change.

Signs of the change could be seen in Roy every time Mrs. Granger told him to do something outside of their normal routine. She told them to wash their hands and face, and even inspected them before they were allowed to sit at the table to eat. Then she made them say grace, and hounded them about eating all the peas she'd made to accompany the macaroni and cheese and hot dogs.

Brian became more tense and nervous as the meal went on; it got to the point where he was shaking and spilled a spoonful of peas all over the table and floor.

"You little..." Mrs. Granger said, her face growing red as she tried to hold in her words and anger. "You just did that so you wouldn't have to eat them!"

"No, I didn't!" Brian cried, trying to clean the mess up quickly. "It was an accident."

Without saying another word, the old woman pushed herself up from her chair, stomped over to the cabinets by the sink, opened one of them, and withdrew a new can of peas.

"You're going to eat this whole can of peas by yourself," she declared, slamming it down on the counter. "You'll sit at the table all night if you don't. That will teach you to waste perfectly good food."

Brian piled the peas on his paper napkin and stared down at his plate. He could feel a knot building in his throat and tears stinging his eyes – he swallowed hard and blinked rapidly, trying to fight back his emotional reaction to the unfairness of this woman who didn't know him.

"No, he won't," Roy said calmly, still eating. "It was an accident and he doesn't have to eat anymore peas than what he already has."

Mrs. Granger paused and turned to face the table, leaving the can of vegetables sitting beside the electric can opener.

"What did you say to me, young man?" she snapped.

"I said he's not going to eat them," Roy said, looking the old woman in the eyes. "He's not sitting here all night stuffing those green pieces of shit into his face because you're a bitch."

Mrs. Granger gasped and stared at Roy in shock – he was still eating calmly, looking straight at her.

"How dare you speak that way to me – your elder!" she sputtered, her face turning so red that it was almost purple.

"I'm going to wash your mouth out with soap, and send you to bed."

"Please don't," Brian whispered, the tears he'd been trying to fight flowing freely now. No one knew who he was talking to for sure, and both the other people in the room ignored him, too focused on the struggle of wills between them.

Roy snickered and pushed his plate away with food still on it.

"I'd like to see you try, you old hag," he taunted, standing and placing his hands flat on the table.

For a moment there was silence between the two as they stared at each other, waiting to see what their opponent would do. The only sound that invaded the silence were the pathetic sobs of Brian, who was sitting completely still, staring at his plate, crying and shaking. He knew what was coming, even though Mrs. Granger didn't; she didn't have a chance.

Suddenly Roy stood up straight, turned, and walked out of the room.

Mrs. Granger was soon after him, following him down the hall yelling at him, calling him a 'little bastard'.

Brian stood up and followed too, racing after the old woman. He caught up to her just as Roy turned the corner into his bedroom – she was about half way down the hall. He gripped the sleeve of her sweater and tugged hard.

"Please don't!" he cried out loudly. "Please leave! You have to leave!"

She shook off his hand with a disgusted grunt and continued down the hall. Just as she reached the end, Roy re-emerged...holding a small hatchet in one hand.

He raised it above his head and brought it swiftly down on the old woman's right shoulder while she was still ranting – she'd been so focused on her anger, she hadn't noticed his weapon.

"No!" Brian called out, just as the sharp metal blade sliced

41

through the old woman's clothes and soft flesh to stop suddenly with a dull *thump* as it met bone.

Roy, ignoring Brian, yanked it back out, slinging blood down the hallway, and raised it again.

Mrs. Granger fell to the floor, screaming and clutching her arm. Blood seeped from the wound to soak her sweater and the light blue blouse she wore underneath.

"Shut up, bitch!" Roy said, complete calm; he spun the hatchet in his hand in midair as he swung it down at her face, striking her jaw with the blunt end.

Brian flinched and fell to his knees when he heard the *crack* of the bone.

Mrs. Granger's cries and screamed were reduced to agonized whimpers; her bottom jaw was now broken, and hung at a sickening, slack angle from the top one.

"That's better," Roy said, raising the hatchet again and swinging the sharp side back down toward the shoulder injury he'd just inflicted.

This time when the metal connected with the bone it broke through.

Mrs. Granger's entire body jerked as her shoulder was severed and shattered all at once.

Roy kept hacking at the same spot, flinging muscle and skin tissues – along with blood – down the hall. The walls closest to the carnage were running with black chunks and thick, red blood; it pooled on the floor beneath the elderly victim.

Brian watched his brother in horror as he severed Mrs. Granger's arm, picked it up, and started beating her with the bloody end.

"Don't you ever," Roy screamed while he pummeled the woman with her own arm, "ever, be mean to my little brother!"

Once he'd had enough of the flailing, severed limb, he threw it aside and started on the other arm with the hatchet.

Roy's face and clothes were now coated in the red blood of

his victim, but he didn't seem to notice. He also didn't seem to notice the continued noise and cries from the old woman on the floor.

"Just pass out..." Brian muttered, sniffling; he wanted to look away but he couldn't. It was like all the other times – he was too scared of not knowing what was happening, and so he stayed where he was and witnessed the violence being unleashed from his brother's soul.

Once Roy had the other arm – severed the same way as the first – he beat her with it again, screaming about how she should have kept her 'bitch mouth shut' or ate the damn peas herself.

Brian couldn't help but feel this was all his fault – if he'd just been more careful at dinner this wouldn't be happening. In the depth of his heart he knew his guilt was misplaced. Roy had done the same thing numerous times for various reasons; it wasn't like this was a stand out occurrence. The psychologist who'd seen Roy had assured them it wouldn't happen again however – he'd put Roy on medication to prevent it. The pills apparently weren't working, because here he was, repeating the behavior the medication was supposed to help control.

Roy, after tossing the second arm aside, took the blunt side of the hatchet to Mrs. Granger's kneecaps; her body jerked violently with each blow and she groaned loudly even with her jaw broken.

Brian couldn't figure out why she was still conscious. The amount of blood she was losing was enough to send her into shock or kill her. The walls of the hall were drenched with blood splatter, and the puddle on the floor beneath the old woman was almost an inch deep and spreading further and further out by the second.

Once Roy had shattered both of Mrs. Granger's kneecaps, he started hacking at her knees with the blade.

"Get over here and help me," he huffed, glancing at Brian

when he had the first of the legs almost cut through.

Brian shook his head, took a step back, and whimpered.

"Don't be a baby!" Roy snapped, standing up straight and glaring at his seven-year-old brother; the blood on his features and his angry, crazed eyes made him look horrifying.

Brian whimpered again. He didn't want to assist his brother – he'd never asked him to do so before – but he didn't want to piss him off more. The possibility that Roy might turn on him scared him more than what was happening now. That fear prompted him to walk slowly forward.

Roy smirked and bent back over to grip the limp leg he's almost severed.

"Grab on," he said when his little brother reached his side, "and we'll pull it off together."

With shaking hands, Brian did as he was told; they counted to three and yanked as hard as they could.

Brian's shoes slid through the pool of blood and he fell sprawling when the leg broke loose with a loud *snap*. He landed flat on his back in the deepest part of the blood puddle, sending a splash of dark, thick liquid shooting out to coat ever more of the surrounding wall space.

Roy bent over double, roaring with laughter.

"You...should..." he said between gasps and laughter, "...see...your face!"

Brian scowled and tried to get up, only managing to flip over and fall face first in the bloody muck. When he pushed his hands down against the floor he felt squishy tissue fragments as well as the cooling, congealing blood against his small hands.

"It's not funny!" he cried, slipping and sliding his way to his feet.

"Ah," Roy said, giving him a brotherly punch on the shoulder, "you'll be all right – it'll wash off!"

Brian nodded and wiped a tear away that was running down his face, but only succeeded in smearing more blood – which

44

was all over his hands – on his cheek and nose.

Roy picked up his hatchet and went to work on the other leg.

Brian noticed that Mrs. Granger's moans and cries of pain were lessening and becoming weaker. He was glad of this; it meant she would be dead soon and Roy would stop.

By the time the boys had yanked off the other leg, Mrs. Granger was dead.

"What are we going to do with the body?" Brian asked, almost scared to learn Roy's answer.

"We could set the place on fire..." Roy said, and laughed.

Brian didn't laugh. Roy had done that before and more people had died as a result.

"Please don't," he whispered.

Roy sighed. "Okay. How about the dumpster out back?"

"Do you think we can get her there without anyone noticing?" Brian asked, skeptical.

"Does it really matter?" Roy asked, rolling his eyes. "We'll just move again and no one will ever know it was us!"

Brian nodded his head yes. He didn't want to get caught outside with a dead body. It was bad enough they had to relocate every time Roy had one of his outbursts – they didn't also need to be hauled into juvenile court. He knew he would probably get off easy, but Roy would be sent to a mental hospital to get help. The end result of the scenarios was the break up of their family and none of them wanted that, so they kept moving and kept hoping it wouldn't happen again.

"Maybe we should call Mom," Brian said, smiling. "She'll know what to do!" He was really scared and wanted the reassurance of their mother – he only truly felt safe when she was around.

"That's a good idea," Roy said, grinning.

Brian nodded, momentarily unsure because of how easily Roy had agreed. He'd expected Roy to tell him to stop being a baby again, and that they could handle it. He hadn't expected for his older brother to be so agreeable about having their mother help pick up the pieces.

"I'll call her," Roy said, as he darted down the hall still holding the hatchet in one hand. He slid as he made the quick turn into the living room, since blood coated the bottoms of his house slippers, and giggled.

Moments later, Brian heard the sound of Roy's voice as he spoke to their mother on the phone – he sounded excited and happy. Treading carefully, he made his way down the hall and peered around the corner, just as Roy was hanging up the phone.

"What did she say?" he asked tentatively.

"Not much," Roy said, and shrugged, "other than she'll be coming home as soon as she can."

Brian nodded. "What are we supposed to do until she gets here?"

Roy looked around.

"I guess we can watch TV."

Brian stepped out into the living room and stood thinking for a moment. He thought it was strange that Roy was still carrying the hatchet around, and that he'd been so happy on the phone; it seemed like he didn't have a care in the world even though he'd just murdered someone...again. He also couldn't believe his brother wanted to sit down calmly – still holding the murder weapon – and watch TV. Although this had all happened before, the little things that were different were really standing out to him. He knew something wasn't right.

"Have a seat," Roy said, motioning to the couch with the blood dripping hatchet.

Brian did as he was told, moving slowly.

Roy plopped down next to him and picked up the remote from where Brian had put it before dinner. He turned on the TV and started going through the channels. Once he found something he liked he left it there.

They sat and watched the show for a while, and when nothing else exciting or strange happened Brian began to relax – he found himself laughing at the puns from the characters, and felt his body melt slowly into the couch cushions. Eventually, he fell asleep.

*

Brian awoke with a start when he heard a woman scream. He sat straight up on the couch, blinked rapidly, and looked around.

Roy stood close to the front door – that stood wide open – with the hatchet raised above his head. Before Brian could utter a word, he swung it down and sank it into their mother's chest with a wet *thud*.

"No!" Brian screamed, standing and throwing the entire weight of his little body against his brother.

Roy spun as Brian collided with him and slammed into the wall.

Brian, realizing what he'd done, became terrified of the possible repercussions. He jumped back as soon as he regained his balance and stared at his brother's back with wide eyes full of fear.

Roy didn't turn around immediately, but took a single step back with his head down. After a few gasping breaths he turned to face his little brother – the hatchet blade was buried in his chest.

Brian's eyes grew ever wider with shock as he realized what had happened.

Roy took two slow, difficult steps toward Brian, reached out with his hand as if to grab him, and then gasped his final breath before collapsing on the floor.

Brian, still in shock from all of the events of the night, stood in the middle of the living room with his mind reeling. He didn't know what to do. There were three dead bodies in his home. He wondered if he should call the police, an ambulance? Run away? He didn't know.

Lost, and seeking what little comfort he could from his world, he knelt down by his mother's side and discovered she was still breathing.

"Mom!" he screamed, and shook her – she didn't regain consciousness.

Knowing there was some hope, and he might be able to save her, he turned and ran to the phone. He called 9-1-1 and told them to hurry. They kept asking him to explain the situation, but he couldn't – his brain kept freezing up when he thought about all that had happened. He carried the handset with him and sat on the floor by his mother's side while he waited for help to arrive, holding her hand in his.

Help didn't arrive in time. Five minutes after he made the call, his mother took her last labored breath and left him alone in the world. Tears streamed down Brian's face as he sat on the floor staring at the woman who'd always taken care of him and loved him. His young heart was shattering with anguish.

When the authorities arrived – just minutes after his mother had died – they started asking questions. Brian knew he had to tell them. He had to tell them the truth about the past and how it had lead to this. He knew he had to tell them about the murders his brother had committed, and how his mother had always covered it up to keep them together. That didn't matter now. What was left of his family had been torn apart by insanity.

CHEAP FARM LABOR

DUSTIN WALKER

The Plymouth rumbled into the dirt parking lot of Alice's Place, kicking up rolling clouds of dust in its wake.
Jack and Sam shuffled past the cracked glass door and slumped into an orange corner-booth. Bacon popped and sizzled, the rich scent of coffee filled the diner. Sam waved the waitress over.

"We can't stay too long," said Jack, finally meeting his friend's red-veined eyes.

"We can't just drive forever either. It's been about nine hours now; he won't find us."

The plump waitress brought over two cups of coffee and some cream, grinning awkwardly as she approached the table. She looked about 20 years old, around the same age as her new customers.

"You guys look wiped, so I brought you coffees," she said, blushing as she lowered the cups. "I mean, if it's OK. I can get you something else if you want."

"No, that's fine," said Jack. "And we'll get some bacon and eggs too."

She smiled and disappeared around the corner.

"So no regrets, right?" Sam stared dopey-eyed over the rim of his coffee mug.

"Yeah, no regrets."

But the truth was Jack regretted a lot. He didn't regret swiping four kilos of cocaine from their ex-dealer, Curtis, as the guy lay passed out on top of a hooker. He didn't regret teaming up with his buddy Sam to pull off the heist. No, Jack regretted having to act out of desperation in the first place. He had managed only a couple months of sobriety before dropping out of college, blowing his student loan and falling back on old habits. Habits that led to dumb mistakes. Jack would have never swiped the coke if he had known that Curtis knew he was from Ontario. Sam had filled him in on that detail just an hour ago.

"You're not still pissed at me are you? I honestly didn't think it mattered that I told him. Ontario's a big motherfucking province."

Not big *enough*. Jack pictured Curtis frantically calling every gang member and thug he could think of in the area. Heading back to Ontario didn't seem so smart. They needed a Plan B.

The front-door chimed as a handful of men in blue jeans and John Deere caps filed into the diner. They each shot Sam and Jack a curious look before settling into a booth.

"Not as many folks drop by during harvest season," said the waitress, returning with the food. "Too busy to socialize here. Too much work to do."

And perhaps enough work to go around.

"So what's your name?" Jack offered a sly grin.

"Mary. Who wants to know?" She smiled back, twirling the strings of her yellow-stained apron.

"I'm Jack and this is Sam."

"Well, hello Jack and Sam. What brings you guys to Cheselton?"

"Job-hunting, actually. Know anyone hiring?"

Mary rubbed her chin. Her big green eyes darted toward the table of farmers. They sat hunched over their coffee mugs and scrambled eggs, mumbling to each other. One man kept glancing over his shoulder at the two outsiders.

"Not a lot available actually. Not *here,* anyway."

"We're not picky," Jack said.

"Well, gimme a second." She went over to the counter at the front of the restaurant and picked up the phone.

"What are you doing?" Sam asked. "We're going to Ontario, not to shovel shit in some farmer's barn."

"Curtis will find us in Ontario. This is *perfect*. Just for a while, until things die down."

Mary returned. "My dad won't be back until tomorrow. He might have something for you then, though."

"Oh, OK. I guess we could hold tight." Jack's smile slipped away.

"If you guys wanted to wait until about three we could hang out, maybe. And if you don't mind camping, there's a good spot on our property."

"It's a date," Jack said.

*

They parked the Plymouth behind Alice's Place and slept away most of the morning. At noon, they each snorted a pick-me-up line of cocaine and went for a walk down what passed for Main Street.

Sam took some convincing that a seasonal gig as a ranch-hand was the smartest, and safest, route. But he came around.

"A fucking *farmer*. Christ. This wasn't part of the plan," he said, as the pair strolled along the dusty, traffic-scarce road with the August sun beating down.

The highway didn't run through this neck of the woods, and the handful of buildings that comprised "downtown" weren't aimed at tourists. Just a few shreds of white paint clung to the turn-of-the-century post office, the single-pump gas station had a window boarded up and the hotel/bar looked more like an elaborate shed.

A red pickup truck headed toward them hauling a camper-like trailer with bars on the windows. Jack stared as it went by, trying to catch a glimpse of any livestock inside. A human hand grasped one of the bars. Jack flinched and almost stumbled off the sidewalk.

"Whoa, man. Stuff not agreeing with you?" Sam asked.

Jack gawked at the trailer as it swayed and shimmied down the street. He shook away the image of the hand. That was it. Once they sold off their coke stash, Jack would check himself back into rehab. A good facility this time; none of those government-funded shit-holes.

"I'm OK. Just starving," Jack said.

They went into the gas station to find some grub. The rapid tempo of a country song flowed from a radio somewhere in the store. No clerk at the till to guard the case full of smokes.

The pair headed toward the coolers at the back. Same old mystery subs and plastic-wrapped cheese sticks. Jack let go of the cooler door and it slapped shut louder than he expected.

"You back already, Bill?" The voice of an old woman crackled over the shit-kicking country tune. She hobbled through a door in the back corner of the store.

"Oh," she said, coming to a stop. "Didn't know I had customers."

"No problem." Jack smiled and went to the till.

Long, leathery hands squished the sandwiches a little as she picked them up to check for a price. It made Jack less hungry.

"We don't get many people passing through here."

"We're actually going to be staying a while. For work."

"Is that so? Tradesmen are you?"

"Nah, just laborers. Helping with the harvest."

"Helping with the harvest?" She eyed Sam as he plunked a pair of sodas onto the counter. "Huh."

Jack paid the woman, thanked her and headed out the door.

"Good luck with the harvest, boys," the woman called after them. Her grin revealed blackened teeth. He couldn't be certain with the music in the background, but Jack thought the old hag chuckled as they left.

Back at the car, Sam devoured his sub of limp lettuce and sweaty cheese. He wiped a blob of mayonnaise off his cheek.

"I think being a farmer may not be that bad," Sam said between bites. "Get baked, feed some chickens and cows."

"I don't think there's any chance of us finding a cover job around here," Jack said.

Sam furrowed his brow, but kept chewing.

"Didn't you hear that woman at the store laugh at us when I told her we were helping harvest? It's all done by machines, and unless you have some mad tractor skills I don't know about, we're not going to get a job operating one of those big fucking combines."

Sam slapped his sub on the dash, already cluttered by a coffee cup and two empty pop cans.

"So why the fuck are we still here?"

Jack rubbed his chin and leaned back against the seat.

"We've got an in, that chick *likes* us. She knows her dad won't hire us, but she wants us around anyway. So we milk it, stay on the farm for as long as we can."

"Guilt her about not having a job and shit," said Sam, nodding. "Maybe you can bang her a few times and we can move in for a week."

"That'll be *your* job, bitch." Jack whipped an empty pop can at Sam, who blocked it with an open palm. Both men laughed.

"Nah, she likes *you* bro. I'll be feeding cows and shit."

They finished eating. Sam did another rail on the back of a CD case.

Jack realized he was just repeating old habits. Manipulation became part of the drug game and he was damn good at it. Get what you want and fuck everyone else. Simple as that. But he desperately wanted out. He wanted a regular job and a regular life. All that would have to wait until they sold off the shit they had stolen. Then he could start fresh. No more coke or booze or drug-fuelled midnight heists. And, unfortunately, no more Sam.

*

Mary walked out of Alice's Place wearing blue jeans and a T-shirt that fit snug against her chest, like plastic wrap squeezing those double-D's. Her long hair framed rosy cheeks and bright red lips that popped.

Jack and Sam leered as she crossed the parking lot.

"Hello boys. Just follow me."

She hopped into a rusty Ford pickup. It roared and spewed black exhaust before fish-tailing onto the road. Jack fired up the Plymouth and chased after her.

They followed Mary down a side road leading to a small, wooden house with a gap-tooth roof. The truck slid to a halt in the gravel driveway.

"You guys will have to ride with me." She called out from the window. "That shitbox you're driving won't make it through the bush."

Sam got out of the car but Jack hesitated. He didn't want to leave the coke unguarded overnight, but he couldn't unload the stuff from the trunk in front of her. Mary shot him a puzzled look as he rapped his fingers on the steering wheel. He would have to come back later.

The pickup lunged forward as Jack pulled his door shut. A field of golden wheat spread out to their left; a sparse forest of thin poplar trees stood to their right. The truck bounced through potholes and climbed over a few logs before arriving at a green tent nestled in the woods.

"Thank God." Sam said as he got out, rubbing his back. "I think that little trip bruised my ass."

"Well, maybe I'll have to take a closer look at it later." Mary winked before kneeling to fiddle with a tent peg.

Jack raised an eyebrow at Sam, who went red and struggled

to suppress a smile. Jack didn't have the hots for Mary, but still, he was a bit disappointed that he wasn't her first choice after all.

Mary grabbed her backpack from the truck.

"You guys up for partying tonight?" She took out a large bottle of rum.

Sam laughed and clapped his hands together. "Now you're talking."

"Damn right I am. Hard liquor and hard drugs. A perfect combination."

Both men went quiet for a moment.

"You've got some hard drugs too?" Jack's voice wavered.

"Don't give me that crap." Mary said. "You strung-out fuckers didn't do a good job of keeping your voices down at the diner. I must have heard the word 'blow' pop up three or four times before you left. I know you guys got something." Jack's stomach sank. How much did she know? Exactly what details did they blab about at the diner? He couldn't remember.

"Yeah, we got a little bit of blow." Jack pulled their small plastic bag of "personal use" coke from his pocket. "Can't be too careful about narcs, you know."

"Oh, I agree." She cracked open the rum and took a long swig, shaking her head a little afterwards. "But I sure as hell ain't a narc, so how about hooking a lady up with a line?"

Sam was on it. He dusted three neat rows of powder onto the back of a map he found in the tent.

"So what really brings a couple of city kids like you to the sticks?" Mary poured shots of rum into plastic cups. "You guys get chased out of town or something?"

Christ. Did she know about Curtis too? Were they that out of it this morning?

"We're not a couple of thugs or anything like that. We just needed to get out of the city for a while," Jack said.

"Hey, I'm not one to judge." She smiled and handed them

both a drink.

For the next few hours they hit the booze hard and snorted an eight-ball of coke. Sam and Mary would press faces every now and then, brushing clumsy lips together as if by accident.

"OK, confession time." Mary splashed more rum into her cup. "There's no work for you guys."

They already knew this, but for some reason Sam felt he had to twist his face in a feign-shock expression.

"Yeah, the woman at the gas-station kind of filled us in," Jack said.

"I just, you know, thought you guys were cool and wanted to hang."

"And hone in on a little free blow?" Sam smiled at her.

"Whatever, *fucker*. You guys apparently need a place to lie low, so here's the deal: I'll let you camp here as long as you guys let me party for free. You *must* be holding more than a just a couple grams of that shit. What do you think?"

They clinked plastic cups to seal the deal.

Maybe this girl was cool after all, Jack thought. He felt even more ashamed about their plan to use her. In a way, it would have been similar to how Curtis took advantage of those crack-thinned prostitutes who frequented his apartment. The comparison made Jack shudder. It was yet another reason to go clean; he could leave all the lies and con jobs behind him. Start fresh. Live right.

Mary stumbled to her feet and swayed her hips back and forth, sloppy like a dive-bar stripper. The light from the campfire silhouetted her curves as she danced. Jack fell asleep with his head on his jacket.

*

Jack jolted from his drunken slumber. His brain throbbed. "We gotta go man, right now, right now." Sam kept shaking his friend even after he woke up. "Someone's coming."

Jack groaned and climbed to his feet. Flashlight beams flicked back and forth in the distance.

"Oh shit. Where's Mary?"

"In the tent zonked. *Fuck* her man, they don't want her."

Jack had no idea who *they* were. Curtis? The cops?

"Let's head that way." Jack pointed toward the forest. Moonlight streamed through the anorexic trees.

They kept a hurried pace through the brush, pressing through skeletal branches that scratched at their faces. Jack's head pounded. One flashlight beam still lingered nearby, but they stopped anyway. Jack didn't think they were in any immediate danger of being spotted.

"What if they got *dogs* or something?" Sam asked.

"We'd hear barking, they don't."

"Think it's Curtis?"

"I fucking *hope* not. Let's keep going."

They continued through the trees, much slower now. Sam led the way. The panicked adrenaline-fuelled sense of urgency disappeared and that allowed Jack's hangover to really sink in. Actually, he was still a little drunk.

Sam came to an abrupt stop and cocked his head to one side.

"What's wrong?" Jack whispered.

"You see that?"

Jack stared hard into the darkness. After a few seconds, he could make out someone standing a couple dozen feet ahead of them. A swaying shadow among the trees.

"He doesn't see us," Jack said. "We can sneak by him."

They reduced their movements to a slow-motion pace. Sam stepped on a branch sending out a sharp crack. The shadowy figure turned and shuffled toward them.

"Let's go," Jack said.

"Nah, we gotta fight him, knock him out. He'll tell his buddies where we are."

Sam walked toward the figure.

"Goddamn it." Jack picked up a baseball-sized rock and followed about a dozen feet away.

The figure charged through the bushes and tackled Sam. A couple short screams shattered the night silence.

Jack leapt forward and swung the stone. It connected against the person's head with a soft, hollow thud. The assailant collapsed.

"Sam!" Jack kneeled by his friend. Blood spurted from a tear in his neck. "Jesus Christ, did that guy fucking *bite* you?"

Sam sucked in quick bursts of air. Jack put his hand over the wound and warm fluid pooled between his fingers.

"Hang in there man, hang in there."

Jack heard shuffling footsteps behind him. Before he could turn around a hand grabbed his hair and smashed his face into a tree. Front teeth tore loose and his jaw went slack like a busted hinge. The side of Jack's head collided with a log as he hit the ground. His vision blurred and the star-freckled sky spiraled above him.

He heard a muffled groan; a wet smacking sound.

Jack struggled to sit up and blinked away the distortion. The shadow man had buried his face into the side of Sam's neck, prying open the wound with gnarled fingers. Even in the dimness, Jack could make out the gaping crater in the side of the guy's skull.

How is he still going? How is it still alive?

Jack tried to scream, but it came out as a soggy moan. The thing in front of him lifted its face from Sam's lifeless body, and turned toward Jack. Gore drizzled off its chin.

Jack stumbled to his feet. He ran out of the trees and into the field, thrashing his way through waist-high grain. It didn't matter who were carrying those flashlights anymore. He tripped and fell a few times, once twisting his foot in a hole. A motor revved in the background. He kept going, albeit at a slower pace and with a slight limp.

Headlights roared out of the darkness. A spotlight swept back and forth through the field and then pounced on Jack, holding him its blinding-white gaze. He dropped to one knee, gasping for air.

"We got 'em," a man called out from the truck. He sounded young.

*

Who are these people? Cops? Please let them be cops.

Jack tried to talk but his pulsating jaw wouldn't follow instructions. He mumbled and sprayed blood into the searing light. Truck doors opened and slammed shut. The field rustled with footsteps.

"Let's get 'em loaded up."

A rope slipped around his neck and drew tight before Jack could react. His mind reeled as he pawed at the noose and the metal pole connected to it.

What are they doing to me?

Fabric pressed tight against Jack's face and everything went black. Fingertips tugged and pulled at his cheeks until the holes on the hood aligned with his eyes. A drawstring synched it snug around his throat.

Jack's jaw exploded with pain as the men dragged him to his feet and forced him into the back of a pickup truck. They killed the spotlight, but its blinding effects lingered. He slumped in the corner of the truck bed; someone sat on the other side holding the pole attached to the noose around his neck. Like animal control securing a feral beast.

Jack took a deep breath. He concentrated as he mouthed the words "help me," but it came out garbled.

"Yeah, yeah." His captor shook the dog-catcher device.

Jack's hands curled into claws as he moaned. He kept still

and quiet after that.

After a few minutes, the truck stopped and his handler shoved him out. Jack fell face-first into the dirt.

No moving means no pain. Just stay put.

A swooshing sound kept a steady rhythm in the background. He raised his head from the soil and his eyes adjusted to the scarce light. About a dozen people swung Grim Reaper-style blades in the pale glow of a pair of spotlights. The stench of rotten meat mixed with diesel fuel.

"You got Camp Three's runaway?" An old, smoky voice called out.

"Yep. He's masked and ready to work." The young voice. Jack could make out a few of his features now: mangled ball cap, flannel shirt and blue jeans. The guy looked about 18 or 19.

"I'll call them and let 'em know we got their runner. Gear him up."

They flipped Jack onto his back. A man in a cowboy hat pressed a long scythe against Jack's chest while someone grabbed his left hand. The cowboy wrapped rope tight around his wrist, binding it to the smooth wooden handle. He did the same for Jack's right hand.

They pulled him to his feet and lead him to the workers, who also wore ski mask-style hoods and had the same sinister-looking tools bound to their limbs. They sliced away at the grain with mechanical perfection, each stroke smooth and exactly the same.

The man on Jack's right wore a crumpled business suit with one pant leg ripped off. His head hung limp against his shoulder, flopping around as he swung the blade. A woman in a blood-soaked dress hacked away on Jack's left. Everyone worked in silence.

"Let's see if he remembers." The old voice.

The noose went slack and lifted from around Jack's neck.

He tried to scream, hoping to yell this nightmare away. Soggy mumbling spewed out instead.

"Doesn't seem like he remembers. Put 'em down?"

Jack's body quivered as he lifted the scythe, drew it back and swung it forward. Again and again. The coarse rope rubbed against his wrists, shredding skin. His heart pumped and fresh blood dribbled down his chin. Wet cloth clung to his face making it tough to breathe.

"Don't let him work on the end of the line, get 'em to the middle."

The noose sprang out of the darkness and slipped around Jack's neck again. They pulled him a few dozen feet to the right before letting go. An obese pre-teen worked shirtless next to Jack. The kid's fat rolls quivered with every stroke he made. Fluid dripped from a fist-sized wound near his kidney.

"He stopped working again Frank."

"Give him a second." That smooth, older voice.

Jack's arms sagged; each swing became slower and shorter. The joints in his wrists popped under the twisting ropes.

I can't keep this up.

As Jack raised the scythe again he stumbled backward, nicking one of the kid's fat rolls with the edge of the blade. Blood and pieces of gelatinous meat slipped out of his stomach like melted cheese. The stench made Jack gag and he fought to keep from vomiting inside his mask.

"What the fuck's he doing now?" It was Frank.

"I dunno. Never seen one do *that* before."

"Just get rid of him already."

The noose slipped back around his neck. They hauled him out of the light and slammed his limp body against the door of a pickup.

Just fucking end it. I'm done.

They aimed a small spotlight into his face. Jack clenched his eyes.

"Remember to use the silencer. We don't need to create any more pain-in-the-ass runways."

"Alright, where'd you put it?"

A cellphone rang and Frank said hello. His voice faded as he spoke.

"Bah, hurry up old man."

No Frank, take your time. But Jack knew that would just delay the inevitable. He let the weight of the scythe drag him to his knees and slumped against the wheel of the truck.

I have to find a way to show them I'm alive.

Any facial expression that could prove his humanity – a smile or sticking out his tongue – would be hidden by the hood. His bound hands prevented any gestures.

I should have tried harder in the truck. Maybe flipped the guy the bird, anything. But I had to be such a damn pussy about my jaw.

Jack tapped the handle of the scythe against the ground in an ignorant attempt at Morse Code. He tried humming a few sloppy bars of O'Canada; the moist mask blocked the sound. He sucked in big, exaggerated gasps of air. Nothing. Jack wasn't even sure the men were paying him any attention.

A cellphone snapped shut.

"So get this, Crew Three says they caught their runaway."

"So what do we have here?"

Not a fucking zombie, that's for sure. Come on guys, put it together.

"Must be from Two or Four, I guess."

Guess again Frank, please guess again.

The chatter of a diesel motor drowned out their conversation. Jack didn't know shit about engines, but that barking rumble sounded familiar.

What if it's Mary? She would go looking for her new friends, wouldn't she?

The motor cut out.

"Now what." More muffled conversation.

"Mystery solved," Frank called out. "Mary knows what happened."

Yes, oh thank fucking God yes. Mary, I love you.

"Yeah, that's the one I saw. I recognize his clothes." Her voice came from just behind the light. "It was heading east, scared me to death."

What? What are you doing Mary? Tell them!

"This is exactly why I don't want you camping out here during harvest. How many times do I have to tell you?"

Tell them Mary! Tell them I'm alive!

"I know dad, I'm sorry."

"Two runaways in a single night. Do you know how lucky you are? Now go home."

Jack realized that the keys to the Plymouth were no longer in his jeans pocket.

She knew about the blow. That heartless bitch.

"It probably slipped away from Crew Two. Those guys never have their shit together," the teenager said. "I'll take care of it."

A click of metal, a muffled pop and Jack's head snapped back. The blasting-white spotlight dimmed. A fuzzy silhouette stood over him.

"You know, I don't think I want to bother with this crap anymore," Frank said. "It's such a bloody hassle."

"Here we go again." The teenager laughed. "You may use the combine a little more each year, but you always end up doing a few quarters the old way. I think you'd be the last one to break tradition."

"Yeah, I know, but every tradition has gotta end sometime. That's it. Next, year I'm only dealing with living workers."

A final bullet ripped through Jack's skull.

GREASE PAINT AND MONKEY BRAINS

DUSTIN READE

Here is something you probably don't know: Grease paint itches like the devil when it dries.

The peeling and flaking makes your skin feel dried out, skeletal, dusty. It is awful. It can drive you crazy. You are out there, wearing several layers of baggy clothing, sweating beneath the spotlights, crammed in that damned tiny car, and all the while your face is coated in an itchy cream that feels like a heavy layer of tight skin. And you can't scratch, either. Heavens No! To wipe would be to smear, to scratch would be to smudge. To attempt in any way to alleviate some of the torture taking place on your face would be to destroy the illusion. The fantasy and atmosphere created by the paint. Children fear clowns enough as it is, imagine how they would react to a clown with a violent streak of smeared paint spread across his face.

So, you find a way to ignore it.

You go someplace else. Someplace in your mind, and you stay there until the show is over. The problem is, when you let your mind wander, it doesn't always come back. Not all the way, at least.

I mean, you already have to be a little crazy to end up a circus clown. It helps.

But there are two kinds of crazy: good crazy, and bad.

Those who start out good crazy do not always stay that way forever.

I first began eating live animals a few years ago. It happened after a particularly difficult performance on the outskirts of a little town in Texas. It was August, the middle of Summer, and the town was in the grips of a two-month heat wave. Bonkers and I had been playing the old "save the baby from the burning building" routine, which did not help with the heat situation.

Bonkers was up in the building, his face painted with a big blue frown, shooting tears out of his eyes through two small tubes taped to the side of his face. I was running around with a few other clowns at the foot of the building, passing the bucket back and forth so it would be empty by the time it got to the building and whatnot. Typical clown business.

Only, what happened after—once the big top was shut down and the crowds had gone home—was far from typical clown business.

I guess the heat really got to old Bonkers that day. Being up in that faux building, surrounded by flames on the hottest day of the year, it did something to him. Something bad.

See, after the performance we clowns like to unwind a bit. We take off our oversized shirts and shoes, and hang around our tents drinking champagne in our undershirts and suspenders. That night, though, Bonkers didn't join us. The two of us usually played a few rounds of blackjack after a big show, and I had been waiting for about an hour when I decided to go look for him.

First, I checked the Big Tent. The trapeze artists were in there, practicing a new routine for the next day's show. I asked Eliza, the lion tamer, if she had seen Bonkers and she said she had seen him over by the animal tent when she had gone in to get the lions. I walked over and pulled back the entrance flap.

The inside of the tent was dark, and the heavy smell of animal waste assaulted my sense almost immediately. I thanked the circus gods for the thousandth time for not making me a wheelbarrow clown. Wheelbarrow Clowns are those clowns you sometimes see in parades which follow the horses and clean up their droppings. It is the lowest job in the circus, even lower than pit crew.

I walked into the darkened tent, listening to the animals stir in their sleep, the shuffling of hay and the soft laughter-like whimper of the chimps. It was a cool night, and I walked slowly through the tent, savoring the feel of the cool night air against my exposed arms.

That's when I saw Bonkers. He was huddled over something near the monkey cage, a single Coleman lantern hung from the tiger cage beside him. The way his shoulders moved indicated he was eating something, but in the dim light I couldn't see what it was.

"Bonkers?" I said. "What are you doing in here? Why weren't you in the tent?"

He spun around and I saw his face and chest were smeared with blood. There were long strings of something I couldn't identify slung over his shoulders and a furry patch of animal hide hanging from his mouth.

"Jesus, man," I gasped, staring at the chimpanzee corpse lying on the ground before him Its chest had been ripped open, exposing the broken ribcage beneath. The entrails were strewn about haphazardly, staining the dirt a dark brown in the light of the lantern. The chimp's face had been ravaged, large holes seeped thick blood where Bonkers had torn into the fleshy muzzle.

Bonkers climbed to his feet and held his arms out in supplication.

"I couldn't stop!" He screamed. "I…I came in to work on a new act and…and, I snapped! I just…"

"Whatever, Man," I said, backing away. "You don't have to explain. It's fine. Why don't you just, uh, go get cleaned up and meet me back at the tent in a little while, eh? I'll clean up here. Don't talk to anyone until you see me, alright?"

Sobbing, Bonkers nodded. He pulled the coil of guts from around his neck and threw it beside the corpse. I don't know why, but I didn't think he was crazy, and I wasn't really afraid of him. I had only backed away because I didn't want him to get any blood on me. I realize that now. As he walked out of the tent and I turned to clean up the dead ape, I realized I understood completely why he had done what he had done.

In fact, as I dug my hands around in the still-warm guts of the dead beast, I found a strange stirring welling up within my own. Life was not precious, as people so often said. It was *more* than precious, it was sacred, incredible. To live and experience the world was some kind of incredible miracle. It was magic. Like the circus. And like the circus, life went away sometimes, but the memory left behind was one of infinite sadness, but also of majesty and embrace. Death was like a circus train leaving town. It was beautiful and tragic at the same time. Women had the ability to create life, and that was a blessing. But the ability to take life belonged to everyone, man and woman alike, and in its own way it was also beautiful. I understood all of this as I lowered my head down towards the corpse. I breathed in the dank aroma of animal hair and hot blood. I thought of how it had lived, cooped up in its cage, except for the brief moments when it was performing a unicycle act to the delight of thousands of children in hundreds of small towns across the country. Burying my face in the splayed cadaver and tearing into the thin exterior of the stomach, I understood completely.

From that moment on, I was hooked. Addicted. The bright lights that killed me at every performance could no longer be suppressed by mere mental exercises. I needed something stronger, something to take the edge off. It started slowly at first, with Bonkers and I taking turns. We killed one animal each, two days a week. We kept it to the smaller animals for a while, often picking up a rat or puppy at some pet store in one

61

of the towns in which we stopped. Then after the performance we would hide behind the Freak Trailers and eat it.

The killing bites were the best, but they were even better when they were delayed for as long as possible. It took some control at first, trying to start at the back legs, or the tail, instead of going straight for the throat where the blood shot out the warmest and heaviest. Often, I would get only a few bites into the back section when the urge would hit too hard to be ignored and I would just rip into the furry flesh of the neck. The tendons and veins would snap and bleed thick rivers of warm blood down my throat, and my eyes would roll back in ecstasy as I felt the last of the heartbeat fade away in my hands. From there it was a simple matter of throwing the mutilated corpse into the lion's cage to dispose of the evidence.

The problem with addiction is the same as madness: once you find you are deep enough into it, you can only go deeper.

Rats and puppies were not enough. We soon began "shopping" at local Humane Shelters, picking out the fattest strays for a few dollars and gorging ourselves on their meat after the show.

In one town, when we couldn't find a pet store or humane shelter before the show, we improvised by sneaking into a pasture under cover of night and eating a small calf we found sleeping beneath a dead cherry tree. Its cries brought me near orgasm. Unfortunately, they also brought the farmer who owned the pasture and the cows, and he in turn brought his shotgun. He fired off several shots, I assume into the air, as neither Bonkers nor myself were injured. But still, the incident instilled in us a great fear of being caught.

From that moment on, we decided to restrict our relaxation techniques to the animals at the circus. It would mean a drop in quantity, as we would once again be forced to eat only the smaller animals, and no longer the large dogs and calves we had grown so fond of, but we were convinced that, if were very careful, and only chose animals of which there were many, we could carry on without incident.

It sounded logical.

The problem is, when one is addicted to something, one can have all the logic in the world and it wouldn't make any difference. A heroin user is often aware of the dangers of his habit, but that isn't going to help him quit. An alcoholic may realize he has a problem, but the glass will be at his lips nonetheless, and the drinks will continue to get stronger and stronger until they produce the desired effect.

The problem with addiction is that, even though no one sets out to become addicted to something, once they are they can justify it to themselves by blaming outside influences for their habit. A man does not drink because he is an alcoholic. A man is an alcoholic because the world *makes* him drink. He cannot handle his lifestyle without a little help. It was the same for Bonkers and I. We did not eat animals because we were sick or addicted. No. We ate them to help us unwind after a hard day's work.

We killed everything: dogs, pigs, cows, sheep (the carnival also boasted a tent of livestock and a petting zoo), as well as the numerous rats and crows that seem to follow circuses wherever they go. We showed little in the way of control. The only constraint we showed was in our habit of waiting until nightfall, when the performance was over, to feed our habits.

Word soon got around that something was not quite right with the circus. Too many animals were disappearing for it to be coincidence. At first, the Foreman thought it was some sort of animal rights group. The circus was always being threatened with lawsuits and protests by various groups and organizations over way it treated its animals. I always thought that was foolish. The animals were treated better than most of the performers. They ate better and they were only required to perform one act, once a night. Hardly mistreatment, if you ask me.

Extra Security was brought on for a while, and during that time Bonkers and I kept our habits quietly to ourselves by once again shopping for our late-night morsels at local pet stores and shelters. It wasn't much, and our performance suffered for it. We were often sluggish during shows, and more than once I missed my cue and threw a pie or a bucket of confetti into the crowd instead of into the face of a fellow clown. I was often reprimanded and told I would suffer pay cuts if it kept up.

Luckily, one of the security guards really did catch a group of kids sneaking into the circus one night, and they were of course blamed for the disappearances and the security was lessened after they were dealt with.

Bonkers and I ate a horse that night in celebration.

We passed it off as the work of the kids that had been arrested. Saying they must have done it before being caught. It didn't make sense, but Circus Folk tend to stick together, and the issue was dropped. Though the scare had put the fear in me something fierce, and I decided right then to stop eating the animals once and for all.

And I did. The first weeks were difficult, and I was once again threatened with pay cuts. I worked extra hard at my act, throwing myself into my work to keep my mind off of the near-crippling urge building up in my bones for fresh blood. The desire was so intense at times, I could barely walk. I had to eliminate every animal from my set, as I found it too difficult to be around them without wanting to shred them with my teeth, to feel their fur and flesh pulling away from their muscles as I bit into their rough hides. But still I pressed on, and soon I began to feel like myself again. My performances improved, and I felt the urge grow less pronounced with every passing day.

I was fit.

I was relaxed.

I was happy.

For a while.

I was helping dismantle the big tent after a decent performance. The pit crew was a little short-handed, so a few of us performers were lending a hand with the tear down. This was not uncommon. The Pit Crew Guys are usually not the most reliable types. You know that old thing about "running away with the circus"? Well, when someone does that, chances are they wind up working on the pit crew. It is hard, back-breaking work, and very few people choose to stay with it for very long. Most of them just use the circus as a means of getting from one place to the other and making some quick coin on the sides. We get a lot of pit boys jumping the train between stops.

When that happens, most of the performers are not against lending a hand where needed. I didn't usually join in, as I have to work on my act most nights, but I needed something to fill the void left by the animals, so I jumped at the chance to do some mindless work for a few hours.

The main tent had been lowered, and we were just about to start pulling pegs when Bonkers tapped me on the shoulder. He had a big grin on his face underneath a painted one.

"Come with me," he said. "I got to show you something."

"It's not another animal is it?" I asked. "Because I already told you, I am not doin' that shit anymore. I've gone straight."

He just chuckled as he led me away from the circus. We walked past the tents and the Freak trailers, beyond the equipment trucks, and out into the darkness. The night air was cold, and there was a heavy fog on the ground that made it hard to see where we were walking. I tripped a few times and wanted to go back, but Bonkers just kept going, his hand never leaving my arm as he led me to whatever clandestine thing he had tucked away beyond the fairgrounds.

We came to an isolated patch of dead cherry trees beside a

small stream. Bonkers pointed to one of the trees.

"There," he said. "Look."

I looked. Bound to the tree, unconscious, was the man that had gone missing from the circus that morning. He was naked, covered in bruises and blood. His clothes hung from the gnarled branches of the cherry tree.

As I stood there, staring, unsure of what to do or say, the man's head moved and he made a sort of gurgling sound.

I leapt back.

"Jee-zus, Bonkers!" I screamed. "What the hell is this? What are you doing? I thought he jumped the train, or something..."

Bonkers cut me off by holding a pair of pruning shears up to my face. His makeup had smeared horribly, his eyes were enveloped in purple smudges, and his rubber nose clung desperately to the tip of his nose. The green hair ringing his head was matted with blood, clinging to his cheeks in veining strands.

I looked at the shears.

"What are you going to do with those?"

Bonkers laughed.

"I'm going to *relax*!" he whispered.

Slowly, he began to approach the man. I took another tentative step back.

"Bonkers," I said, my voice seeming distant, dreamlike. "Don't..."

It was no use. As I watched, Bonkers placed the open blades of the pruning shears up to the man's collar bone. Using great force, he started closing the blades, wrenching his arm up and down as he sawed through the heavy rod of bone just beneath the flesh. The man awoke with a start, screaming into the multi-colored rag stuffed in his mouth.

I wanted to help. I wanted to grab a cherry branch and club Bonkers over the head, spilling his brains onto the dried roots of the trees. I wanted to save the pit boy fighting to stay alive as a sadistic clown with a cannibalism fetish cut through his tendons with pruning shears. Yes. I wanted the screams to stop…but, mostly, I wanted to taste him. I wanted to put my lips against his jugular vein as it gushed dark red blood onto his chest. I wanted to feel the muscles separate from his ribcage as I bit into and peeled away the meat from his pecks. I wanted him dead, dead, dead.

The shears closed with a bone-snapping crack. The sound seemed to echo off the trees before being swallowed up by the babbling stream beside us. Bonkers dug his fingers into the wound, fishing around while the man slipped in and out of consciousness, finally pulling what looked like a long extension cord covered in blood and bits of fatty tissue from the ragged wound.

I took a step closer.

"What's that?" I asked.

"The jugular vein," Bonkers said. His tongue emerged from his painted lips and licked the vein tenderly. His eyes rolled back into his head as he slurped the marrow from the exposed collar bone.

I was horrified to discover those old familiar feelings coming up again. I had done so well! I had quit! Hell, I had even returned to those stupid late-night rounds of blackjack in the clown quarters. I didn't need this anymore! Did I?

As my floppy feet dragged my barely-resisting body towards the bleeding pit man, I knew I would never be able to quit, not for real. The urge was just too strong, and the demands of the job too stressful, for me to ever succeed going Cold Turkey.

As I leaned to deliver the killing bite, I realized it really didn't matter whether I quit or not.

Not really.

Not anymore.

I mean, pit boys jump train every day.

HUMANS EAT FREE

JAY WILBURN

The smell of the blood soaking into the dirt was driving them mad.

The fences buckled under the weight of the bodies pressing against them all around the perimeter. The steel connectors strained audibly on the posts. Concrete around the bases of the fence posts began to emerge from the dirt. The unsettled dead reached boney fingers and discolored tongues through the holes in the bulging chain link.

They were riled by the recent activity. They wanted to taste the mud. They wanted to fertilize the Earth with more of it.

They growled and moaned with hunger. Fluids leaked out of open, unhealing wounds as their bodies were pressed on all sides. Their teeth raked against the metal links ringing into the compound grounds.

They looked on the empty fields of withered crops. Their searching eyes passed over the collapsed well and the burned-out windmill. They listened to the wind rattle the loose metal on the structures.

They did not comprehend the meaning of the wavy, yellow line painted over the dirt and concrete from one leaning fence to the other through the middle of the bloody, delicious grounds.

The tin door to one of the structures banged open.

The creatures closest to the fences went silent as the air was pressed out of their lifeless lungs. Gummy mucus oozed from their nostrils and over their broken teeth. They stood motionless as the monsters behind them tried to walk through

74

them to get to the new action and sound.

Mack Coy dropped the point of his peg leg into the dirt after he used it to knock the sheet of tin aside from his hiding place. He had not slept well. The groaning corpses made it difficult to hear danger approaching.

He was hungry. The crops had failed and their supplies had run out. He had made a deal with his survival partner over rationing and Mack had been betrayed.

He brought out the new blade he had spent the night sharpening. It was folded tin and used a broken piece of pipe and duct tape for the handle. It was crude, but it would do nicely.

Mack began crossing the grounds toward the yellow line. He left one sneaker print and one, round peg print in the moist dirt with every other step. He tried to look for movement in the other buildings on both sides of the line, but the heat lines rising off the metal into the air and the compromised fences were distracting.

He ignored the bandages over his left eye and around his gut on the same side. They smelled like the bodies around the fence lines. The cloth had started to hang loose and was stained black and yellow. He had ceased trying to change them.

The collapsed hood over the broken well burst up behind him as he approached the yellow line. She had been hiding on his side of the line all night.

She fired her harpoon gun at his back from the exposed mouth of the well pumps. Mack tried to dodge, but took the barb into his left shoulder. He felt it grind against the bone through his back and he knew he was in trouble.

He tried to run for cover on her side of the yellow line. As he ran, he heard and felt the chain rattling out as he pulled it along behind him with the harpoon shaft.

She had been busy during the night too.

"Don't do it, Hatty," Mack yelled over the groans and pops

from the fences. "Don't do it!"

Hatty Fields stumbled out of her nest and fell on to the concrete at the base of the well. She spit out blood she couldn't afford to lose. If she still had her front teeth, she would have lost those again in the fall and probably would have bitten off part of her tongue. Fortunately for her, Mack had knocked those out for her with a pipe from the burned windmill two days ago.

Hatty almost lost the end of the chain as she struggled to get back up. She was hungry and it was making her sloppy. She nearly lost the advantage from all her work of setting up the ambush.

She quickly hooked the chain over the twisted rebar sticking out of the broken slab and heaved it into the busted well cover.

The chain clanked loudly and repeatedly as it was drawn down the open shaft into the dry darkness. Mack was jerked backwards off his feet. He tried to spear his sword into the ground to anchor himself, but his hands were pulled away from the handle as it wavered abandoned where he had planted it in the dirt. He was dragged backwards and unarmed across the ground. His foot and peg plowed uneven furrows through the dirt. As he scraped over the concrete section he screamed, leaving skin from the open tears in his clothes smearing his flesh over the yellow line.

He only had one chance to turn the situation around. He knew Hatty and she wasn't just planning to let him disappear down the well. She wanted him too badly to let that happen.

As he was flung toward her, Mack rolled over and whipped his peg leg around to Hatty's side. She tried to bring the metal lip from the well hood down on his head like a guillotine.

She has been very busy, Mack thought as he jammed his peg into the grimy flesh over her ribs.

He felt something snap below the skin. Hatty gasped for air and staggered backwards over the silent pump housing. Her guillotine missed his neck and connected with the side of the harpoon. The spear bent and tore loose from his back ripping out a section of bone locked on the barb as the weapon clattered down into the well.

The dead on the perimeter writhed against the barrier as the fresh smell of blood hit the air.

Mack's left arm went numb and fell limp. He struggled to use his right arm to get up before Hatty could rally.

He advanced on her and then dove out of the way.

Sparks flew off the pipe when Hatty swung the modified shearing saw as she cranked it.

"You've been hoarding fuel, Hatty," Mack yelled as he stumbled up against the blackened frame of the windmill.

Hatty rose up to find Mack, but stayed behind the cover of the scarred pipe as she spoke over the buzz of the saw.

"You got nerve," she huffed, "accusing anyone of hoarding, Mack."

Mack circled around the well without backing up. He did not give her room to step out in the clear.

He said, "This all comes down to you keeping your promises, Hatty. We had a deal. This could all have been avoided, if you just contributed your fair share."

"You would like that, wouldn't you?" she accused. "You would take it all just like those beasts on the fences."

He rounded the well and approached the pumps and piping from the other side. She swung the saw and sent sparks off the pump vent as she grazed the slats. He backed away and kept circling.

"We had a plan," Mack said. "We needed to ration what we had left. We needed to eat to survive."

"You would have just kept going until there was nothing left to—" Hatty was cut off as her feet were jerked out from under her.

The wire had wrapped her ankles and bit through the skin as

they were drawn together. The saw barked and jumped against the pipe as she fell backwards hitting her head. Sparks flew and the saw pulled loose from her hands. It continued to run as it chewed at the dirt and concrete pulling itself along the side of the well and out into the grounds.

She put a lock on the trigger, Mack thought.

"God, she's good," he whispered.

Mack jumped over the pipes and drove his knee into Hatty's sternum to keep her beaten to the ground. She gagged up stomach acid and blood with the impact.

Mack tried to wrap the wire around her neck, but his left hand wouldn't cooperate. Hatty kicked, but Mack slid over her knees and locked his knees on both sides of her chest.

Blood ran down the back of his arm. Some of it was absorbed into his fouled bandages, but the rest dripped into Hatty's eyes and mouth. She tried to wriggle loose, but failed. As she struggled, she licked her lips to lap up the blood. Her eyes rolled back in her head from pain and from the ecstasy of the salty taste.

"Enjoy it while you can," Mack grunted as he looped the wire behind her neck.

Hatty screwed her body around under him and slid her head under the pipe to keep Mack from wrapping the wire around her throat.

How could I have been so stupid to let him get the drop on me like that?, Hatty thought as she tried to writhe her body free.

Mack braced his knee against her chest and wrapped the wire around his right palm as his left arm hung limp.

He said, "It's a shame you waited until your breasts withered away with starvation. I could have used those."

He pulled the wire over the curve of the pipe and yanked her face up into the under side of it. He couldn't see it, but he heard her skull connect with the metal. She spit out more blood.

Hatty hissed. "Eat yourself."

"We already did that, you selfish witch."

Mack slammed her face back up into the pipe. The wire sliced through the skin of his palm as it tightened. He bled down over the metal rings welded to the pipe supports. The wire slid back through his blood as it dropped back along the edge of one of the rings and welded bolts.

Hatty mumbled through her swollen, split lips. "It was a waste, Mack. We could have cut ourselves up until there was nothing left. It's a bad plan."

He jerked her face up into pipe again and let her drop back down to the bloody mud.

We should be done here soon, Mack thought.

He said, "You sure didn't stop me from serving up my leg for dinner and you ate your entire helping as I recall, Hatty."

He pulled up on the wire again. It snapped apart over the support ring and Mack fell backward off of her.

Hatty pulled herself out under the pipe. As she stood up, she pulled the wire out of the cut along the back of her neck. Her nose was twisted and flattened into her face. Her lips and eyes were puffing out badly.

Hatty ran.

Mack scrambled up to follow her, but got jerked back by the wire embedded in his bloody hand.

"You owe me a leg," Mack yelled after her. "I'm getting that and every bit you have left as interest."

Hatty paused on the concrete over the yellow line. She used her broken nails to scrape up the pieces of skin Mack had left behind when he was dragged toward the well. She pressed the bits through her purple lips and over her exposed gums.

Mack growled when he saw it. He unwound the wire faster out of the deep laceration in his hand. He reached under the pipe and peeled off the layer of skin from Hatty's nose. It wasn't much, but he sucked it down to try to keep things even.

Mack ran after her across the grounds. Hatty was spitting grit out from the sides of her teeth as she worked to separate the gravel from the road rash she had eaten. The bodies along the fences cracked their teeth trying to bite through the metal. The noise of the shearing saw continued to buzz across the ground.

Mack caught up with her. As he grabbed at her hair, she whirled around and cut his left arm off at the elbow. She had his tin sword.

Jesus, he got this thing sharp. He was good, Hatty thought as she saw the blood spurting into the ground from his stump.

Mack staggered back and tried to cover the bleeding. The blood spurted through the fingers of his right hand.

Hatty went for the severed arm on the ground.

"That's mine," Mack screamed.

He lunged for her and Hatty stabbed the tin sword into Mack's belly through the bandages. He groaned out as he shook with pain.

Hatty spat out more grit. "I'm going to eat it while you watch."

Mack took his hand off his stump and aimed it into her face. The stream of blood sprayed in her eyes and her hand came away from the pipe handle of the sword. He pulled the blade out of his gut with a drawn whine.

Hatty wiped her eyes and then licked her hands. Mack turned the sword around to use on Hatty.

She grabbed up the arm from the dirt and turned to run. Mack swung low and sliced through the back of her ankles. She screamed as she collapsed to the ground.

Mack rolled her over as he tried to decide what piece of her he wanted first. She was already chewing the meat from his left forearm off the end of the bone.

"It's delicious," Hatty mumbled over the meat.

Mack raised the sword up to drive down into her chest. Hatty kicked out, snapping off his peg leg in splinters. Mack fell to his side in the dirt next to her.

She was chewing on the arm again.

Mack growled. He drove his stump into her throat, letting the blood run down both sides of her neck. She ignored him as she ate with her eyes closed. He used his remaining hand to bring the edge of the blade down along the side of her face. He sawed and carved her cheek off exposing the teeth that were chewing up the pieces of his arm. One fingernail fell out of the hole as she chewed.

Mack dropped the sword so he could snatch up the slice of cheek for himself.

*

Across the grounds from where they ate, the shearing saw finally pulled itself along until it connected with the bottom of the chain link fence. It bucked away twice, but finally sliced through the bottom linked and walked itself up into the next link. One of the creatures grabbed the moving teeth and sliced off all its fingers. Another stepped on it and removed its gangrenous foot. The tool continued to eat through the fence as the bodies pierced themselves on it one after another. Intestines were diced and sent flying into the air on both sides of the fence.

The saw was finally knocked loose from the chain link as the first bodies pressed through the folded gap in the damaged section. The saw rolled three times before it buzzed against the ground again. It slowly dragged itself across the grounds in another direction.

More of the dead monsters staggered through the sharp opening, cutting themselves on the wire. They failed to bleed as they moved toward the thick smell of fresh blood deeper in the compound.

*

Hatty drove the point of the sword through Mack's good leg until she felt it grind against the bone. His teeth would not release her shoulder as he whipped his head from side to side.

She picked up the broken piece of his peg leg and stabbed it into his neck. He shuddered, but his teeth clamped down harder as blood coursed out from the artery in his neck. Hatty forgot about her shoulder and pressed her swollen lips to the wound at the base of the wood stake and began drinking. The blood oozed out between her teeth through her open cheek.

Mack and Hatty never noticed the others gathering around them even after they locked on to the couple's warm skin with their own broken teeth and cold lips.

DEAD MEN AND THE DAMNED

R.W. HAWKINS

Two riders under an ashen sky, and the wind wailed across the Badlands. Thunder roared in the east. The occasional shafts of sunlight speared the dark clouds, yet it was a weak light, diseased and lethargic. The ground under the horses' pounding hooves was hard and unforgiving. The soil needed rain. Only the hardiest of settlers made their homes out here, where the way of the gun prevailed in the scattered settlements and ramshackle towns. Every soul, every man, woman and child was judged by a bullet.

Elgin and Abernathy lived by that same code. They hunted the sinners and the faithless; the murderous and the unjust. And although they were Christian men, their payment was coin, whiskey, and clean whores.

Elgin pulled up his collar against the cold breeze and ran his hand over greying stubble. He narrowed his eyes against the swirls of topsoil kicked up by the wind. His wide-brimmed hat sheltered his head from the elements. The holsters carrying his twin pistols creaked as his body swayed with the horse's movement beneath him. He was a haggard, cynical man, lean and tall and wiry.

The Great Fires had destroyed much of civilisation nearly twenty years ago. This was a new America, forged from the ashes of a dead world. The religious elite ruled the remaining states with the cold ruthlessness of the Old Testament God they worshipped. The Time Before, when planes had flown through the skies and ships had sailed the seas, and free speech was not a sin, was a distant memory.

83

Elgin's ancestors had been slaves, although the creed of their identity had been lost from his skin before he'd been born. He was Louisiana stock and proud of it. He scanned the horizon, watching for signs of their quarry. The outlaw Enoch Lime wasn't stupid, but he was careless. Careless enough to be tracked. Elgin and Abernathy had almost caught him back in a small town in Ohio. Murphy had died that day, shot in the stomach by Lime. He had died slowly in the ruins of an old farm, crying for his wife and son while Elgin held him. They had burned Murphy's body upon a small pyre; they would have lost ground on Lime if they'd taken the time to bury him. Elgin missed Murphy. He missed a lot of things, but that was life, and life had no sympathy for men like him.

Abernathy raised the binoculars to his eyes.

"What is it?" said Elgin.

"A homestead."

"A farm?"

"Yeah."

"How far?"

"Two miles." Abernathy put away the binoculars then took a drink from his canteen. He splashed some water over his heavily-bearded face, shaking it off like a dog would. One of the few survivors from the Virginian Plague Zone, he was long in the jaw and short in the temper; the kind of man who'd pick sweetcorn out of shit if he could profit from it. But Elgin trusted him in a fire-fight; that was all that mattered in their line of business.

"Let's go," Elgin said, and they kicked their horses into a gallop.

When they reached the farmhouse it seemed deserted. A clothesline of clean washing flapped in the breeze. A crucifix had been ripped from the front door and smashed into pieces. Abernathy went to search around the back of the farmhouse while Elgin stayed out front, one hand poised next to his pistol.

Elgin had a bad feeling in his bones.

Abernathy returned a few minutes later.

"What is it?" Elgin said.

Abernathy spat. "I've found something."

*

On the grass at the far side of the house a thin, red-haired man had been pinned to the ground in the shape of the crucifixion, his hands impaled by wooden stakes hammered through his palms. His guts had spilled onto the grass, but he was still alive. When he noticed Elgin and Abernathy he started to giggle.

"That's not all," said Abernathy. He gestured to Elgin's right. A woman, probably the man's wife, was hanging on a rope from a tree branch. She had been beautiful in life; now her skin was cold and grey. Her eyes were open, bulging in their sockets. Her tongue hung limply from between blue lips.

"What happened here?" Elgin said.

"The Devil's work," said Abernathy, bowing his head. The red-haired man was still laughing, spit flying from his mouth and falling back onto his face.

"Did the woman stake him to the ground?" Elgin said. None of this made any sense.

"I don't think so," Abernathy said. "

"That means there's someone else here."

Soft footsteps on the grass behind them, and they turned around. A little girl with blonde hair and a bloody dress stared at them. Her face was contorted in an animalistic snarl. She chewed her lower lip, drawing blood. Her eyes were wide. In her hands were a hammer and a large knife dripping with blood.

"It's all right," Elgin said, trying to placate her. "We won't hurt you."

"I don't think she gives a shit," Abernathy said, unlimbering his automatic rifle.

The girl screamed at them. She was feral. Her limbs were trembling. Elgin tried not to think of his own little girl killed by cholera five years ago.

The girl ran at them, the knife raised in a tiny hand. Before she got within five yards, Abernathy shot her in the chest and she was thrown backwards, crumpling into a mess of hair and limbs. The rifle's report throbbed in Elgin's ears.

"Why did you kill her?"

Abernathy grunted. "She wanted to kill us."

"We could have captured her."

"And then what? Take her along with us? She would've killed us first chance she got. Look what she did to her father."

"You gonna kill him as well?"

Abernathy calmly walked over to the man and shot him in the head.

Elgin spat on the ground. A flock of crows were perched on the roof, watching him. He cursed under his breath as he marked the farmhouse's position on the map with a pencil. He drew in a breath and tasted the sour air. This place made his teeth itch. This was tainted ground. Abernathy was right – the Devil had been here.

They said a prayer for the family, but left them as they'd been found. No point in burying the corpses. The scavengers would feed well for a while.

The men moved on, riding into the gathering storm.

*

They travelled across the wastelands. Elgin felt uneasy about the girl's death. He'd done some terrible things in the past, but he'd never been complicit in the death of a child, even one that seemed to have been possessed by something demonic.

86

According to the creased and tattered map, the nearest settlement was about three miles away. They reached the town, called Mercy, around midday. It was a squalid, provincial shithole with all the charm of a leper colony. Elgin had been here before, five years back, when he and Abernathy had been hunting a child molester. The streets had been full of criminals, whores and other wretches shunned by civilisation back east. This was where the unwanted and the forsaken sought refuge. But today the dusty streets were empty and deserted. Store signs swayed and creaked in the wind. Buildings stood dark and silent.

"What happened here?" Elgin said. "Where're the townsfolk?"

"Did they hear we were coming?" Abernathy wiped his mouth with the back of his hand. His eyes were nothing but dark slits within his weathered face. His free hand was poised near his holstered six-shooter.

"Let's take a look around," Elgin said.

*

Elgin was first to see the naked, fat man sitting cross-legged in the middle of the street, chewing on a dead buzzard. Feathers were stuck around his mouth, moist with spit and blood. More feathers had collected by his feet. His bug-like eyes regarded Elgin and Abernathy as they halted before him.

"You seeing what I'm seeing?" Abernathy said.

The fat man grinned at them, gnawing on a ragged wing. The bird's thin bones snapped under his chomping teeth. He made a terrible smacking sound with his lips, as if he had never eaten such a delicious meal.

"Sick son of a bitch," Abernathy said. "I've eaten buzzard before...but I always cooked it first."

"Yeah, I remember," said Elgin. "And it still tasted like shit."

Abernathy leaned forward on his horse. "You OK there, friend? Drunk too much moonshine?"

The man didn't reply. He discarded the tattered remains of the bird and then burped.

"Think everyone around here's gone mad?" Elgin said.

"Hope not," said Abernathy. "I know a lovely piece of ass here; she can suck an apple through a shotgun barrel."

The fat man stood up, unsteadily, swaying a little on his feet as he straightened his flabby legs. He was well over six feet tall with hunched, hairy shoulders like columns of rock covered with moss. His hands balled into fists, and he chewed on his lower lip, just like the girl at the farmhouse had done. The grin vanished from his face. He was breathing heavily through his nose. His cock dangled like a dead cephalopod.

"Looks like he wants a fight," said Abernathy.

The fat man charged at them, hands outstretched, letting loose a bloodcurdling scream. If it wasn't for the insane look on his face he would've appeared quite comedic, with his staggering gait and his rolls of fat jiggling as he kicked his legs.

Abernathy took out his pistol and put a bullet in the man's chest.

The fat man stumbled but then righted his course and kept coming. Abernathy shot him again, but the man didn't stop. Abernathy put three more rounds into him, and the man fell down, finally, sprawling in the dirt. He coughed and spluttered. Elgin finished the man by shooting him in the head. A mercy kill.

"Nice one," said Abernathy.

"We didn't have to shoot him," said Elgin, reloading his pistol and holstering it. "He was unarmed. You got any honour, Abernathy?"

Abernathy shook his head. "Not since I took this job. Look at the state of him; he might have been sick. Wouldn't have been a good idea letting him get too close. The girl at the farmhouse was crazy. Maybe it's some kind of plague."

"Maybe Enoch Lime had something to do with this."

"Wouldn't put it past the shit-kicker."

A scream rang out. A woman ran at them from an alleyway, dressed in a bloodied nightgown. She clutched a crowbar, cursing at them in an awful, nail-scraping voice. Her bare feet kicked up plumes of dry dirt.

"What the hell?" said Abernathy.

Another woman shot out from the opposite side of the street; Elgin turned to her just as she launched herself at his horse. She bit at the horse, sinking her teeth into its flesh, and the horse reared-up on its back legs, shrieking. The woman screamed, flung backwards as Elgin kicked her away. She fell onto her back.

Elgin aimed his pistol at her. "Don't fucking move."

The woman moved, springing to her feet like an insect. She growled. Elgin shot her in the face and she went down. He turned to see Abernathy batting away the other woman with his foot. She swung the crowbar and hit Abernathy on the shin, and he cried out, more in annoyance than pain, and shot her twice in the chest. She fell down and stayed down.

Elgin checked that his horse wasn't too badly injured. The woman's bite had been weak, barely breaking the skin. He patted the horse's neck, cooing softly to the frightened animal.

"What's wrong with these people?"

"They're fuckin' mad, is my guess," said Abernathy, and he reloaded his pistol, lazily, as if he were out shooting pheasants on a Sunday morning.

Elgin looked at the dead bodies on the ground. Something cold in his stomach uncurled itself and wrapped around his spine. There would be more corpses by nightfall.

*

They went deeper into the town, past dark passageways between dilapidated buildings and crumbling shacks somehow holding together against the elements. There was no question of turning back and heading east. Their employers would be displeased.

Somewhere far away a dog howled. The streets were haunted by drifting shadows and the creeping whisper of the wind.

"I reckon a plague's driven everyone crazy," Abernathy said. "Seen it before. Remember that town in Kentucky?"

"How could I forget?" said Elgin. "But if it was a plague, there'd be more than just three infected people; if the rest of them are dead, there'd be piles of corpses. Plague pits."

Abernathy nodded. He took out a piece of jerky from his bag and started chewing on it.

They rounded a corner onto the next street. They stopped in the middle of the street.

"God in Heaven," said Elgin.

Men, women and children had been hung up on the fronts of buildings like executed criminals. They had been eviscerated. Their eyes had been removed. Elgin counted twenty-three bodies. He said a prayer for them.

"You hear something?" Abernathy asked, tilting his head to the side.

Elgin listened but could only hear his heart hammering in his chest. His horse snorted, trembling beneath him.

"Easy girl," said Elgin, stroking the horse's neck. He looked down the street, attracted by movement. A man stumbled around the corner at the far end of the street. His clothes were torn, and caked with dark fluids. He held a butcher's hook in his left hand.

Abernathy sized him up. "You gotta be fuckin' kidding me…"

The man's shoulders heaved with excitement. He pointed at them and then screamed.

"He's mine," said Abernathy, taking out his pistol.

Then more of the townsfolk came roaring around the corner, filling the street, crammed in like ants. They quickly caught up with the man and surged up the street. They screamed and growled and snarled.

Abernathy dropped his piece of jerky.

"Oh shit," said Elgin. He and Abernathy turned their horses around and fled down the street, away from the horde, until they met another mob of townsfolk swarming towards them, baying for blood. Most of the townsfolk carried makeshift weapons – pitchforks, sickles, knives and other tools – raising them in the air like some forgotten tribal army.

"It's a trap!" said Abernathy. He shot two men running towards him.

"Here!" said Elgin, spotting an opening between two buildings. "Quickly!"

They rode through the passageway, barely making it through. Elgin's feet scraped on the buildings' sides. The roar of the townsfolk filled his head. They emerged onto the next street, but many of the townsfolk were already there waiting for them. A man bolted towards Elgin, brandishing a wooden club. Elgin shot him in the head.

"Fucking maniacs!" Abernathy said, shooting a skinny woman rushing towards him, holding a scythe.

The swarms had now blocked both ends of the street, and more townsfolk spilled out of the buildings and passageways, flowing like oil, intent on the two riders. Elgin unleashed his shotgun, cutting down droves of crazies with hot buckshot. Blood stained the ground beneath them. Ribbons of red upon the dirt. Death-screams filled the air. The swarms closed in on all sides. Abernathy was firing his automatic rifle into the masses, cutting them down. Elgin did the same with the shotgun, dropping many of the townsfolk. But they kept coming, fuelled by some supernatural or insane urge.

Elgin's shotgun clicked empty. His horse cried out as a woman plunged a knife into its side. Elgin kicked away the woman, producing his twin pistols, and he shot her in the neck; she went down clutching her throat. He marked his targets, taking them down with the efficiency of a seasoned hunter.

Two men grabbed at his horse, trying to drag it to the ground. Elgin turned, put a bullet into each man's brain, but not before they'd pulled the horse off-balance. More people slashed at the horse with knives and rusty tools. A girl no older than fourteen cut Elgin's thigh with a jagged piece of glass. Elgin pistol-whipped her across the face, breaking her nose. She wheeled away, blood seeping through her fingers as she covered her face.

The horse went down.

As Elgin was thrown to the ground he saw the same happen to Abernathy. Elgin punched and kicked at anyone that rushed at him, but it was a losing battle. He holstered his pistols and took out his hunting knife and tomahawk that'd been strapped to his legs. Manic, wide-eyed faces crowded him. Blades cut at him. Blunt weapons battered his head and shoulders. Fingernails raked his skin. Rotten teeth bit at exposed flesh. The stink of unwashed bodies enveloped him. He hacked blindly with his knife and tomahawk, as if he was cutting his way through an overgrown sea of vines and weeds. Blood splattered upon him, partially blinding him. He tasted it in his mouth. He screamed as he ended lives with the keen edge of the tomahawk, slicing-open skulls and severing heads from bodies.

"Grenade!" shouted Abernathy. Elgin was ready. Abernathy always kept a grenade on his person in case they fell into a *really* dire situation. Elgin flung himself to the ground and covered his ears.

The explosion was deafening. Shrapnel flew in every direction, slicing through flesh and bone. When Elgin stood up, he saw many dead and injured. His ears rang. This was his chance. His heart sank when he realised Abernathy was dead.

He stumbled away, clearing a path through the mob. His horse was torn to pieces as the demented townsfolk recovered and swamped the poor animal. He had loved that horse.

Somehow he barged his way through the insane hordes, hacking at anything in his way. Men, women and children fell to the knife and the tomahawk. Multiple cuts, bite-marks and wounds marked Elgin's body.

An old man with withered arms and a cleft palate attacked him with a pitchfork. Elgin parried the man's feeble attack then disembowelled him in two swift moves.

But others were chasing. For each lunatic he killed, another took its place. A rabid dog launched itself towards him, bared teeth aimed for his throat. He ducked as it flew past him; when it charged back at him, he dispatched it with the tomahawk.

A woman with a crying baby wrapped in a blanket bolted towards him; she screamed at him and then threw her wailing child at him like a grenade. Elgin dodged the baby-bomb and watched it get swallowed up by the horde chasing him. The mother charged at him, and he silenced her feral screams by cutting her throat.

An awesome roar filled the air. Elgin stopped, his weapons held ready. An ancient, rusting lorry came crashing down the street, clipping buildings and mowing down townsfolk as it rampaged towards him.

The driver was waving his left hand in greeting from the cab. His face was a picture of madness. He was grinning.

The townsfolk tried to flee from the lorry, but many of them were pulverised underneath its massive wheels. Its front grille was covered in fresh blood and gore. Bones crunched and snapped underneath its massive wheels. Skulls popped like water balloons bursting.

The lorry headed straight for Elgin; he waited until the lorry was almost upon him, then he dove out of the way. He turned around to see the lorry lose its grip on the ground as it went too fast into a turning. The driver lost control. The lorry tilted onto one side, its wheels kicking up dust and dirt. A screech of metal and brakes, and the lorry careered into a group of huts and tipped over, crushing them underneath the trailer. Diesel leaked onto the ground. The driver was screaming. The wheels continued to spin even as the lorry lay stricken.

Elgin stood up, aching and hurting from bites and cuts and bruises.

The lorry exploded, sending Elgin and the townsfolk sprawling, knocked down by the blast.

Elgin got to his feet, quickly, and watched the tall plume of smoke rise into the air. The lorry was an inferno. Heat on his face from the fire. He could smell burning metal and fuel. What remained of the townsfolk regained their 'senses' and returned their attention to Elgin; he faced them, daring them to come at him. He twirled the tomahawk, flashing them a grim smile. Many of the townsfolk were dead or injured, bleeding and broken, cradling shattered limbs and crushed bodies. They wailed in pain.

They ran at Elgin; he turned and fled down the street towards the burning lorry. The horde screamed for his blood. He was flagging, his limbs growing tired. His heart felt like it wanted to burst through his chest. His vision blurred and swayed. He glanced back just in time to see a man closing on him with a claw hammer. Elgin stabbed the man in the stomach, and the man fell down clutching his guts.

As soon as the man was dispatched, an elderly woman with a harpoon gun hobbled out onto the street. She fired and the lethal projectile flew towards Elgin, skimming the top of his head as he dove and rolled to evade it. The woman was thrown backwards by the harpoon gun's kick, falling onto her backside.

Elgin kept running. The lorry driver, a screaming, stumbling figure of flame, bolted towards him from the inferno that had been the crashed vehicle. Elgin dodged the burning man, kicking him away. He fell back into the flames. He stopped screaming.

Elgin rounded the corner onto another street.

There was a small church ahead at the end of the street. Salvation loomed teasingly. Elgin used the last of his energy to stumble towards it, kicking his legs hard and praying the door wasn't locked. A house of God might protect against the evil pursuing him.

He slammed into the door, and it opened. He shut it and shot the bolt just as the horde crashed into it, snarling and cursing him. He managed to push one of the wooden pews against the door. It wouldn't hold for long. He fought to control his breathing. The shotgun was lost. The blood of those he'd killed mixed with his own, dripping from his clothes. His hands were bloody and covered in tiny scraps of human flesh. He took in deep breaths of stale air as he surveyed the church's interior. It was a humble place of worship. Candles burned in the corners. Crude depictions of the Jesus-Man watched him from the walls. Elgin sighed, dropping to his knees and finding some comfort in such simple things, even as the townsfolk hammered and clawed at the door. He prayed for salvation, and he prayed for Abernathy's soul. He cursed the hordes outside. If he had enough bullets he'd wipe them all out.

"Welcome," a voice said from the altar area at the front of the pews. A voice he recognised.

Two men emerged from the shadows: the town's priest, a short man with his eyes removed from their sockets. The other man was the outlaw Enoch Lime. He was emaciated, white-haired and dark-eyed. He looked more like a lizard than a man.

"Greetings, Mr. Elgin," Lime said, smiling a rotten smile.

Elgin stood up, gripping his weapons. "Enoch Lime."

Lime's smile didn't falter. "So you've met the people of this fine town?"

Elgin grunted. "Yeah, they're real friendly."

"I take it Abernathy didn't survive…"

"You'd be correct in assuming that."

"Such a shame. We could've used him." Lime closed his eyes, and they moved underneath his eyelids. The hordes outside stopped banging on the door.

"What the fuck's happened here, Lime? You have something to do with this?"

Lime opened his eyes. He held out his hands, palms upwards, and shrugged his shoulders. "It wasn't me, Elgin."

"Then who was it?"

"Something more powerful than anything you've faced before."

"What's that supposed to mean?"

"Look above you."

Elgin looked up at the church's ceiling, where a shadowy mass lurked and writhed, its black tendrils dancing in the air. It was like oil and smoke combined, covering the entire ceiling. He could feel the dark entity groping at his mind, searching for secrets and memories.

While Elgin was distracted, the eyeless priest charged towards him, a knife held between bony fingers. Elgin looked away from the shadow-thing just in time to evade the blade arrowing for his throat. He countered by kicking the priest in the knee; there was a sharp crack. The priest cried out and fell down. He thrashed the knife through the air; Elgin batted the blade away and then stabbed the priest in the chest. The priest let out a shallow breath, almost as if he was relieved, and went limp, slumping to the floor. Elgin put his foot on the man's body and pulled out the knife.

Lime was clapping his hands. "Very good, Elgin. But you have no idea what you're up against. You're in the presence of something magnificent."

"That thing on the ceiling?" Elgin said, wiping his weapons clean on the dead priest's garments. "Don't look too magnificent to me."

"It is the Root," Lime said. "The wrecker of civilisations. The source of every corrupt soul upon this earth."

"Bullshit," said Elgin.

Lime's grin was unnatural. "It is the Root of All Evil. He is a god."

"That thing's not a god."

"You're wrong," said Lime. "I used to be like you, trudging blindly through the dark, worshipping a false deity…but now I'm enlightened. I've seen the wonders and miracles of the Root. I am its messenger and prophet. I will help us into a new age. A new order. It converted this entire town in hours, Elgin. There is no limit to its power."

"So what about the people hung up on ropes?"

"They were non-believers. They didn't have the required faith. So we dealt with them."

"You mean they were immune to the Root's corruption?"

"In a way, yes," said Lime. "Now it's time for you to be… judged. My lord has given me free reign to do with you what I like."

Elgin noticed Lime's right hand drifting behind his back.

Just as Lime snatched the pistol and drew it, Elgin threw the tomahawk; it flew through the air and embedded in Lime's forehead, almost slicing his head into two parts. Lime's pistol fired, and the bullet caught Elgin in the face, blowing away the right side of his jaw. Both men fell simultaneously, only one of them breathing. Elgin cried out, his hands trying to stem the flow of blood from his face. He breathed in fast, shallow gasps. Several broken teeth fell from the hole in his face. The pain was unbearable. He shut his eyes and concentrated, willing himself to fight the pain, to control it.

The hordes began hammering on the door again.

The Root crept towards him, gliding down the walls like fog. Elgin grabbed the knife. He rested it against his throat. His pulse quickened under the cold blade.

Then he stopped.

The Root was inside his mind, searching and probing. It descended on him like a bird-of-prey. It found memories of his family.

"Leave me alone," Elgin said.

The Root's black tendrils caressed his skin, soothing him. He thought about his dead wife and daughter.

The Root spoke to him, its voice a softly-sung lullaby.

It'll be all right, Elgin. Everything will be all right. Its voice reminded him of his mother. *I admire you, Elgin. You are strong. You are a man of faith. You are stronger than Enoch Lime ever was.*

The pain in Elgin's face faded a little. The Root's insipid influence touched his mind, whispering sweet promises and rewards.

"What do you want from me?"

I want you to be my prophet and my messenger. I will heal you and you will live a very long life in my new kingdom. You will replace Enoch Lime. You will help me rule this land. Humanity will have a new god.

There was a pause to let the words sink in.

Will you worship me, Elgin? In return you will see your wife and daughter again. I promise this to you. Your god took them away, but I can bring them back to you. You'll never be alone again.

Two figures were now standing over him. He smiled at them. His wife and his daughter smiled back at him. His face didn't hurt anymore. He felt no pain. They had returned for him. They weren't really dead, were they? He was confused. If he could get them back, then everything would be alright again. Life would be good and peaceful, and he could give up being a bounty hunter. They'd go home and be a family again.

That's right, Elgin. Everything will be alright. I'll make sure of that.

Then the pain returned, and things became clear. His family was dead, and they were in the ground. Bones and dust. The cholera had taken his daughter. His wife had shot herself not long after.

He laughed to himself, bitterly.

What's so funny, Elgin? Do I amuse you?

"It amuses me that you think I'd fall for some cheap mind-trick. That isn't my family; they're waiting for me in another place. I'll meet them again. You can't convert me."

No, Elgin, don't be irrational.

"Sorry," he said. "But fuck you."

No!

Elgin drew the knife across his throat, creating a crimson smile. He cut deep through skin, muscle and flesh, severing his windpipe. The pain was intense but fleeting, and the life seeped out of him as his blood spilled onto the floor around his body. He let out a low gurgle as he slipped into the darkness.

And he died smiling.

SHANGHAI ED

WAYNE C. ROGERS

Shanghai Ed Kulczynski could still hear the distant sound of gunshots as the current of the Yangtze River carried him further away from the tramp steamer. Though he couldn't make out the *Lady Jenna* through the thick fog, he could still see the occasional flashes of gunfire and knew everyone aboard the ship was being massacred.

Unable to wrap his mind around the unbelievable events, Ed concentrated on holding onto the life preserver with his good arm, knowing the river would suck him under if he lost his grip. He had to get as far away from the ship as possible. Certain death was behind him and life was ahead, beckoning to him like a siren calling forth to her lover. It was the unexpected sound of a small outboard engine that forced Ed to face his present situation. The *creatures*, or whatever they were, couldn't allow him to escape.

They were coming after him.

Throwing his injured arm over the old preserver, he began to paddle his feet beneath the water, heading to where he thought the north shore was. It was difficult to tell with the fog surrounding him. Still, he'd been a seafaring man for over twenty years and knew the sound running water makes when close to land. There was also the fact that if he wanted to stay alive, he had to reach the river's bank before the boat got to him. He wouldn't have a chance if they caught him in the water. To keep his mind off of how tired and scared he was, Ed allowed his thoughts to gradually return to the steamer and what had happened twenty minutes ago.

*

It had been after midnight when Ed had come off his six-hour watch. He'd been guarding the precious cargo in the bay area of the steamer and was now ready to relax and get something to eat.

He knew the captain of the steamer was transporting weapons and ammunition to the Marxist rebels in the west of China. It was a quick way to make a lot of money, unless you encountered the soldiers of the Kuomintang political party, who were fighting the rebels for the control of the mainland. And, if that wasn't enough, there were also the river pirates who found the steamers and other boats going up and down the river easy prey. They were more dangerous than Chiang Kai-shek's soldiers because they didn't take prisoners. The pirates had developed the ugly habit of killing anyone aboard a captured boat to insure a lack of witnesses.

Once Ed had been relieved of his station, he'd gone down to the galley to get some ham and scrambled eggs. He had just sat down at the table and had been in the process of sticking a forkful of eggs into his mouth when he'd heard the sound of gunfire coming from the main deck. Ed forgot to put his fork down as he jumped up from his seat, rushing to get topside and see what was happening. As he ran up the narrow flight of stairs, he shifted the fork to his left hand and used his right to pull out the Colt .45 caliber semi-automatic pistol at his side. Ed had fought the Japanese during World War II and wasn't afraid of any river pirates. He was ready to kick ass and take names. When he exited the final hatchway and stepped out onto the main deck, however, what he saw caused him to stop in mid-step and to stare in total disbelief. There appeared to be

Chinese men dressed up in old coolie outfits, attacking the crew in a ferocious battle of life and death.

The problem was the attackers looked like men, but weren't.

The inhumanity of the creatures was apparent to Ed as he saw their blood-red eyes and the huge incisors inside their mouths and the long, pointed claws at the end of their fingers. They were what the Chinese referred to as *chiang-shih.* Ed had heard the legends of them on and off for years, but had never given the myth much credence. Every country around the world had its tales of demons, hobgoblins, werewolves, and vampires.

China was no different.

He saw the *creatures* had tremendous amounts of strength, enabling them to tear off the arms and heads of the men defending the ship. The whole scene was like a shark-feeding frenzy as the attackers screamed out with ear-piercing voices. They were murdering the men Ed had worked with as if the tough seafarers were nothing but a bunch of Cub Scouts being offered up for the slaughter. One man got his face ripped off with a fast sweep of a clawed hand. Another mariner had his arm pulled right out of its socket and thrown across the deck like a bare chicken bone.

Ed was so preoccupied with the carnage he failed to notice the *chiang-shih* coming up on him from the side. It was only the creature's loud child-like scream that saved him. Whirling around with the speed of a man half his age, he acted out of pure reflex and stuck the fork into the creature's right eye with his hand. The *thing* howled in rage. This gave Ed the time he needed to aim the .45 and put three rounds into the dreaded vampire's chest.

To Ed's surprise the bullets had little effect on it.

"*Shit!*" Ed said as he fired two more shots, but this time into the *chiang-shih's* face. The two .45 slugs ripped into the creature's fact and exploded out the back of its head, but the horrifying thing still didn't go down.

Shanghai Ed knew he was going to die if he didn't think of something pretty damn quick.

That thought was replaced with a sudden wave of pain shooting through his left arm and shoulder. Spinning around, he saw another creature with blood on its extended hand. It had raked those sharp claws down Ed's left side, cutting open his khaki shirt and tearing the flesh to the bone. He fired the last two rounds into the second *chiang-shih's* face. Then, placing the handgun back into its holster, he high-tailed it across the deck, dodging another creature and trying to think of a way out of this mess.

Tripping over the foot of a dead crew member, Ed hit the deck with the side of his face and had the breath literally knocked out of him. He lay there for a moment, trying to get this his thoughts back together. That was when he noticed the dead man's machete lying three feet away. Scurrying over to it like sand fiddler, he wrapped his fingers around the handle of the edged weapon and managed to get back up as a creature charged him like a wild demon from hell. Ed swung the machete and cut off one of the creature's extended hands.

The vampire stopped to stare in surprise at its bleeding stump.

Ed swung the machete again, this time putting some spit into it. He cut the vampire's head halfway off. It hung loosely from the creature's neck by a thick piece of flesh with its one good eye still open and blinking rapidly. Its long pointed tongue was darting outward as if searching for something tasty to eat. Ed hit the creature one last time and sent its decapitated head sailing through the air with its braided pigtail flying behind like tail end of a kite.

"You don't screw around with Shanghai Ed," he said, looking around for another *chiang-shih* to kill. He saw three of the bastards converging upon him and decided it was time for a swim. "To hell with this shit."

Throwing the machete at one of them, Ed took off toward the railing of the ship. He grabbed one of the life preservers and jumped out into mid-space, falling forty feet to the cold, dark water below. The force of the impact stunned him, and he nearly lost his grip on the preserver. He managed to keep his hold on the flotation device and then pushed his way from the ship, not wanting to be drawn into the rear propellers. That was when he saw a number of junks, floating alongside the steamer. There were more creatures standing on them and one was staring directly at him.

Ed gave the vampire the middle finger and then started swimming away from the steamer as fast as he could.

*

Ed's mind drifted slowly back to the present and his immediate dilemma. He could tell the motorboat was closer. Though he was attempting to be quiet, it seemed as if the creatures knew exactly where he was. Maybe they could hear him paddling his feet. It was either that, or they could smell the scent of his blood in the water. The real question was whether or not to release his hold on the preserver and take a chance at swimming to shore without it. He knew the north bank of the Yangtze wasn't far away. Ed thought he could make it even with the wound. He was strong for his age and had the endurance of a thirty-year old. There was also a possibility that if he released the preserver and allowed it to continue down river, the creatures would follow it and *not* him.

He weighed the odds.

Releasing his hold on the preserver, Ed used the strength in his legs to keep moving through the water toward the shoreline. He kept as much of his body beneath the surface as was humanly possible, breathing in and out through his nose so he wouldn't draw any attention. He listened as the sound of the outboard motor shifted direction and moved away from him, heading west.

So far, so good, he thought.

He kept moving toward shore, breathing in deeply through his nose, pacing himself so he wouldn't lose his strength.

Ten minutes must have passed when he got water up his nose. This led to a frantic fit of hacking and coughing, which caused the boat to change its course.

"*Damn,*" Ed said.

He started swimming harder, determined to make it to shore before he was caught.

The heart-pounding swim took ten more minutes, and Ed was exhausted by the time he crawled out of the water and up the muddy bank to what he hoped was safety. He lay there for a minute on his back, unable to move. It was the sound of the approaching boat that spurred him to action. Turning over and rising hesitantly to his feet, he made his way up the bank to a grassy knoll that overlooked the Yangtze. He couldn't see much in the darkness, except for some thick brush and a few small, scattered trees. Heading north, Ed began to run as quickly as he could.

*

The journey inland turned out to be more grueling than he'd expected. Ed was stumbling and falling and cursing to himself as he made his way through the surrounding brush, listening to the sound of his trackers closing in. They'd made it to shore and had come after him with a vengeance, wanting to put an end to this drawn-out chase. Ed wasn't about to give up. That, of course, was the exact moment he tripped over an exposed root in the ground and fell face first, hitting his forehead on a sizeable rock.

The blow knocked him out.

When Ed came to several minutes later, he could hear the sound of voices whispering to each other in the night. Still groggy from the blow, he stifled a moan and reached around to the left side of his belt, pulling out the fishing knife he always carried with him. The voices were speaking Chinese, and it took him a moment for his mind to translate the words back into English.

The voices belonged to Kuomintang soldiers, *not* vampires!

Their outpost had been notified about the attack on the steamer up river, and they'd been told, as others had, to check the shoreline for river pirates. The soldiers weren't happy about having to trek a mile in the middle of the night.

Ed knew he wasn't off the hook. If the soldiers got him, they'd put his ass in prison or maybe shoot him.

Staying still and not making a sound, he watched as eight soldiers in uniform walked past him. All the men were carrying rifles with bayonets at the end, except for the officer who was trailing behind. He had a .38 caliber Webly revolver in his hand and a Japanese *katana* hanging upside down from the leather belt around his waist.

Ed knew what a katana was.

He'd seen what the Japanese could do with it during the war and the bloody battle in Shanghai. He'd developed an unconscious admiration for them and their fighting skills with a sword.

His eyes followed the back of the Chinese officer, wondering how he'd come into possession of such a weapon. That was when it dawn on Ed that the long sword could be a means to his survival. He'd already seen what a machete could do, and a katana was ten times better. The challenge, however, was getting possession of the sword without being shot or captured.

After the squad of soldiers had passed, heading toward the river, Ed rose quietly to his feet and followed them. He

106

suspected the soldiers were about to run head-on into the vampires. If that happened, he might have a chance to grab the sword. He decided to stay twenty feet behind, watching and waiting for the attack to take place.

It did a few minutes later.

Ed saw three vampires erupt from the surrounding darkness and attack the soldiers from both sides. The eight men were caught off guard and weren't able to react fast enough to keep the creatures from tearing into them with a ferocity that was terrifying to watch. Two of the enlisted men managed to get off a shot with their rifle, and the officer emptied the chambers of his six-shot revolver. Though Ed had already seen the speed and capability of the vampires, he was still amazed at how swiftly they could kill a group of men without breaking a sweat.

Lowering his body to the ground, he crawled at a snail's pace to the dead Chinese officer. Thankfully, the creatures were busy lapping up the blood from the other bodies. Only one raised its head as if it sensed *something* in the vicinity.

Ed froze where he was.

He knew not to move with those red eyes glaring in his direction, searching for anything that meant danger to the group. The creature stared for a full minute before it returned to its feeding. Ed swallowed hard and then reached around the waist of the officer and felt for the two metal clasps hooking the sword's scabbard to the belt. He found them and unfastened the sheath. Then, holding the prize to his chest, he eased back into the darkness, inching his body through the tall grass.

When he was far enough away, Ed rose to his feet and carefully removed the razor-sharp sword from its wooden scabbard. He slid the scabbard down the back of his belt so he wouldn't lose it, and then began to walk back to where the vampires were feasting, carrying the sword in his right hand.

He wanted to catch them off guard. The element of surprise would make the difference in whether or not he survived the confrontation. He circled around the three creatures as he placed the top edge of the sword across his right shoulder.

It's now or never, Ed thought.

He took a deep breath and charged into the group like a maniac needing his medication in an insane asylum. As the first *chaing-shih* lifted its head to see what was going on, Ed decapitated him with one swing of the sword. He didn't wait to see the results, but instead spun around and brought the sword back up so he could cut through another creature's outstretched arm.

The third *chiang-shih* was almost on top of him.

Not having enough time to bring the katana back but for a swing, Ed drove the point of the sword straight into the front of the creature's neck. Pulling the blade from the body, he spun around to face the second vampire. He cut off the creature's head while it was still focused on the missing arm.

Two down and one to go!

The third vampire hissed as it attempted to staunch the flow of blood from its neck.

"You're not going anywhere," Ed said.

He rushed the vampire and then dropped low, swinging the katana at its left ankle, severing the foot from the leg. The creature gave out a howl of pain, but it was cut short as Shanghai Ed rose back up and whirled around, taking off its head with one swift stroke.

The battle was over.

Ed stood there in the middle of the dead bodies, breathing heavily, finding it difficult to believe he was still alive.

"It's time to get out of here," he said to himself. Placing the sword back into its scabbard, he walked back to the river.

An hour later, Shanghai Ed was heading down the Yangtze in the vampire's boat. The fog was already starting to dissipate and by daybreak it would be gone. Ed needed to pull into a town along the river and have his left arm and shoulder examined by a decent doctor.

Luckily, Panzhihua was only three miles away.

*

As the early morning sun arose on the horizon, Shanghai Ed smiled for the first time in several hours as he steered the small craft toward the busy docks of Panzhihua. The boat people along the river were already up and about, washing clothes and cooking food in their woks. The docks were alive with workers unloading cargo from the steamers in port. Ed passed a medium-sized junk with four Chinese men on board. Standing at the bow, however, was a Caucasian male wearing a brown fedora, khaki pants and shirt, and a brown leather bomber jacket. The man nodded at Ed as they passed each other. Ed smiled back, thinking he knew the stranger from somewhere.

Once Ed was on dry land, it took him an hour to find a hospital and to get his arm and shoulder stitched up. Afterwards, he still had enough money left to rent a hotel room for a week. He used the time to rest and to heal his body. Ed also needed time to decide what he was going to do next. Did he want to return to Shanghai or find some work on the river?

He didn't know.

Checking the daily newspaper everyday for information about the *Lady Jenna,* he discovered the authorities knew little about the incident. Another article he came across told about an American archaeologist who was excavating the tomb of China's first emperor. There was a picture of the professor in the paper, and Ed recognized him as the man from the junk. He didn't know a lot about archaeology or excavating old tombs, but maybe there was work to be had. It wouldn't be hard to get a ride back up the river and to locate the professor. In fact, it would be nice to have a job that wasn't stressful or dangerous for once.

STUFFED INNOCENCE

INDY McDANIEL

Ritchie Dunn found the stuffed bear in the dumpster behind the Pump'n'Gulp. It wasn't edible and it reeked of waste and puke, but it sent a spark of happiness through the homeless young man's heart. "It's perfect," he muttered, wiping at one of the more questionable stains that adorned the bear's matted fur. He clambered out of the dumpster, nearly taking a dive into the side of the building, and started down the dark alley. He forgot about his rumbling gut, focused on the ruined stuffed animal he cradled in his arms.

The bear was brown. Or at least it had been originally. There were too many stains on it now to tell. A smear of chewing gum was stuck behind one of its ears. The stitching around its ass was coming loose, allowing some of the stuffing to push free. The bear had seen better days. Far better days.

"Lenore's gonna love you," he said to the bear, tickling its black button nose. The bear didn't offer a response, just stared back at its savior with lifeless glass eyes. Ritchie tucked the bear under his arm and picked up his pace. If he hurried, he could get to the club before Lenore got off.

*

Lenore DiCamillo lit up a cigarette and took a much needed drag. Her skin sheened with drying sweat and body glitter. The crowd tonight was shit. It wasn't surprising. Wednesdays were usually pretty terrible. *You'd figure Hump Day would attract more people to a strip club*, she thought. She tapped some ash on the floor and took a nice, long look at herself in the half-mirror she sat in front of.

She wasn't the typical silicone-enhanced stripper. Maybe that was why she kept getting the Wednesday night shifts while that bitch Busty got primetime slots on Friday night despite being the washed up whore that she was. Her light brown hair was pulled into a ponytail that ran down the length of her back. She had a petite frame but she wasn't anorexic skinny. Multi-colored nipple tassels adorned her small breasts. She didn't have much in the chest department, but she knew how to make the tassels swing tantalizingly enough to pay her rent.

As long as I get something better than a damn Hump Day gig before the first of the month, she thought with a hint of bitterness. Her one-bedroom apartment was a shit hole but at least it was a place to live. Not everyone in Ever Falls was so lucky. She knew that well enough. Her thoughts turned to Ritchie and she felt a blend of frustration and pity. He wasn't much older than she was and already he'd been dealt a nice, steaming shit sandwich of a life. It didn't help that he was hopelessly nuts.

Lenore stubbed out her cigarette and immediately lit up another. Why she'd thought dating a homeless schizophrenic would work out, she had no idea. She'd tried to deal with him and it had actually been working for a while. Once she'd managed to get him past his terror of water and coaxed him into the shower, he'd even made a fairly decent live-in boyfriend. He cooked – surprisingly well, all things considered – and that wasn't a trait to be disregarded in a prospective mate.

He'd been a blast in bed.

Lenore smiled sadly as the memories of their wild hijinks fluttered through her mind. If she focused long enough on the good parts of their relationship, the bad stuff didn't seem so

112

bad.

Except it had been.

Despite his normally sweet persona, Ritchie was still nuts. It varied. From the mostly benign to the potentially lethal. Trying to get her panties off the ceiling after he super-glued them up there had been a pain in the ass – Ritchie seemed to think that's where they were supposed to go – but it was nothing compared to waking up with him holding a steak knife to her throat, screaming about how she was trying to replace his blood with Mr. Bubbles.

Sixteen stitches and a new pack of underwear later and she'd sent Ritchie packing. A better person would have tried to get him some kind of help. At least, that's what Lenore told herself on her downer days. Her rationalization was that she could barely take care of herself. Between rent, bills, food, her drug habit, and the meagre savings she optimistically referred to as her 'college fund', Lenore wasn't exactly flush with cash.

Beyond that, Lenore wasn't exactly mentally stable herself. She wasn't nearly as bad as Ritchie, but her bipolar moods swung from high to low at the drop of a hat. The drugs helped. Her job didn't. Dealing with sweaty douche-bags cat-calling to her as she shook her ass and wiggled her tassels into the wee hours of the night didn't do any wonders for her self-esteem.

No, Ritchie could take care of himself. He'd been doing it before she came along and he could do it again now. Lenore stubbed out the second cigarette and checked her watch. She still had another performance before she could clock out for the night. Fifteen minutes of gratuitous nudity and sticky portraits of George Washington slipped into the waistband of her G-string.

Lenore stood and slipped into her outfit. She took a final look in the mirror. "Time to get your ass out there and make your daddy proud."

*

"I'm tired, Ritchie," Lenore grumbled, fiddling the key into her scooter's ignition. She finished strapping the half-helmet onto her head. "I just wanna go home, take a shower, and crash."

"But I've got this," Ritchie said, holding the soiled teddy bear out to her. "It's for you."

Lenore gave the bear a dubious look. "You shouldn't have. And I really mean that. It looks like it's covered in puke."

"No," Ritchie shook his head. "Not puke." He sniffed it, barely reacting to the stink coming off of the stuffed toy. "No, that's not puke. Just old food. Some soda." He gave the bear a second sniff. "Someone may have peed on it."

"And you want me to have it?" Lenore said with disgust. "Look, I know our relationship could've ended on better terms, but this is just ridiculous. Why don't you just tell me to fuck off and be done with it?"

Ritchie's face constricted and he squeezed his eyes shut as he tried to organize his disjointed thoughts. "It's not like that. It's nice, see? It's like I won it for you at a carnival."

"Except it didn't come from any damn carnival," Lenore shot back. His persistence was getting annoying. Her muscles ached with fatigue and she desperately wanted to wash the stink of the strip club off of her body. She did not want to waste half the remaining night arguing with Ritchie fucking Dunn in an alley. She sighed. "Fine, gimme the stupid bear."

Ritchie grinned widely and handed it to her. Lenore looked it over and tried to fight the urge to be sick. She snagged a plastic bag off the ground and wrapped the bear in it before shoving it into her backpack. "We good now? Can I go home?"

"Can I come with?" he asked, hope in his eyes.

"No," Lenore told him. "Dammit, Ritchie, we've been over

114

this. You can't stay with me anymore. My theoretical health insurance won't cover it."

It took a few moments for that to register with the homeless man. He looked sad but still a bit hopeful. "That's okay. It's a start. I'll get you some flowers." He started surveying the alley, trying to spot anything that might pass for a bouquet. Thankfully for Lenore, there wasn't anything close to floral in the alley.

"Alright, you go do that," she said, firing up the scooter. "I'm gonna go home now." Ritchie nodded, his attention still focused on finding her the flowers. Lenore felt a pang of sadness. "Look, Ritchie, you take care of yourself, okay? Find yourself someplace warm to hunker down. I heard we're in for a rough winter."

"Right," Ritchie responded, still not really paying attention to her. He turned away and pretended to search behind a dumpster so she wouldn't see the tears in his eyes. He offered her a wave. "I'll see you tomorrow."

"I don't work tomorrow."

Ritchie didn't respond.

Lenore sighed and headed for home.

*

Lenore took the plastic bag out of her backpack. She unwrapped the dirty bear and looked it over. It might have been pretty once, but that had been a long time ago. *Goddammit, Ritchie*, she thought. She carried the bear over to the trash can, intending to get rid of it. She paused just before dropping it into the bin, staring into the bear's glassy eyes. The bear stared back.

In a depressingly sick way, the bear was a good representation of Ritchie and their doomed relationship. Hell, it wasn't even a bad representation of herself. She'd been

115

pretty once, too. Still was by certain standards, but life had worn away at her, if not in a physical sense then definitely mentally and emotionally. Letting out a tired sigh, she decided to try and salvage the bear.

She snipped out the dried gum and stitched up its ass then threw it into the washing machine. She dumped two full caps of detergent onto the bear then flipped the settings over to use hot water. Even then, she doubted it would kill all the bacteria dancing around in the stuffed animal's fur. She started the washing machine and went to take a shower. When she came back out, the machine had stopped. She took the soggy bear out and tossed it into the dryer then went to survey the food situation.

Lenore popped a couple vicodin while she waited for the water to boil so she could make the pack of ramen noodles she'd found at the back of the cupboard. She'd have to go shopping at some point. She counted through the wrinkled bills that made up her paycheck of the evening. Just under two-hundred bucks. Not a bad haul for a Wednesday night. She didn't work again till Sunday afternoon. Surprisingly, Sunday afternoons brought in a decent crowd at the club. Plenty of people fresh out of church and ready to rack up some fresh sins.

Maybe things wouldn't be so bad this month.

She poured the boiling water over the noodles and waited for them to soften up before sprinkling the small back of seasoning over the bowl. It was beef flavor. She hated beef flavor. It explained why the pack had been hiding in the back of the cupboard, covered in a thick layer of dust. She felt the pain meds kicking in about halfway through her meal. The aches and pains running up her back dissipated, but didn't drop away completely. She considered upping her dose.

The bowl of soggy noodles grew cold, only half-eaten, and Lenore was well into her vicodin buzz when the grating buzz

116

of the dryer drew her out of her mental lingering. She blinked slowly, trying to remember what the sound signified. "Oh, shit."

Lenore stumbled out of the rickety chair and over to the small dryer. She popped the lid open and pulled Ritchie's gift out. It was still stained and looked like it had been run over by a semi, but it wasn't nearly as disgusting as it had been. Even the rank odor seemed to have faded, for the most part.

"My crazy ex-boyfriend, the romantic sap," Lenore muttered.

She went to bed.

She took the bear with.

*

Ritchie laid out the collection of dead foliage he'd found. To a casual observer, it would look like a cornucopia of old clippings from a gardener's trash bin. To Ritchie, it was probably the most beautiful bouquet of flowers ever imagined in the civilized world. He had no doubt that Lenore would love it. She'd take him back. Finally.

He arranged the 'flowers' and then re-arranged them, trying to decide what order they looked best in. When he was satisfied, he wrapped them in a sheet of wrinkled newspaper and shoved the whole thing into his jacket pocket. Dead leaves fluttered from the bouquet, unnoticed by the homeless man.

Ritchie checked his wrist and remembered he didn't have a watch. He squinted up into the sunlight. It didn't help him gauge what time it was and after a few moments, his head started to hurt. He looked away, blinking the dark spots from his vision. He had to find Lenore and give her the bouquet.

Starting towards the main road, Ritchie felt a wave of nausea hit him. "No," he gasped, clutching his stomach as the world turned grey. "Not now. I'm busy." He stumbled as the bricks under his feet shifted awkwardly. His shoulder collided with the wall of the adjacent building and a spark of pain shot through him. He dropped to his knees and squeezed his eyes shut, trying to will the episode away.

It didn't work.

Ritchie's eyes snapped open. The bright day became overcast in his vision. The world around him seemed to grow taller and loomed over him, pressing in with claustrophobic oppression. He pushed to his feet and scrambled for the alley's exit. As he reached it, the ground cracked open. The bricks grated against each other, sending a cloud of dust into his eyes. Ritchie coughed and tried to wave the dust away.

Spreading from one end of the alley to the other, the ground formed a jagged grin of brick and mortar. Fiery light flickered deep within the ground's maw and it laughed at him with the sound of brick scrapping against brick. Ritchie let out a terrified shriek and spun on his heel, rushing back into the alley. He spotted a row of dumpsters and pushed himself in between two of them, squeezing his skinny, emaciated form between the hard steel.

Ritchie pushed his head between his knees and rocked back and forth, sobbing. At some point, he wasn't sure exactly when, he'd pissed himself. The bitter stench of urine assaulted his nostrils, overpowering in the tight confines between the dumpsters, but he didn't dare move out. He heard things moving out in the alley. Sick, slippery things sliding along the ground, whispering hateful threats as they searched for him.

It's raining, it's pouring, you're gonna be dead in the morning, hissed one of the voices in an eerie sing-song tone.

Ritchie pounded his fists against his temples, trying to force the lurking monstrosities away.

You and your little stripper, too, another of the voices chuckled.

Thursday night was pizza night.

Lenore ordered her usual. Large, thin crust, with extra cheese and extra anchovies. She loved the salty little fish. They used to drive Ritchie crazy. Well, crazier. After a couple pizza nights gone awry with Ritchie trying to set the anchovies free by peeling them off the pizza and flushing them down her toilet, she'd started ordering him his own pie. Small, hand-tossed, with mushrooms and olives.

Lenore shuddered at the thought. Who the hell wanted fungi on their pizza? Mushrooms grossed her out. She didn't even enjoy the magical variety. She'd given them a chance, but after screaming at a crack in the wall for two hours about how it owed her back rent – an argument she'd lost – and then curling into a fetal position in her bathtub, humming songs from the Lion King, she'd decided they weren't for her.

Lenore popped a vicodin, lit up a cigarette, and waited for her pizza to arrive. Her eyes fell on the dishevelled bear Ritchie had given her. It still looked like shit. She still thought it deserved to be chucked head-first into the nearest dumpster. And she still couldn't bring herself to do it. For all his faults, Ritchie actually wasn't so bad.

She wasn't crazy enough to give him a second chance in the relationship department, but if he was still thinking about her then who the hell was she to toss out his attempt at mending the badly scorched bridge between them? The guy had enough problems without her treating him like shit.

Lenore sighed and popped another pill. She checked her watch.

Where the hell's that damn pizza?

*

It was dark.

That was the first thing Ritchie realized when he came around. At some point, he'd passed out and the sun had set.

His head throbbed, his right arm felt numb, and his mouth was dry. Something smelled of stale piss. He remembered that it was himself and sighed. He wrenched his way out from between the dumpsters and rubbed his arm until the feeling returned. He smacked his lips, re-moisturizing them, and looked around the alley.

No monsters, no laughing hole in the ground, no more crazy. He felt relieved. Despite the pain in his head, his mind felt clearer, more focused. That's usually how it worked after an episode. Whatever was wrong with him, it just seemed to build and build until it overwhelmed him and then when it was all over, it receded back into the depths of his mind and waited patiently as it regained strength.

Ritchie pulled the battered bouquet from his pocket and looked it over. It hadn't dealt with being crammed into the tight confines very well, but he thought Lenore would still be impressed.

At the thought of Lenore, a flash of his episode came back to him. The *Things* had threatened him before, plenty of times, but never anyone else. He didn't know what it meant, but he didn't like it. The collection of dried out, half-destroyed foliage fell from his hand, forgotten in an instant. He rushed out of the alley, starting towards Lenore's club before he remembered she wasn't working tonight. He spun around and headed in the opposite direction, towards her apartment complex.

*

"Why do you look so familiar?"

Lenore shoved a wrinkled twenty towards the pizza guy

standing at her door. His name tag labeled him as Ted. "Keep the change, alright?" She took the pizza and started to push the door shut but at the last moment, the pizza guy shoved his hand out and caught it. "Hey, asshole," Lenore grumbled. "A two buck tip is the best I can do. You're lucky you got that much, as long as it took you to deliver."

"You dance down at Fallen Angels, right?" he asked, a leering sparkle in his eyes. He glanced over her shoulder into the apartment then down her body. Lenore shuddered, able to feel him peeling away her clothes in his mind.

"Nope," she said firmly. "I thought about applying there once, but I didn't feel like dealing with horny pervs like you. Do you mind? The pizza's getting cold."

Ted kept his hand on the door, holding it open. He outweighed her by a good fifty pounds. Maybe more. Lenore's mind started drawing up battle plans, in case things went shitty. Chuck the pizza at him, haul ass to her bedroom, grab the revolver stashed in her nightstand, then do her best Dirty Harry impression. *Feel lucky, punk?*

"No, it's you," the pizza guy said, still eyeing her. "I'm down there most nights after work. What's the name you go by down there? Misty something, isn't it?"

"Look, goddammit," Lenore said, raising her voice. "I don't know who this chick you're pining over is, but if I was her, I wouldn't be too impressed with your attitude right now. I've had a hard fucking life and right now all I wanna do is relax and eat some fucking pizza. Ya dig?"

The pizza guy let out a disappointed sigh then shoved the door open. The move caught Lenore off guard. The edge of the door struck her just above the eyebrow and she stumbled backwards, hissing in pain. The pizza fell from her hand, the box flying open and depositing the warm slices onto the floor in a series of wet splats. Something warm trickled down Lenore's face and it took her a moment to realize it was blood.

121

"Son of a bitch!" she hissed.

"I can't stand liars." Ted moved into Lenore's apartment and shoved the door shut behind him. It slammed heavily and Lenore jumped. She tried to remember her plan of attack. Her eyes went from the asshole invading her crummy excuse for a home to the pizza lying splattered over the floor. *So much for phase one.*

Lenore turned and rushed deeper into her apartment, heading for her bedroom. She heard the pizza guy pursue, his heavy feet pounding after her. She didn't dare look back, too afraid to see how close he might be. Her heart thudded in her chest as adrenaline shot through her, putting her nerves on edge. *Shit, shit, shit, shit...*

Lenore bumped her bedroom door open with her shoulder and dove across the messy twin-size bed in the middle of the room. The thick comforter she used to keep warm in lieu of having a heater bundled up under her and she wound up tangled in the thing. The front half of her body fell off the far side of the bed while her legs remained pinned more or less together by the blanket.

"Where you running off to, whore?"

"Fuck!" Lenore hissed, reaching up to the nightstand and yanking the drawer out. The drawer pulled free of the nightstand and flipped. The snub-nosed .38 revolver flew free and sailed clear over her head, landing in the corner of the room. "Goddammit!" She scrambled for the gun but the damned comforter had her pinned. She kicked at it, trying to free her legs.

"Holy shit," Ted gasped. He went around the foot of the bed and scooped the revolver up. "You were gonna shoot me." He stared down at her with dull shock in his eyes.

"I sure as shit wasn't gonna invite you to eat dinner with me," Lenore shot back, giving up on trying to get free. Her eyes focused on the gun. What was it they said about the

122

dangers of owning a gun? That the odds were good you'd wind up having it used against you? *Well, shit, the tree-hugging hippies were finally right about something…*

Ted tossed the gun away with disgust. Lenore heard it clatter out in the hall. She felt a pang of disappointment that it hadn't gone off and sent a stray bullet into the asshole's brain. "I can't believe you were gonna shoot me!" Lenore caught a flash of sneaker as he kicked at her head.

A flash of pain and then everything cut to black.

*

Things got strange as Ritchie rode the rickety old elevator up to Lenore's apartment. The dusty bare bulb shining above flickered and then went out. A moment later and the lift came to a stuttering, screeching halt somewhere between the third and fourth floors. Ritchie stumbled and felt fear creeping up his spine. He reached out, finding the control panel for the elevator and tapping at the darkened buttons.

Nothing happened.

"Hello?" Ritchie called, hopeful that a resident might hear him.

No response.

Panic flooded through him. He wondered if a person had to be born with claustrophobia or if they could just get it. He wasn't sure, but the longer the elevator remained frozen, the more he believed it could be the latter. Cold sweat beaded on his forehead. He kept punching at the elevator's buttons, hoping it would fire back up.

Something dripped into Ritchie's hair. He jumped and put a hand to his head, feeling the moisture. He tried to see what it was, but in the dark his hand was just a dark shadow against a darker shadow. Another drip struck his forehead and rolled down his cheek, leaving an icy chill in its wake.

123

Without warning, a downpour of water washed over Ritchie from the top of the elevator. He screamed, trying to move out of the way, but in the small cube-shaped area there was no place to escape the liquid rushing over him. He crouched down into a ball and clenched his hands over his head as the water slowed and came to a drizzling stop.

Opening his eyes, he looked up to see the ceiling of the elevator was gone. In its place, an endless void stretched upwards. An eerie red light shone down from above, painting the interior of the elevator in a disturbing crimson shade. "What the hell?" Ritchie muttered, staring in awe. *This isn't right*, he thought in a surprising moment of clarity. *Something's wrong.*

Ritchie slapped himself.

It hurt.

He wasn't dreaming.

That didn't rule out another episode, but they never came on so suddenly after another had left. Maybe he was getting worse. Maybe this was life now. But even that didn't make much sense. If he was trapped in his insanity, why was he thinking so clearly? Even in his more lucid moments, Ritchie never felt this sane.

"R-r-r-ritchie…"

The soft voice elongated the first letter of his name into a low purr. He looked to the dark corner it came from. From the shadows, a figure emerged, oozing out of the elevator wall. It crawled on its elbows; head hung low, stringy hair obscuring the face. A slick black oil-like substance smeared across the thing's nude form. Jagged fingernails clicked against the floor then scrapped along it as the thing dragged itself closer to him.

Ritchie remained frozen in his corner, staring with wide-eyed horror at whatever it was inching its way across the length of the elevator. As it reached the center of the lift, it paused. Its head jerked up and it locked piercing eyes with him. The red light from above cast jagged shadows across her face, but even so, he recognized the figure.

"Lenore?"

"What's the matter, baby?" the freakish Lenore asked. She pushed herself up from the floor, revealing her nude chest to him. "Don't you like what you see?" She rubbed her hands over her small breasts, smearing the oil stuff around on her skin.

"Not to be rude, but no," Ritchie replied, although he found it hard to look away from her chest, especially when her fingers flicked against her stiff nipples. "Why are you in here?"

Lenore's face twisted into a playful smirk that looked more predatory than sweet. "I live here, silly."

"I don't mean the elevator."

The smirk dropped away as fast as it appeared. She leveled a deadly serious gaze on him. "I know."

The gaze drew his attention from her tits. He looked back, only now noticing how her eyes were devoid of the emerald sparkle they usually had. Black on black and as deep as the void stretching out above them. "You've never been in my nightmare before."

And like that, the smirk returned. Lenore's hands continued to play with herself. One dropped low, disappeared below the thick curls of her pubic hair. "Times are changin', Ritchie-Rich."

"I'd rather they didn't."

Lenore gave him an innocent, schoolgirl pout as she twisted one of her nipples back and forth. "Aw, why not?" The pout faded into a bored look. She rolled her eyes. "I mean, it's not as if you're living the dream life. Wouldn't you rather stay here, with me?" Her body jerked and swayed, moving to the beat of a silent song as she performed for him. She dropped back onto her ass and spread her legs, running her hands up the insides of her thighs before reaching their apex. "The sights I

125

could show you…"

"Stop," Ritchie said firmly, shutting his eyes and turning away. "You're not real. You're in my head. Get out. I don't want you to see this side of me, Lenore."

Lenore let out an irritated hiss. "Please, I've seen this side plenty. Remember the time I came home from work and you'd doused the entire apartment in lighter fluid? You were trying to figure out how matchsticks work and were about two strikes away from frying the both of us before I stopped you. I've been in here longer than you know."

"That was different," Ritchie argued.

"You're damn right it was," Lenore agreed. "Out there, you could hurt me. You could kill me. In here, we don't have to worry about such trivial things as mortality." She let out a throaty sigh, the one that signaled her impending climax. "C'mon, Ritchie," she pleaded. "Play with me. You know I can't get there all by myself."

"No!" Ritchie screamed. He forced himself to his feet, towering over Lenore. "You're not her! I don't know what you are, but I know you're not her! Now get the fuck out of here!"

She broke into sobs, her performance forgotten. "You're such an asshole," she cried. "I try to be there for you. I try to take care of you."

"No," Ritchie said, calmness in his voice. "You don't. Because you're not her."

The sobbing dropped away. "Fair enough," she said with that bored tone. "The least I can do is thank you for that lovely gift you gave me." Her hands ran over her breasts and down to her belly. Those jagged fingernails dug into soft skin. Thin rivulets of blood ran down her stomach and curved around her thighs. She dug in harder, tearing into her flesh. The wet ripping sound came with a cry of ecstasy from Lenore's throat. She threw her head back and moaned out her perverted orgasm as she tore into her viscera. Coils of slippery guts spilled into her lap.

Ritchie watched, horrified, as Lenore dragged the teddy bear from the cavernous wound in her stomach. She held the stuffed animal up to him. Thick blood matted its fur. The glass eyes stared at him, as black as Lenore's. Then in a flash, they turned red. The bear's stitched smile mouth split apart, revealing rows of sharp teeth. It chittered out a laugh and reached its stuffed arms out towards Ritchie.

Lenore set the demonic teddy on the floor and it scampered towards Ritchie. He screamed as it clambered up his left leg, biting chunks out of him as it went. It reached his stomach and tore through his stained t-shirt before tearing through him. A second pile of guts spilled onto the floor as the teddy bear burrowed into him. Ritchie dropped to his knees, trying desperately to pull the bear free while push his intestines back in.

Lenore lay in front of him, cackling. "Poor, poor Ritchie," she giggled. "Why do you always have to do things the hard way?"

Ritchie didn't have an answer. Dark spots swam in his vision. His head went light. He collapsed forward, doing a face plant between Lenore's splayed legs. He felt the warmth of her gore-covered nethers against his lips as his consciousness faded.

*

"Sick fucking bastard," Lenore snarled at Ted.

She pulled at the ropes binding her to her bed. When she came to, he was just finishing tying her left wrist. He'd stripped her. Not surprising. She was used to being naked in front of complete strangers, but this was different. She tried to pull her legs together, but the knots were firm, rubbing her ankles raw. "When I get free, I'm gonna tear your fucking balls off."

With Lenore secured, Ted turned his attention away from her. He pulled his cell phone out and dialed a number. "She's ready. Come up." Ted hung up and set the phone on the nightstand.

"Got some friends coming up to help you get it up, you limp-dicked piece of shit?" Lenore yelled as Ted began to disrobe. "You hear me? I called you an impotent sack of feces. And I don't give a fuck how many of your friends are coming. I'll fucking take all of you. Hope you like the taste of cock, cuz I'm gonna shove yours down your throat."

Ted turned and leveled a dark glare on her. "Such a foul mouth," he said, shaking his head with disdain. "The Selector has chosen wisely." He took a step towards her and backhanded her across the face. The blow stung and Lenore tasted blood in her mouth. She spat a wad at Ted. "Now keep your whore mouth shut or I'll break your jaw."

Lenore didn't reply, but it wasn't for lack of wanting. She didn't want to risk him telling the truth. After all, it would be hard to bite if her jaw was broken. And if Ted or his 'friends' came anywhere within biting range, she planned on going bloodthirsty cannibal on their asses. She shuddered with disgust as Ted dropped his skivvies.

She heard a knock at the front door. Ted gave her a sad smile. "Sit tight. We'll be starting shortly." He left the room and Lenore went back to trying to get the knots loosened. She wasn't a complete stranger to knots. One of her ex's had been into bondage. It had been fun then. Now, not so much. And regardless of Ted's numerous flaws as a human being or even a sentient life form, apparently tying knots wasn't one of them.

As Lenore struggled to get free, one thought kept running through her mind.

Who the fuck is the Selector?

128

Ritchie snapped awake.

He sat up, finding himself on the elevator floor. The lights were back on, the void above was gone, and the doors stood open, waiting patiently for him to depart. The pit of dread in his stomach concerning Lenore was even stronger. Rising to unsteady feet, he shambled out into the fourth floor hallway and made his way towards Lenore's apartment.

Reaching the door, something felt wrong. Ritchie couldn't see anything specific that stood out. It was the same old door. The same worn brass numbers proclaiming the apartment as number 402. But his stomach flipped and flopped in his belly. He went to knock on the door but paused. Instead, he reached down to the knob and twisted it. It turned easily.

The door was unlocked. Something was definitely wrong. Lenore never left her door unlocked.

Ritchie pushed the door open and moved into the apartment. His foot came down on one of the slices of pizza and he slipped, nearly falling on his ass. He grabbed for the wall and straightened himself. The pizza slices littered the front hall. Ritchie recognized the little slivers of anchovies. Pizza night had gone horribly wrong.

He rushed through the small apartment, quickly confirming Lenore wasn't in the kitchen or the living room. He moved down the narrow hall leading to the bedroom and bathroom. The bathroom door at the end of the hall was closed, but the bedroom door hung open. He moved to the door and looked through, gasping.

Lenore laid spread eagle on her bed, wrists and ankles bound to the head and foot boards. She'd been stripped. Perched on top of her with his large hands clamped around her throat was a bear-man. Ritchie backed away in horror as he recognized the

129

teddy bear he'd given Lenore. It was no longer the small, filthy, lifeless stuffed animal he'd found in the dumpster.

"What the fuck?" he gasped, gaining the attention of the bear. Its large, spherical head turned to look at him. Lenore's bulging eyes shifted to Ritchie as well. She made a weak gurgle, drool slobbering down her chin.

"The Selector," the bear said with eager excitement. "It's so good you could make it. You're just in time." The bear clamped his hands around Lenore's throat tighter. Something in her neck popped and her body gave off a jerk. The life faded from her red face.

"No," Ritchie moaned. His back pressed against the wall and his foot struck something solid that skidded heavily against the floor. He looked down to see Lenore's revolver. Scooping it up, he took aim at the bear-man and fired. Stuffing and brains sprayed against the wall and the bear-man collapsed over Lenore's lifeless form.

Ritchie hurried into the bedroom and shoved the bear-man off the bed. Cradling Lenore's head, he patted at her cheeks. "C'mon, wake up," he whispered, tears stinging his eyes. Anger and sorrow flowed through him as he tried to come to terms with what was happening. "Dammit, come back!" He slapped Lenore across the face. Her head moved loosely to the side, her blank eyes looking away from him. Ritchie buried his face against her chest, sobbing.

"Your tears are wasted, Selector."

Ritchie lifted his head and turned to the bedroom door. Three more bear-men stood in the room, watching the scene through glass eyes. "What?" Ritchie's face scrunched up, trying to make sense of what was going on. Was it another episode? Had his episode ever stopped? Maybe he was still laid out in the elevator. He hoped he was still laid out in the elevator. "What is this? What are you?"

"As if you don't know," the bear-man in the middle said.

"The Teddies have been a part of Ever Falls since its inception. Despite our best efforts, this city has fallen into the depths of depravity." He lifted the soiled teddy bear and held it out to Ritchie. "You found the idol, put it into the hands of a deserving sacrifice, and set the wheels in motion. You performed admirably, Selector." Ritchie took the stuffed animal with numb hands, staring down at it with confusion then back to the trio of bear-men gathered around him. The leader motioned to Lenore. "This one was filth. Exposing her body in exchange for money. Taking drugs. And such a foul mouth. You've done a great service for the preservation of innocence."

Ritchie shook his head. "This isn't real," he told himself, squeezing his eyes shut. "It's just my nightmare."

"It is both real and a nightmare, this world," the bear-man said. "But you've helped us along the path towards ending the nightmare. Your behavior seems a bit conflicted." He motioned to the dead bear-man on the floor. "But that's to be expected. We do not judge an individual on solitary actions alone." He nodded to the soiled teddy in Ritchie's hands. "Choose wisely, Selector. We expect great things from you."

The bear-men filed out of the bedroom. The leader paused at the door, turning back to Ritchie. "The Teddies will be watching, Ritchie Dunn. Make us proud." The bear-man left.

Ritchie tossed the filthy stuffed animal away and pulled at the knots binding Lenore to the bed. He pulled her limp body into his arms, hugging her tightly. "Just wake up," he whispered to her. "I don't want this to be real."

Ritchie waited, begging for reality to return, as Lenore's body grew cold and stiff in his embrace.

REMEDIATION

PATRICK MACADOO

Giant mushrooms, their caps the size of dinner plates, dotted the tall grass of the front yard. Rhonda sank back into the Sebring's driver seat. She was having another one of those moments, couldn't quite bring herself to open the door and get to work, wouldn't be hard at all to drive the 'company' car (really Rick's wife's old car) back to HQ and take the bus home, take this job and shove it.

She closed her eyes against the imminent headache. She saw their genuine smiles, Samuel, Sherylynn, Serena, her babies, kids so good they shamed her into facing her own snobby attitude towards her mother, who scrubbed floors and toilets, who put her through college. She feared her and her siblings' constant complaints about being poor brought on the cancer that ate her mother alive. She supposed the only thing she could do to make amends was to suck it up. She grabbed the handle of the wooden tote crammed with her cleaning supplies and scoffed. For all her pricey education, she was basically doing what her mother did.

She pushed the door open and grabbed her duffel bag with her free hand. At least the heavy gray sky promised a soaking that would give her a valid excuse to skip mowing the damned lawns. She would've never gotten the whole development done today anyways, nevermind the coming storm and the tornado watch, shoot, the job would take a landscaping crew all day, but Rick, cutting costs to keep the company 'solvent,' terminated that contract, as well as the contracts with the

132

housecleaners, the handymen, even the security service. All their former duties fell on her now. She should've known better back when Rick insisted that her business cards read 'Ronny,' instead of 'Rhonda,' or her full first name, which he claimed sounded too 'urban.' She'd love to watch his fat face burn beet red if he ever found out they called him 'P-Rick,' but she supposed she never would, since after the sub-prime crisis she was about the only one left, and she didn't dare call him that, because the consequences would be unemployment, food stamps, welfare. She'd seen close up how poverty ground down children. She'd be damned if she'd let her babies go that way.

The first rain droplets struck her face. She hurried to the front door, glad she'd already changed into her sneakers. Inside the foyer she flicked the light switch up and down. The family room remained gloomy. She hoped the storm had knocked out the power, and Rick hadn't cut that service too.

"*Ohhhhhh.*"

She froze. The groan came from the kitchen. She eased the cleaning tote to the foyer tiles, then fished her Taser out of the duffel bag. She flipped open her phone and punched in 911, and placed her thumb over Send.

"*Ohhhhhhhelpmeeeee.*"

The man's voice, nothing sneaky about it, sounded cracked and raw, homeless. Rhonda's shoulders slumped. Not as frequently as in the inner city properties, but still, from time to time, she'd stumble upon squatters out here, and they were always a hassle. She sniffed, and detected the cloying, unwashed stink, which intensified as she approached, and made her eyes water as she passed through the kitchen doorway.

She muttered, "Oh my Lord," while taking a backward step.

He curled fetal on the linoleum. He convulsed, emitting a constant, shuddery moan. His tangled, matted dark beard obscured the lower half of his face. His greasy long hair spilled out of his ski cap, its fringe pulled low to his eyebrows despite the August heat. The cap's grimy brown matched the soiled shades of rest of his bulky clothing. A smear streaked the linoleum, the thin, meandering trail sticky enough to glisten in the dim gray daylight shafting into the dark kitchen, the rippled smear culminating in a puddle, which goopy droplets, dangling from the saturated seat of his pants before accumulating enough mass to drizzle free and plop into the gruel below, fed.

"Oh, Hell no!" Rhonda backpeddled away from the fecal stench while hitting the Send button on her phone. She scooped up her duffel bag, had her hand on the front door's knob, barely registering the operator's apology that the tornado was significantly delaying response time. Could've been a rapist hiding in the kitchen. Could've been a murderer. Screw P-Rick, screw this job … meant screwing her babies. She glanced at the cleaning supplies. The paramedics sure as hell weren't gonna clean up that mess.

She rummaged through the tote, found a paper dust mask and strapped it on. She returned to the kitchen doorway and said, "Lord. What you been eating?"

A series of hacks shook his torso. She found herself bending her knees, reaching out to him, but rancid wisps penetrated her dust mask and made her recoil. Her voice pitched soft, she said, "You got any friends around?"

He raised a shaky hand and clutched his beard, the tremors traveling up and down his arm, rills of drool spilling onto the floor. On the back of his neck, an egg-shaped lump swelled, pulsing larger, larger. She retreated to the doorway, afraid that the ballooning goiter was gonna burst and spray her with God knows what foul nastiness. The goiter expanded oblong, like a potato, straining, stretch marks splitting the flesh around its base, then it imploded, collapsing into a pocked growth, a monstrous wart. The man gurgled, more darkish drool dribbling from his beard and lips.

134

"I-I'm sorry," she said, while backing out of the kitchen. She headed for the first floor bedroom. The paramedics could deal with *that*. While she changed into her sweats and baggy tee-shirt, and laid out her skirt, blouse, and jacket on the bed, raindrops began to pelt the roof.

A thump rattled the bedroom door in its frame. She jumped, fumbled for the Taser, then snatched up her phone. "Back off! I got a gun!" She wished she did, wished the builders had used better materials as the door bowed in its frame, her warning doing nothing but spurring the man to more violent efforts. A busy signal answered her 911 call. She darted to the bathroom door, hoping its lock was more heavy duty. She pulled the door open. The resultant backdraft gusted a gagging stench into her face. She slammed the door shut, but not before she caught a glimpse of the shadowy bathroom. Slime on the walls, the counters, the floor, the ceiling, the sick man must've been using the toilet for days.

She strapped the dust mask across her mouth and nose. Assuming the shoulder-width stance the self-defense instructor taught her, with both hands she pointed the Taser at the buckling door. When he stumbled through, she pulled the trigger. The tines struck dead center and the voltage caused him to jerk all the way down to the carpet. She gave him a few extra seconds of juice before she took her finger off the trigger.

She stood over his twitching body. White, wearing baggy, soiled clothing, but a shorter beard, not the same man. Nobody else looming in the gloomy family room. She grabbed her duffel bag and edged around the twitching man. A huge wart protruded from the side of his neck. *Disease.* She checked the seal of her dust mask. She had to get out of here.

She peered out of the bay window into the angry blue-gray downpour. She tried her phone again, but the storm had knocked out service. She ground her teeth. Most tornado watches turned out to be nothing, but the rain sheeted so hard she couldn't make out her car. From the kitchen, the sick man moaned loud. God knew how many contagious folk might down in this unit's basement. She had to make a break for the next unit, which had no water service, and so the squatters probably hadn't bothered with it. She skirted the sick man in the kitchen and stood at the back door. The damned rain was gonna ruin her weave.

She took the extra tee shirt out of the duffel and tented it over her head, and she dashed for the next unit's back door. To the north, clouds funneled high in the sky. The wind snatched at her makeshift umbrella and flung hard raindrops against her body. She averted her face. Algae choked the surface of the model unit's backyard pool. She frowned. Just last week, or maybe two weeks ago, she'd cleaned the pool to a spotless and cool blue.

She unlocked the back door and stamped her wet sneakers on the first section of linoleum inside the unit's kitchen. No footprints, no streaks of … whatever, marred the linoleum. She stepped out of her sneakers. She wasn't gonna have to scrub this floor if she could help it. Even in the premature darkness, she saw the stain on the wall.

Mold.

The stain spread from the corner of the ceiling to halfway down the wall. In the huge blotch on the textured white paint, she saw the end of the company. P-Rick finally declaring bankruptcy. Unemployment for her, foodstamps, welfare, a cramped apartment in a horrible neighborhood, her babies struggling through the worst school in the district.

God damned Rick.

The prick had plowed ahead, even as the market began to tank, with the development, believing that things were gonna turn around, that the first slips were just momentary blips, and as things went from bad to worse, he kept going, cutting costs by skimping on materials, and on treatments, and on fillage,

136

they built the damned development on swampland, for God's sake, what did he expect would happen? The development was a damned mold farm.

She rubbed her eyes. She exhaled a shuddery breath. Maybe the other units were clean. She had to stop jumping to the worst case, the stress was eating her up inside. She still had a job. *Worry about getting through today, then worry about tomorrow.*

She stepped back into her sneakers and fished the flashlight out of her duffel bag. She found the basement door and started down the steps, inspecting the walls for damage on the way down. With her other hand, she kept trying her phone.

Her soles scuffed along the concrete, the flashlight's beam found no mold on the unfinished, sheetrock walls. Relief loosened her muscles. She dropped her arm, and the flashlight's beam flashed into the far corner, illuminating a figure huddled against the wall. Rhonda yelped while pouncing back.

The girl waved her hand. "Hi. You're not a cop, are you?"

Rhonda huffed out a breath. Long dark hair spilling out from under her backwards baseball cap, small nose, pierced lip, baggy earth-colored clothing, big clunky black boots, the young white girl seemed clean, but she looked homeless, like those packs of kids that roamed downtown, teens too busy running wild to get a job or go to school.

The girl smiled. Her teeth gleamed bright. Rhonda said, "I'm not a cop."

"I hadda get away for a little while. I hope's alright."

The girl's slurry voice nettled Rhonda. The girl's scumbag pose could not disguise her refined beauty, the product of spas and boutique toiletries. Probably the daughter of some Meridian Hills hotshot. The girl drew her skinny thighs tight against her torso, wrapping her arms around her shins, and rested her forehead on her kneecaps. She muttered, "So sick and tired …"

Rhonda bowed her head. Might be a poor little rich girl, but Rhonda supposed her parents were worried sick about her. Rhonda shined her flashlight on the girl's neck. No huge wart. Her lethargy, her apparently self-imposed isolation, looked to Rhonda like the girl was on a long, slow comedown from some crazy-steep high. "What you doing here, girl?"

The girl didn't raise her head. She mumbled, "Roger said free trips …" Her voice rose into a whine while saying, "But then they wouldn't let me *leave*!" Her voice fell back to a mumble while saying, "I don't feel so good." She lifted her head, which lolled back and forth. "I gotta get back."

Rhonda didn't need the girl to spell it out for her. Last few years of high school, a bunch of her friends got flushed down the drug toilet. She knew what happened to a pretty girl, lured out to the edge of town, pumped full of dope, a roomful of sleazy men, the math worked out the same every time.

The girl scraped her back against the sheetrock on her way up to her feet. She swayed. "Whoa, headrush."

"You don't have to go back. Just wait out the storm here, and I'll drive you home after."

The girl hugged herself. She shivered. "N-no, I gotta get back. *Damn*. I *hurt*." She took a couple shaky steps.

Rhonda reached out to her, felt the mask shift on her cheeks, then withdrew her hands. "There's a tornado coming. You can't go out there."

The girl ignored her, continued on her meandering path towards the stairs. Rhonda aimed the flashlight's beam in front of the girl, afraid the junkie would stumble and fall, and sue … Rhonda muttered, "Damn." No way in Hell was she gonna touch the girl, but she couldn't let her tumble down the stairs, much less wander out into a tornado. She cleared her throat. "Girl, you can't go out there. Tornado's coming."

The girl, tottering up the steps, waved the back of her hand. "S'alright. Stopped raining. I know a safe place. C'mon."

Rhonda frowned. She followed the girl upward, meaning to make sure she made it to the ground floor. After that, the girl was on her own. Rhonda winced. What kind of person thought that way? How'd she ever get so callous? When did she become a Sunday Christian? She glared at the girl, who was approaching the top step and holding her hand out for the door knob. *The goddamned junkie*. Oblivious to the fact that her thoughtless actions were putting Rhonda's own children in danger of becoming motherless.

Rhonda screamed, "Stop!"

The girl's hand closed around the doorknob. Rhonda pounded up the steps. The girl pushed the door open, and bright sunlight shined into the basement. Rhonda stopped in her tracks. She shielded her eyes with the back of her hand.

The girl, in a cheery tone, said, "C'mon."

Rhonda followed the girl up into the kitchen, and out the backdoor. Under the awning, Rhonda saw nothing but blue sky, but stepping out into the yard, into an unobstructed view, she saw the bruised clouds swirling stupendously high, constricting all horizons. *The eye of the tornado*.

The girl slid the glass backdoor of the next unit open. Rhonda shook off the fact that the door was unlocked. She dashed forward and grabbed the girl, warts or no warts, and hustled her into the kitchen. The girl whined, "*Hey.*"

"Move it, girl!"

The girl shook her arm free and said, "You gotta be careful–"

Rhonda felt the groans of the kitchen floor through her sneaker's soles. Mold mottled the kitchen's walls and ceiling, not just stains, but having burst forth into rolling green swathes. The floor listed, then, with a splintery *ratttch*, gave beneath Rhonda's feet. She screamed.

She plunged into a spongy mass, her left leg bending beneath her, her right leg spearing through the mass, which trampolined under her weight, her head bobbing, at its peak maybe a foot below the kitchen's floor original level. Moans, wheezes, and coughs surrounded her as people shucked broken boards and rotted flooring, thick mold coating the undersides, off themselves.

"Awww, harsh, man,"

Rhonda's darting eyes focused on the quavery voice of a man near her. The white guy, his clothes blending into that unwashed shade of homeless brown, sprawled on the bed of porous green. His scraggly beard hid most of his face, but he seemed mildly peeved that the falling shards of floor had disturbed his nod. Other squatters, all white, by the looks of them all homeless, maybe two dozen, roused themselves enough to clear their own little personal lounging zones, then began to resettle into their stupors. The fact that the floor had collapsed on top of them, one intact beam running the kitchen's width with fractured crossboards spaced down the beam's length like a brontosaurus spine, didn't seem to trouble the stoned-to-the-bone squatters.

Rhonda spotted the girl, who knelt, her belly on the spongy green, her face hovering above, her nose grazing the petals of a pale green bloom, her eyes closed. The flower quaked, then disgorged a mist, which the girl inhaled, then she sighed, curled up on her side, and stuck her thumb in her mouth.

Rhonda spotted blooms, pale green circlets dotting the darker green, beside each squatter, the white guy nearest to her twisting his face above a flower, inhaling its misty discharge, then relaxing his head back on his patch, sighing, "That's better." Something about the way he craned his neck … Rhonda blinked, refocused her eyes, but the sight didn't change. The mold had seeped up his backside, coating the first few inches of his clothes, fusing his legs and torso into place.

140

Rhonda scanned the rest, and some, like the poor little rich girl, lazed free on the fibrous surface, but others languished half-submerged, the texture of the growth around immersed limbs sludgy, one bedraggled woman sunken to her waist but still hunching over a pale bloom, and, in a corner … a bald man, a beatific smile stretching his lips, petals tickling his nose, his body swamped to his chin, the mold blotched green up his cheeks.

The green-mottled bald man dropped a bit lower, the sudden motion slapping Rhonda back to her senses, back to awareness of her own disposition, her right leg encased to her hip, her left leg pinned underneath her, her body tilted, her palms flattened against the mossy carpet, which softened, moistened, against her fingers.

On reflex she pressed against the vegetation in order to wrench up her trapped leg, but the mold gave and her hands plunged to her wrists. She yelped and tore her hands free, ripping slender runners twined around her fingers from the mass. She lunged towards the nearest wall, towards a jagged section of intact floor. She clutched the ragged linoleum, which pulled loose, and an undertow dragged her left leg under, dragged her backwards, towards the center.

Darkness rolled in. *Tornado*. She snatched the flashlight from the surface of the mold. The duffel bag banged into her ribs, the bag still slung over her shoulder. They were all gonna die. She was gonna die. She cupped the dust mask with her free left hand. She flicked on the flashlight. She whisked the beam around her. An uneven hoop of bulbs circled her. The bulbs opened, their petals glistening, their cores compressing in preparation for a burst, the collective on the cusp of soaking her in that psychedelic mist.

Instinct forced her to jerk downward. She plunged into the softening mold. Pitch black engulfed her. The gritty pulp scraped the dust mask from her mouth and scoured her cheeks and lips. She gasped, her mouth filling with bitter wet fiber, then her knuckles jammed against something hard. She ran her hands over the curving hardness, rending pulp away from its slimy surface. She punched the flashlight's butt against the surface, and again, felt it pock, and she smashed her left fist into the weakened spot. The surface split, and she fell headfirst, her shirt snagging on the crack, and she flipped and landed flat on her back, the knobby surface beneath her pounding her kidneys, knocking the wind out of her, the fibrous mush in her mouth geysering from her scratched, bleeding lips.

She retched. She flipped onto to her belly and pressed herself up to her hands and knees. She groped over the bumpy, hard ground and found the flashlight in a pool of warm slime. She had to shake the flashlight a few times to get it to turn on. She gaped.

On all sides bulbous pods tapered from the tufted mass above to thick, trunk-like stalks growing out of the hard, lumpy tier she knelt on, and within the pod that she spilled out of, albino strands were already plaiting over the crack in its rind. She shook, watching those wiry, hairy strands weave over the wounded rind. All those pods, the poor wretches above, slowly sinking … *digested*. Under her damp clothes, her skin tingled, the tingling intensifying to near painful, then a wave of dizziness washed over her, left her numb.

She mumbled, "So hard." It was hard, so damned hard. The job was too hard, P-Ricky only kept her around because she took his shit with a smile and a 'thank you.' So hard not to smack him across his big fat face. So much easier to lay back and forget about everything. But the ground was too hard. Too hard to get comfortable on the hard surface. A headache, faint throbs, grew insistent. She fluttered her eyelids, her babies' faces flickering.

She growled as she levered her torso upright, her growl ending in a guttural, "*No*." She swept the flashlight's beam against the deep green ceiling. She could climb up, maybe break through, but the juice, the mist, she'd lose herself for good, drugged out while this … *organism* devoured her, bit by bit.

She thrust her knees into the matted fabric beneath her and elicited some spring from the cellular roughage. She rose to a crouch and squeezed between the solid shells of the tuberous pods, making her way toward the wall, angling towards the corner that she judged to lie above the cellar doorway to the cement stairs that climbed to the back-patio hatchway.

She reached a rounded recess behind a pod. Weedy growths choked the recess, dangling from above, and the walls consisted of the same dry, spongy material. She rotated, sucking in her gut, groaning against the hard pod pressing against her breasts. She shifted till her back was against the pod and she lowered herself. She unzipped her duffel bag and rooted around, though she knew there was nothing in there she could use to dig her way to the bottom.

She removed her hand. She blew her lungs empty, the last wisps coming out as wheezes. She pulled the collar of her tee-shirt over her mouth and nose. She started digging with her bare hands. First couple of inches, and her faux nails snapped off, the mold coming up in huge flakes, which she cast aside, and she slitted her eyes against the dust wafting up in the air. When she'd worked the hole a foot or so deep, she bent over and stopped. She closed her eyes. The crud was coming up easy, she could make it to the door, she knew it. But where then? Probably the cement stairwell was choked too, and if she managed to dig her way out without suffocating, surely by then she would've breathed in so much mold dust that she'd be dead in a matter of … what? Months? Weeks? Days?

"What's the use?"

The tingling returned to her skin. She felt the weight of the dust caking her damp clothes. If she made it outside, the tornado was waiting for her. Better to curl up and die. Better still, rip open a pod and let that crap rain down on her, put her out of her misery, let the trip carry her away while her body dissolved to nothing.

She raised her head. Where was this shit coming from? Her whole goddamned life … suspensions, teen pregnancy, deadbeat *dads*, working her way through school, her mama's death, Samuel's 'behavioral' problems, and goddamned P-Rick, P-Rick and his goddamned development, the goddamned land so cheap because it was goddamned swampland, and now, she laughed, the rumors about toxic waste, not the nuclear kind, no, but the medical waste kind, or the pesticide kind, yeah, that made sense … but whatever caused this growth, she'd been through Hell and back. The drug stuff was getting into her head, making her forget that she was a fighter.

She bared her teeth and resumed digging. In a matter of seconds, she punched through to a pocket. She shined the flashlight into the haze. Green streaked the gray of cement. She lowered herself into the pocket. She dropped down to the concrete. Hunched low, she found the cellar door, had her hand on the doorknob, but she had to look. She pivoted, the flashlight's beam showing the underside a few feet above the cement floor, puckered holes perforating the rugged expanse, no doubt marking the position of the stalks above, clusters of thin white vines trailing out of those craterous green sphincters, bones encasing the lower ends of the vines, she blinked, no, not encasing, but the vines penetrating the marrow, sucking out every last bit, leaving nothing but shards and small piles of white dust on the basement floor.

She turned to the door and pushed it open. Mold coated the passageway's walls, the steps, the ceiling, but just a coating, no blockage. She took a step into the passageway. Those bones back there … she knew goddamned well where those bones came from. She couldn't leave the girl.

144

She started up the stairwell. She wouldn't leave the girl. She'd call … somebody, the authorities. She could picture the house cordoned off, hazmat-suited technicians combing the grounds, the government seizing the land, the company going bankrupt. She exhaled. She actually felt a little lighter, seeing where it was all going. She'd go to the hospital, and P-Rick was gonna foot the bill. Hell, she was gonna sue his fat ass. She managed a tight smile, and, reaching the top of the stairs, she pressed her ear against the hatch. Sounded quiet on the other side.

She shoved the hatch open, not at all surprised to find the doors unlocked. The sun glared down on her. A breeze, cruising from the east, brought the scent of callow corn from the rolling fields. She staggered up to the patio. She wheeled. The sliding backdoor was open. The trapped squatters lolled, the girl was still curled up in the far corner. Rhonda took a breath, then swooned.

She backpeddled, trying to maintain balance, then went down to one knee in the tall grass. She waited for the headrush to pass. She stood up too fast, reeled, and finally got her feet underneath herself in the middle of the street.

"Oh my God."

She performed a slow turn. The tornado had touched down in the development, crisscrossing the lot, she guessed, by the path of destruction. Units had been torn open like tin cans. Mold riddled the exposed innards of every unit she could see, one particular growth had reached the second floor of a freshly de-roofed unit.

"How many …"

Had to be hundreds digested to sustain that much mold. On that roofless unit, monstrous pale-green blossoms, as large as her car, waved in the breeze, discharged small clouds of spores, that floated on high, towards Indianapolis.

Pain flared in her stomach. She pressed her hand to her belly, felt the growth, knew what it would look like before she raised her shirt, saw her skin swell, a lump, a roundish tumor, stretching her skin several shades lighter, then the implosion, and the sharp agony drove her down to her knees. And she knew. She knew this development might be ground zero, but the mold had been spreading for a while now, and there were plenty of other developments standing empty around the city, the region, the country.

She took her phone out of the duffel bag. The display showed four bars. She called Stella, her sitter. When Stella answered, Rhonda coughed, felt the sprouts wending up into the back of her throat, then said, "Get the kids out of the city. Take 'em to your sister's place in Rockford."

"What?"

"Just do it Stella, I don't have time to explain."

"Where are you, what's goin' on?"

"Do it, now! I … I'll meet you there, and I'll explain everything. I gotta swing by work first."

She flipped her phone shut. She yearned to talk to her babies, but every second counted for them, and she herself probably didn't have much time left, and she had to have a little chat with P-Rick, face to face.

SHRIEKING FOULLY FOR RELEASE

JOSHUA DOBSON

Spider-web cracks crawl across the surface of a grimy mirror, capture the reflection of Becky's zit encrusted, pus-filled face, and puke it back at her in compound fly-vision.

"Cliiit-face, cliiit-face, cliiit-face," an oily singsong voice trailing off into hissing oblivion mocks her.

She pinches a crimson zit on her right cheek. As it pops, pus and blood spray across the mirror in a buckshot pattern and a small yellowy-white maggot oozes from the wound in a seething trickle of pink pus. She winces.

She pinches a crimson zit under her left eye. As it pops, pus and blood fleck the mirror and a large, rubbery, yellow worm oozes from the wound in a seething trickle of pink pus. She gags.

She pinches a scarlet zit on her forehead. As it pops, more pus and blood splatter the filthy broken mirror and a small, dead baby hummingbird oozes from the wound in a gush of pink pus, leaving a sunken crater of collapsed flesh in the center of her forehead.

Becky jerks awake with a dying fish gasp and peels the damp faux-satin covers from her sour, sweaty flesh.

The whirr of the shifty-eyed, black plastic kitty cat clock feels reassuring. But wait a second, hadn't she donated the shifty-eyed, black plastic kitty cat clock to the Salvation Army because it had seen too much? Goosebumps bloom down her skinny arms. She'd heard of lost cats finding their way home, but this was . . .

Gurgle, rurgle, gurgle.

The veal cutlet dissolving in her witch's cauldron of a gullet was putting up a fight, clawing at her insides, shrieking foully for release.

Gurgle, wurgle, gurgle.

The human body is a leaky garbage bag.

With a reluctant sigh, Becky wrenches herself from the warm womb of bed and lurches bathroom-ward. Something crunches under her bare size nine. Not stray cereal. Something gooey inside.

She raises the lid and parks her fat ass on the toilet seat. The new toilet seat. The new toilet seat which never seemed to be cold. She came home from work one day a few weeks back and her toilet seat had been replaced. She asked the super with the lazy eye why he had replaced her toilet seat, he swore up and down he didn't know what she was talking about, and she believed the lazy eyed bastard.

Her anus dilates and several pebbles of shit plop, plop, plop into the bowl. Water splashes on her ass, which sends a shiver shuddering through her. Rabbi on the news said the water supply was riddled with copepods, yucky, tiny little sea-monkey crustacean critters she most definitely didn't want touching her ass. Becky didn't like to touch or be touched by anything that laid eggs. It gave her the creeps. She had lately taken to boiling her bathwater.

She tears off a square of toilet paper and wipes the slimy mystery goo from the bottom of her left foot.

She squirts out a dribble of piss and all the neighborhood dogs began to howl as if in answer. Lately dogs howl every time she pisses, and there was a dog pound right down the street so the racket was nigh on apocalyptic. She has two theories as to why this was happening, either:

A. The fury of the dogs was inflamed by some scent or

148

pheromone in her piss. (The flaw in this theory was that the phenomenon of the pissed off dogs had begun to occur only recently, and she had not altered her diet or medication regiment in any appreciable way.)

or,

B.   Her urethra was shaped such that when urine passed through it a whistling sound, inaudible to humans, much like those silent dog whistles, was generated. (The flaw in this theory was that the phenomenon of the pissed off dogs had begun to occur only recently, thus it would mean that the shape of her urethra had somehow changed recently.)

The prognosis of both scenarios = not good.

The hair on the back of her neck is standing up. She hates dogs. As a teenager, she'd gotten part of a hot dog stuck in her vagina while masturbating with it. Telling her mama why she had to go to the emergency room was the hardest thing she'd ever had to do in her life. After that mama would have her Chihuahua, Mr. Blisters sniff Becky's crotch a couple times a day. Mama said Mr. Blisters could smell anything that went on down there, even if it was just her touching herself sinful like.

She hates her bathroom. The pipes make funny noises and the water smells weird. The bathtub is bizarre. It has clawed feet. Incredibly detailed clawed feet with tiny corns, bunions, and blisters sculpted on them, even tiny toenail weevils visible only with a magnifying glass. And if one stares long enough at the pistachio-pudding-puke-green walls of the bathroom, one begins to see horrible leering faces hidden in the swirls of the plaster. The perpetually grimy yellow tiled floor bears the greasy stains of greenish-blackish web-toed footprints that can't be scrubbed away no matter the amount of cleanser and elbow grease expended. The stains are incredibly detailed; she can even make out the swirling grain of the friction ridges on the long spindly webbed-toes. The perpetually grimy yellow tile reminded her of one of those dance floors with the steps diagrammed on them; the footprints staining the floor had the regularity of dancing. Her goddamn bathroom door has an accursed crescent moon carved into it, like a motherfucking outhouse door. She had been forced to use an outhouse once as a child, during a family trip to a dude ranch. She was afraid a little girl in China was gonna poop at the same time and Chinese diarrhea full of lil' maggots of rice was gonna splatter all over her bare butt, and the maggots would crawl up her butt-hole and lay eggs inside her.

Plop, plop, plop.

One day a few months back, walking home from work, she glanced up at her bathroom window and sure as shit, someone was standing in her bathroom. He seemed to be sucking on the wall. Her first thought upon learning there was an intruder in her bathroom: He'll find the aquarium net by the toilet; he'll know I use it to scoop out the foamy mousse-textured, half-digested Vicodin I sometimes vomit up and he'll know I eat my own puke out of the toilet. She saw red. She rushed inside, taser at the ready. No one there, but the smell could've gagged a maggot. And almost all the peeling yellow lead paint was gone from the walls exposing the pistachio-pudding-puke-green plaster and the horrible leering faces that would emerge from the swirls if one stared too long.

She threw out her douche, in case the Phantom had replaced it with acid, like that freak in Texas a few years back. She pitched all the toilet paper and washed all the towels in case the Phantom had rubbed poison ivy all over them, like that freak on the news a few months back. She threw out the toothpaste and liquid anti-bacterial hand soap in case the Phantom had jizzed off into them, like that freak in the paper a few weeks back. What if he put her toothbrush up his ass? Kept thinking of things he could've tainted. Hard, but she had to force herself to say: Fuck it, better to die than to live in a world where you have to buy a new toothbrush.

Plop, plop, plop.

Her eyes have adjusted to the darkness. Her belly so resembles rising bread dough that she has to fight the urge to punch it down. She stares in abject fascination at her flabby thighs. They put her in mind of bloated, torpid sea creatures. Sitting as she was smooshed the fat out and made the cellulite bubble up, mashed potatoes beneath milk-skin. Her flab is like Silly-Putty. If she sat on the Sunday comics section of the paper she could exhibit herself in carnival sideshows as the fat-tattooed-ass lady. She pinches a dollop of fat between her sausage link fingers and squeezes as hard as she can, until the she can't stand the red-white waves of pain for another second.

She can feel a whopper coming . . . ppbbffftt. Just a mighty cheek-rattling fart that makes her curl her lip up like Elvis and smells so rank she thinks it might set off the smoke detector.

The panic was beginning to set in. Every time she took a shit, and that seemed to be more and more frequent lately, she had a panic attack, spurred by the fear she might have to puke and would summarily throw up all over her naked lap. She's flushed and the tingling cockroaches are crawling all over her face.

She leans forward and screeeaks the window up like the blade of a guillotine.

Warm, greasy rain, like the drool of an idiot god, splatters against the rotten windowsill. She signed the lease for this apartment during winter. During summer, the smell of burning cat fur from the crematorium smokestacks of the dog pound down the street wafts through every window left open.

Plonk, plonk, plonk.

A flash of lightning illuminates the vista outside Becky's bathroom window. There is some kind of thing clinging to the rotten, crooked, Missing Child/Missing Pet flyer encrusted telephone pole across the street. 'It' looks sorta like a really big dude, wide as a Cheshire grin and tall as a gallows, wearing some sorta fleshy yellow SCUBA suit and a gas mask. It clings to the black pole, about a foot below the humming electrical transformer, directly in Becky's field of vision. It has a huge, rubbery, orange cock with a tip like a bioluminescent pineapple. The second she laid eyes on it she knew she would never tell anyone ever, but she found her tiny self overwhelmed by the unholy fear that someone would somehow find out about her unnatural discovery and proceed to name the thing clinging to the crooked, black telephone pole after her. It seems to be looking up at the buzzing transformer mounted atop the crooked, black pole. She prays with all her might to a god she doesn't believe in that it won't turn in her direction it's wrinkly, yellow head with the obscene dangly thing where the mouth should be. Even if Becky hadn't been taking a shit naked as a jaybird, she wouldn't have wanted whatever the fuck that thing is looking at her, even if she was bundled up like an Eskimo.

She feels a fart, a great big thunderous one, welling up behind her weak, puny little sphincter. She bites her lip trying to hold it in, but alas it is of no avail. She emits a Hiroshima fart that splits the night.

PWWWWAAAAAAAAKKKK

The creature on the pole swivels it's oddly shaped head and regards her curiously with a pair of enormous, glowing red amoeba-eyes, like those Precious Moments knock off children in the tacky '70's thrift shop paintings.

A high-pitched tinny whining noise fills her ears and she suddenly and inexplicably grows as eerily calm as the eye of a hurricane. Those burning bejeweled, ruby red orbs are hypnotic, better than Vicodin. Those eyes, they are the whole world. She feels as if she is falling from a great height. Nothing matters 'cept those big, bloody crimson eyes. Not even the, what under ordinary circumstances she couldn't help but regard as horrible, ghastly, and utterly loathsome gurgling,

152

splashing, and bubbling noises emanating from the suddenly vibrating toilet atop which she sits, nay, not even these matter when those shimmering scarlet eyes look upon her and she upon them.

When the long, thin, ice-cold thing with the consistency of something one would find growing on a rotting log began to caress her goosebumped ass and probe at her sweaty snatch, it was like it wasn't even real, it was like she was playing herself in the made for TV movie and she was being confronted by a lame-ass recreation of a trauma she'd experienced years before.

Shoulda put the blue stuff in the water more religiously, she thinks, just before the cold, jellied tentacle from the toilet plunges into her pussy. She winces in pain and somehow she can taste it, calamari and compost, lutefisk and sewer sludge. Her eyes slam closed like guillotines. The slimy strip of sewer calamari pumps in and out of her cunt several times. The cold, fungoid stalk swells and pulses inside her, stretching the walls of her pussy like the Pear of Anguish, a medieval torture device resembling a metal pear of interlocking leaves, which with the turn of a screw, unfolded, like a blooming flower of steel inside you.

She can feel the hot bile welling up in her throat. Her face is on fire. She tries to fight it, but alas, it is of no avail. She vomits warm, half-digested orange sherbet all over her naked lap.

The kraken-cock tentacle suddenly explodes inside the damp embrace of Becky's cunt-folds. Literally explodes. It was like a firecracker had gone off in her pussy. Her ears are ringing. She now knows how the proverbial M-80-cat felt. Dry heaves wrack her.

When she opens her eyes, the thing is gone from the pole, and though she is mostly blessedly numb down in her nethers, beneath the pinprick tingle spreading out from between her legs, she can faintly feel part of the sewer-tentacle still wiggling deep inside her violated cunt.

She spends a timeless time trying to force it out with sheer will. It doesn't work.

She explodes from the toilet, stumbles to the kitchen on rubbery, traitorous legs, and is fumbling with the silverware drawer containing the gleaming chromium barbecue tongs, when the tingling grey numbness wraps around her like mummy linens, and the mouth of nihility gobbles her up amidst the clatter of the silverware drawer's contents raining to the floor.

The sticky, yellow linoleum is cold against her goosebumped skin when she awakes.

She can't feel the wiggling thing inside her pussy anymore.

Her pussy itches something fierce, like its being gnawed by a swarm of termites. She pulls herself up to a sitting position, naked flesh peeling away from the filthy, yellow linoleum with a zipper sound. Crouching like a frog, she spreads her thighs, lowers her head, and examines her crotch. It looks like someone has thrown acid on her red, raw snatch. She feels an intense desire to scrub her pussy with a bleach soaked sponge. She scratches her bush; thick clumps of hair fall out with each stroke of her finger and drift lazily to the filthy linoleum floor.

Her ass itches too. She scratches her butt like she had just had a cast removed as she trots to the bathroom. Uses a hand mirror to look at her fat ass in the mirror over the sink. Her ass was a pretty revolting specimen to begin with, looked like a pumpkin made of bleached moon-cheese which had been shot repeatedly with a BB gun, and the splotchy, yellow-pink mold-rash which had sprouted wherever the toilet-tentacle had touched certainly did nothing to help the situation.

The itch is maddening, like her ass is being gnawed upon by poisonous locusts. She feels an intense desire to fill a piecrust with calamine lotion, sit on it, and wiggle her butt around. Speaking of pie, was it her, or was her belly starting to balloon

154

up a wee bit? And hadn't her belly button been an 'innie' when she showered this morning?

She suddenly craved pickles and can feel phantom teeth gnawing her sore nipples.

As she stares in stunned disbelief, her belly begins to swell before her very eyes. As her belly grows bloated and distended, wicked ugly lil' purple varicose veins begin to writhe and crawl beneath the stretching skin. The twisted little veins seem to spell something in some strange unknown alphabet. The swirls and slashes have the regularity and repetition of writing.

Pain pickles her pussy as foul green goop begins to ooze from it, and trickle viscously down her flabby thighs. Her breasts, in addition to her belly, have begun to swell, and her erect nipples, in addition to her cunt, now begin to disgorge foul green slime.

Becky pukes thick yellow bile down her swelling tits.

The accursed thing in her belly strains against its fleshy fetters, the ball of fornicating snakes that must be its misbegotten head visible beneath her stretching skin, a lamprey encrusted fetus being eaten by that beach ball from the old Prisoner TV show. Goddamn thing was liable to chew its way out of her.

An avalanche of junk cascades from the shelf of the closet when she opens the door. Becky grabs the vacuum cleaner, a bottle of vodka, and a tub of Vaseline from the secret hidey hole behind the paneling of the shelf.

She'd bought her vacuum cleaner at a po-leece auction; someone had scrawled, "NATURE ABHORS" across the bag in black permanent marker. She slides the wand nozzle on the ironic vacuum's hose attachment.

She debates popping a Vicodin, but she decides against it, cuz she fears ripping her insides apart and not even feeling it.

She pours vodka over the wand nozzle and gulps down as

much as she can stand.

She lubes up the wand nozzle with a fistful of petroleum jelly.

"Dirt Devil don't fail me now," she gulps.

She begins to insert the greasy wand nozzle into her suppurating cunt.

Too late.

Her navel tears open and ejaculates black slime, just before her belly splits apart like a blooming flower, an extremely moist carrion flower, and slimy black tentacles unfurl from the bloody cunt-like wound. A squiggling tentacle curls around the wrist of her abortin' hand. Becky fights with all she has and manages to pull the stretchy tentacle to her mouth. The tentacle tastes like rotten goat meat boiled in diarrhea and it unleashes a gush of bitter ooze as she bites it in twain.

Her eye pops as she slams the wand nozzle into her eye socket with all her might and flips the vacuum's switch, attempting to suck her brain from her skull. Hoping with her last breath the blackness inside her body would die with its host.

CREATING A BEGINNING

PHILIP ROBERTS

"And here it is."

Jessie Moeller stepped aside and gestured for Spencer to enter. Both squinted their eyes against dusty air. Thin slits of light pierced through the cracks of boarded over windows, Jessie's own flashlight darkened in his hand, the decayed room kept purposefully dark for Spencer's benefit.

A wall had once divided the living room from the kitchen, and the shattered remains of it could be seen, a gap of gouged wood between the carpeted living room and the tiled kitchen floor. Age had turned the couch into a sunken corpse, fluffy innards pouring from slashed fabric. In the center of the plaster ceiling wires revealed where a light had once shined.

Spencer moved further towards the kitchen and the rusted appliances still pressed against the wall beneath the boarded window. The fridge drew his eye and the yellowed papers stuck beneath plastic covered alphabet magnets.

A B+ math assignment, the words Good Work! written in dark red along the top corner, the barely visible crayon drawing of a girl and a dog, both shapes reduced to smudged colors, and other relics of the past remained. Spencer ran his fingers over the drawing.

"What did you say happened to them?" he asked without looking back at his guide.

"Way I heard it, husband caught the wife cheating, cut her up, kid saw the whole thing and died like, I don't know, eight years later or something. You know, offed herself. Usually how

157

it goes." Jessie brought a cigarette up to his lips as he spoke, lighter nearly to the tip when the dry, aged wood caught his eye. With a shrug he put the lighter away, cigarette still stuck between his lips.

Spencer turned back towards Jessie. "You know this?"

"I heard it. Most the people in the area know that one."

"Yeah, but is it true. I don't, you know, feel anything or nothing like that."

"Look, I brought you here. What the hell you expecting? Look in the closet, maybe there'll be a finger or something along the floor."

A thoughtful smile plucking at his lips, Spencer did just that, fingers groping over dirty floorboards in search of proof. He stood up frowning.

"I mean, you really expect you're going to find anything here? What is this, five places I've shown you now? We've hit almost every haunted place in the area. Besides, you're supposed to move in or something, you know, live here for a bit and then it all drives you crazy. Least that's how I heard it."

"Yeah, I guess." A hopeful look coming over his face, Spencer glanced back over. "Know any others?"

"Not within walking. Hell, for the same going rate meet me next weekend and I'll drive you over to Wilbur. They're supposed to have a few places you might like. You done here?"

Spencer took another glance around, frowning, before nodding. "Sure."

Jessie gestured his head towards the door and waited for Spencer to go first. They left through the door Jessie had broken open, and as they walked through the dark suburb and away from the last of the houses for the night Jessie took a long look at the boy he'd been given good money to show around.

Though Jessie himself had never cared for the stories of demonic abandoned homes in his youth, and had rolled his eyes at the wide, frightened eyes his once younger friends had shown at the prospect of taking a peek into such a structure, he still found Spencer's fascination a tad disturbing. Jessie fully admitted a bit of prejudice behind his dislike. When the factory on the north end of the city moved its operations elsewhere, people like Spencer's dad lost their jobs, and the whole area dipped into a poverty it had never crawled out of.

The white trash, as Jessie had no qualms calling them, had a look about them, one prevalent in the seventeen-year-old Spencer's lanky, muscular body, his long face, and his dirty clothes. How he had scrounged up the fifty to pay Jessie for these little tours was something Jessie preferred not to know.

He hated too that the boy seemed less fascinated by the notion of a haunting, and more by the violence that led to them; always searching for proof it happened.

"You know the place you showed me a few weeks ago, one off of Woodbury?" Spencer said as they walked beneath an unusually dark overcast, removing any hint of moon or stars. "It was all a load of bull. Searched through forty years of newspapers and not a word about anything. Even talked to the company trying to sell it, and they said they didn't know about no legend or murders. I bet most of these places don't have anything special about them. Just broken down homes."

"Why you care so much about this shit?" Jessie pulled out his lighter as he spoke, finally lit his cigarette.

But Spencer didn't answer, smiling, and Jessie decided to let it go, figuring the less he knew about the kid the better.

They stopped in front of Jessie's own house. "You walking home?"

"Sure," Spencer said. "Look, I'll meet you next Saturday to drive out to Wilbur, okay? Make sure you find some real good ones, you know, like big families killed, or, hey, maybe we can find an old asylum. I see that shit in stories all the time."

"Whatever you want. I'm going in. Talk to you later."

He stepped up to the rather modest two-story building he

159

called home and waved at Spencer walking away.

*

Three people lived in Jessie's home: Jessie, his brother Daniel, and his brother's wife Roberta. When Jessie awoke some time after three in the morning to see Spencer's smiling face hovering right above his in the darkness, the cool, sharp knife already pressed against Jessie's throat, he thought of his family first.

"What are you," Jessie began to whisper, but Spencer pressed the tape against his mouth before he could answer. Handcuffs already bound Jessie's wrists and his ankles. The shock of the moment prevented him from trying to struggle when Spencer dragged him off the bed and into the dimly lit living room.

Daniel and Roberta had already been seen to, both tied and gagged along the far wall, their eyes wide, muffled cries increasing at the sight of Jessie.

From out of his pocket Spencer poured the pictures onto the floor in front of Jessie. Violent death filled all of them; the age, gender, or race of the victims varied throughout.

Spencer's face appeared in front of Jessie again. "I didn't kill these people if that's what you're thinking. Nah, just got them online. But see, they got me thinking about a few things, and I think I've been going about it wrong."

He pulled up and moved over to Roberta's bound form, curly brown hair falling over her tear-reddened eyes. Daniel attempted to lunge for Spencer, but bound as he was, he merely fell to the hardwood floor, cried muffled protests, and impotently watched his wife dragged into the middle of the room.

"Why go looking for this stuff when I can make it happen. People will be talking about this afterwards. I bet you some

160

kids from the high school sneak in here, you know, few years from now, seeing who has the guts."

Jessie tried in vain to talk against his gag but the tape wouldn't let his lips open. Spencer seemed to understand and moved towards him. Before reaching for the tape a harder look fell over the youth's face. "You scream and I'll hurt you bad, you got it?"

The tape tore from Jessie's raw lips. "Please don't do this."

"It's good saying stuff like that. Way I figure it, most these stories always have some kind of passion to them, like, fit of rage and stuff. But I don't hate you. Hell, I don't hate most people, but if I want this to work, I need some real emotion in here. That's why I thought of you."

Though something in Jessie thought he knew what Spencer meant, he still asked, "What the hell are you talking about?"

But Spencer saw the understanding in Jessie's eyes, smiled at it, pulling upright with the blade held tightly in his hand. "I know about that guy you knifed. Why you think I came to you to begin with? Never met anyone else who killed a guy. Friend of my bother who was in the army says he killed a guy, or thinks his bullet did it, but he wasn't too sure, so I don't think that counts. Besides, gunning a guy down ain't the same as knifing him and seeing his eyes up close." Spencer knelt down again; so eager he fidgeted, holding in the excitement. "What was it like? You look him close in the eye as he died? Got to tell me you did."

He had. They'd called it self-defense, and so Jessie had been able to go free, but in truth the self-defense was a blessing, because Jessie would've killed the man no matter who had hit first, or pulled a weapon first. Age had tempered the anger that had once led him to thrust a knife into another man's stomach and spit in his face as he died with his eyes opened so wide.

"I can show you more places," Jessie pleaded.

Spencer scowled at him and pulled up. "I bet there wasn't

161

shit that happened in those places. I want a real haunting, something I know is true, and something that can live on. If we're talking about these places where nothing happened in, just think of what people will say about your house."

"It doesn't have to be this way," Jessie pleaded, tried to think of anything he could say, anything to stop Spencer as he knelt in front of Roberta and grabbed hold of her hair.

"Afraid it does," Spencer said. He stared right at Jessie, held his gaze with total calm, and drove the knife into Roberta's neck.

She bucked against his grip, robe pulling loose, blood spilling across her bare chest as Spencer cut deeper into the skin without ever looking down, his eyes never leaving Jessie's face, smiling at him. Spencer pulled her head up, let Jessie see the spasms, the neck splitting open, her eyes rolling back in her head while behind her Daniel crawled across the floor, face wet with tears, his muffled cries the only sound in the living room.

Spencer let go of the hair and let the body fall face first onto the floor. Blood crawled outward, almost seemed to stretch towards Jessie, he thought.

Jessie didn't speak. He leaned his head back against the wall and closed his eyes. He tried to force the image of Roberta's face out of his mind. Spencer's hands grabbed hold of his hair and jerked his head forward, made him open his eyes to stare into the madness leaning in close to him.

"Need to see it all," Spencer said.

Jessie leaned in closer himself, nose practically touching Spencer. "You want me to see, you cut my eyes open, but I'm not helping you with your fantasy." He closed his eyes again, heard Spencer pull back, thought maybe the boy would follow his suggestion, and Jessie didn't know how far his bravado could take him, but the pain never pierced through his eyelids. Instead he heard something being dragged across the floor, and heard Daniel's muffled cries get louder.

Then the feet stepped calmly up to him and he smelled the stink of Spencer's breath blowing across his face. "You're right. Why didn't I think of it? It's like in the stories you hear, about a kid in the other room, or something, maybe in a closet, and he, like, hears it all, but he can't see it. Shit, that's pretty good. You keep them closed."

Then it came. Jessie clenched his mouth so tightly closed he felt his gums ache, felt pain as the cuffs cut into his wrists when they jerked against the metal, but that was nothing compared to the muffled shrieks his bother uttered. Mixed with the cries Jessie could hear the sound of flesh being cut, a wet, sickening quality to it, and with each sound his mind offered him what might be happening right in front of him, along with his brother smiling, the two of them kicking back with a beer, walking to school as children, huddling close in the bedroom when their father came home stinking of liquor.

He told himself the sounds weren't real, a nightmare Spencer's odd obsession had forced upon Jessie, and any moment he'd wake up. When the cries finally ended something in him almost believed he'd only see his bedroom ceiling when he opened his eyes.

Hands grabbed hold of him and shoved him to the floor, pressed his face against it, lifted his hands up. His eyes didn't open until he felt the cuffs pop free. Then he stared at the wood floor and the red stained into it. He pulled himself up, seeing without allowing his mind to fully grasp the image of his brother's body pushed against the wall, stomach cut open, blood spread all over the white walls.

Jessie let his attention turn instead towards Spencer standing in the doorway smiling at him. A bloody knife waited at his feet. Jessie knelt down and grabbed hold of the blade.

"Now you do me," Spencer said. He pulled off his shirt and motioned towards his bare, skinny chest.

"What?" Jessie asked, his left eye twitching.

163

"You have to kill me next. That's the way this works. I got it all figured out."

The knife fell from his fingers and struck the floor. Spencer barely had a chance to see it fall before Jessie leapt forward and took them both down. He saw himself from far away hammering Spencer's face, rocking it to the side, splitting open his lip, breaking his nose, sealing off his left eye. Something in him understood he couldn't kill Spencer and give the freak what he wanted. He needed this guy to go to jail and suffer the rest of his life for the lives he'd taken. Killing him now would only let him off easy, give him a role in the game, yet Jessie kept hitting, reducing Spencer's face to little more than a pulpy mound of bleeding skin.

The two shots brought everything back to reality. The world snapped into focus with those shots, and though Jessie could see the red oozing out from his chest where the bullets had ripped through him, he felt no pain. Even when his lungs refused to suck in air and he stumbled off of Spencer's body, he still couldn't feel anything, could only stare at Spencer pulling himself off the floor with the gun in his hand. Though the face was battered almost beyond recognition, Jessie could see the smile in Spencer's eyes.

"Knew you'd come through for me," Spencer garbled out, forced the words through his bleeding lips. Jessie fell onto his back, gasping, his left hand clutching his chest. Above him Spencer knelt down closer. "I know you didn't think much of me, like most people don't, figuring I can't work most shit out in my head, but I got this one good. I like you Jessie, no matter what it looks like here; I value what you done for me.

"Can't just be a stranger come in killing people. Sure, people sort of talk about that shit, but it has to be a family member, you know, cause that's the way this is. With your prints on the knife and people knowing what you did, just makes things as it should be. I even told my dad I was coming over here, staying the night so you could take me to more of those places, ones you know about where people supposed to have died, and so I say you went crazy, killed them, tried to kill me, but I brought a gun, cause this neighborhood ain't the best, and so I stopped you."

Jessie coughed, tasted what he could only assume was blood in the back of his throat, finally feeling a fire burning inside his chest.

"I'll make sure people know your name," Spencer said, whispering into Jessie's ear. "Don't have to worry about that."

Jessie had no thoughts, mind unable to conjure them in those last minutes as he stared up into Spencer's face and tried to speak, to reach out his hand and grab hold of the guy's arm, though he didn't know to what purpose. His hand fell away before it ever reached him.

*

Spencer leaned against the brick side of a house and took a long drag on his cigarette while the boy in front of him shook his head.

"I've heard that crap before," the boy said.

"I'm telling you," Spencer said, pointed across the street towards the empty building. "No one has lived there in fifteen years. Look it up, cause there were a lot of reports about it at the time. Most places, you know, people say something happened, but you can't find anything on it. That ain't true for this one. The guy butchered his brother. Practically spread his insides across the room." He smiled at the boy's pale expression, took another drag.

Hesitation flickered across the boy's face before he tried to shake it off. "You're just making that up."

Spencer shrugged. "Takes you five minutes to look it up, maybe less. Every word of it is true. Bet you can even find

165

pictures if you look hard enough. I've seen them."

He watched the kid roll his eyes, continue on down the sidewalk, one of many Spencer had spoken to over the years. The boy tried to shrug it off, act like he was too tough to care, but in Spencer's mind he could just see that face lit but a computer's glow, leaning in close as he read the truth, smiled in fear and fascination. Spencer smiled himself at the thought.

For two more hours he stood up against the building, going through half a pack, watching the sun begin to sink and the streetlights flicker to life. When the darkness crept a bit closer Spencer finally pushed off the wall and started on his way home with the empty windows of Jessie's home watching him go.

DARKEST DREAMS

ZOE ADAMS

When I was first employed by Madame Infliction, I was shocked and appalled. It was bad enough the club looked seedy from the outside, with its tacky neon lights, but inside it was even worse.

The chairs had handcuffs hanging from the armrests and legs. Many of the tiny mahogany tables were broken from the girls climbing atop them in chunky shoes. The bar was always kept clean, but the alcohol supplied to the club was either deathly or... well, it didn't bear thinking about. A silver mirror ball hung from the roof, while the stage lighting looked as if it should belong at a children's birthday party. Across the back wall hung a plain velvet curtain, separating the back world of the club from the metal pole in the centre.

I was hired two years ago, when the great recession of Great Britain hit. I barely had the money to pay for the tiny flat I lived in and I'd skip meals because I couldn't afford it. I got sick and struggled to pay the medical bills. I sold possessions to greedy pawnbrokers in a pitiful attempt to survive, until I barely had anything left to sell.

It was the most awful experience of my life.

Madame Infliction changed all that. I'd been tap-dancing for money in the city centre, singing outside of large department stores where the rich still could shop. She took me to a greasy spoon café, and pressed a hot drink into my hands. As I sank my teeth into a squashed sandwich, she explained she was a manager, looking for some hard-workers.

To look at Madame Infliction, you wouldn't guess what she

did for a living. A woman of grace and style, I thought she was a model. Oh how wrong I was.

When I first saw Darkest Dreams, my mouth hit the floor. You thought about selling your body, this is no more degrading, I thought. Ten other girls sat with me, either nervously checking their hair, or broadly explaining how many men they'd had sex with and what positions they'd been in. One girl, no older than sixteen, claimed she'd been through the Karma Sutra more than once.

When it was my turn, I stumbled onto the stage barefoot. Once the pole was in my hand though, I forgot about the gaping girls and let my imagination run wild. After years of studying dance, I was finally putting what I had learnt into practise.

Madame Infliction hired me on the spot.

Just two years later and I'm one of the most popular girls at the club. I work every night without fail, either waitressing or entertaining. I get big tips and the occasional date offer. The flat is warmer now than it has ever been. I'm healthy, and my possessions are back where they belong.

When I am in my flat, wrapped in my thoughts, my name is Rachel, university graduate, timid as hell. When I take to the stage, I am Ravish, and I aim to please.

*

It was blowing a gale as I left for work that night. My gym bag was filled to bursting with costumes and accessories. The weight of it slowed me down; I'd been for an audition with an uprising dance company, and I'd just made the call-backs. Getting to London for the call-backs would be expensive and I needed all the money I could get.

I stumbled along as best as I could, until I reached the bus stop.

I perched on the bench, lighting a cigarette. Madame Infliction kept asking me to quit, but as long as I scrubbed up well, none of my customers noticed.

An older man came out of the growing fog. He kept his head down as he walked towards me, huddled into a leather trench-coat.

I moved further up on the bench, giving him more room for his hulking frame. He nodded in greeting, his breathing laboured.

The bus lurched to a stop. I moved forwards, dragging the bag as I went. As I climbed onto the bus, my bag strap caught and my clothes tumbled to the ground.

"Fucking hell!"

I scrambled to pick them up, but Trench-coat was already there. He started to pick up the laciest pieces of underwear. I bit my lip. If he had anything to say, he kept his mouth shut as his fists clenched in the revealing dresses.

"I think these are yours."

"Thanks." I stuffed the clothes back into my bag and pushed my weekly ticket at the driver's partition. He jerked his thumb back and I headed for the first empty seat I could find.

The old woman who'd been spying at me from the window gave me a disgusted look and moved closer to the window, her hands gripping her reusable shopping bag.

Stupid old bitch.

When Trench-coat got on the bus, it wobbled with his weight. When he'd finally found a seat near the back, the bus got underway. It jerked and spluttered as it carried on down the road, hitting potholes as it went. Some snotty-nosed little kid opened a back window, and the smell of wet fish invaded. I clamped my lips shut and pulled the collar of my jacket up to cover my nose.

Finally we stopped outside the Oxfam charity shop. The graffitied shutters were already pulled down against the night. I grabbed my belongings, nodded my thanks and headed straight for the side street. A quick walk through, and the club loomed before me. Dodging the traffic, I reached the doors to let myself in.

Alyssa was already sat at the desk, her most alluring secretarial costume in place. She signed me in, before ushering me through to the dressing rooms.

The rest of the girls were already stuffing themselves into babydolls and pulling striped socks over their knees. When the sounds of happy revellers filtered into my ears, I knew I was ready to go. I'd been scheduled as a waitress that night, and even I think I look enticing. A skin-tight leather dress, with stockings that reach my thighs. I can strut with the best of them in my sky-high stilettos. My hair is backcombed and I've layered up on the black make-up like some rock goddess.

The new girl twirled on the pole, bending in places that left nothing to the imagination. She had already gathered a number of fans, from the young to the old. I took the tray of complimentary drinks that was waiting at the bar, and made my way to the full tables. Money fluttered at me and I slipped the notes into the top of my stocking. I batted my false eyelashes and pouted my lips at a group of boys, fresh off the wagon.

"Any chance you're on the pole tonight?" a regular asked as I passed his table.

"Not me no. I'm just your friendly neighbourhood pot girl." I winked as I took his glass.

I was used to the pain of wearing stilettos but today my feet ached more than usual.

I leant against the bar, massaging my ankles as Brett started making up the orders.

"A guy was asking for you earlier," he said, as he upturned a bottle of vodka.

"What do you mean?"

"Said he knew you. *Sean*, I think he said, but I couldn't be sure."

I shook my head. "I don't know anyone called Sean. How did he ask for me?"

"Ravish." The drinks tray was loaded and I pushed the name to the side as I set back around the club, delivering glasses and shots.

On my way back to the bar, I spotted Trench-coat. He nursed a bottle of beer in one hand, while the other grasped the side of the stage. His eyes roamed over Mina's curvaceous figure, finally settling on her gyrating hips.

"Is that him?"

Brett squinted at the back of Trench-coat's chair. "I can't tell from here. Sorry doll."

I sighed. "Listen I'm taking an early break. Let me know if this guy comes back, okay?" I left my tray on the side, and hurried to the staff bathrooms.

I raided the First Aid kit for the painkillers. My ankles ached and the start of a headache was imminent. I dry swallowed the two capsules, before reapplying my lipstick and pushing the pins in my hair back into place.

Sean. The only Sean I could think of was Sean Bean.

Brushing it off, I headed back out. Madame Infliction was sipping champagne at the bar, looking every inch the lady and sexual predator. Her dress was hiked up over her knees, and the sleeves hung from her shoulders.

"Ravish!" She slid from the bar stool, greeting me with an air kiss to the cheek. "You look wonderful, as always."

"Thank you Madame."

"I have a proposition for you."

"And that would be?"

"A member would like your services." Her thin eyebrows arched, waiting for my reply.

My mind went blank. "I thought Eternity was servicing tonight."

171

Madame waved her hand, as if shooing away a persistent fly. The bangles on her wrists clattered against each other and her diamond ring caught the light.

"Eternity has called in sick. Again. But I have it on good knowledge that she's currently shacking up with some high class barrister while his wife's away."

I knew which barrister she was talking about. He flattered all the girls, but of course, only Eternity would be stupid enough to fall for his tricks.

"I understand you've had a busy day, but this would be a favour to me, and of course you will be properly paid."

"I'll do it."

Madame beamed at me. "That's what I like to hear from my best girl." She pressed the key into my hand and curled my fingers over it.

She gave me another air kiss and headed towards the reception area, champagne flute held high.

I took the water bottle that Brett offered, and headed towards the back rooms.

The club isn't just a place to ogle a pole dancer or get a sexy drink. In the back rooms, certified members are allowed to touch the girls on offer. The first starter members are too shy to let their mind's run free, and ask for the simple things like a hand wrapped around them, sometimes a hot wet mouth.

And then, you get the regulars. The ones who come in, expecting a girl to climb on top of their bodies and show them what talents they're hiding.

I've been a back room worker for three months, and in that time, I've done things that would make your toes curl. And I assumed tonight would be no exception.

Kay was sat by the curtains, in nothing but a pair of French knickers. Bottles of chilled wine surrounded her, topping up glasses as a few customers waited in line.

I gave a seductive purr, as I stood before them. One man

gulped. *Newbie.*

"Welcome gentlemen. Now, who's first?" I trailed my hands to my hips, where I gripped them softly.

"Somebody's waiting for you inside," Kay said, as she uncorked a fresh bottle.

I nodded, and pushed through the curtains into the hallway. It was lined with photographs of the girls, "hard at work". I grinned as I passed mine – I'm wrapped around the pole, bending backwards, a gentleman's tie between my teeth.

To my surprise, Trench-coat was waiting outside the room. His wallet was clutched tightly in his sausage-like fingers.

I rolled my eyes. *Just my luck.*

"Ah a customer!" I said, widening my eyes slightly.

He looked up nervously.

"Come through here." I unlocked the door, ushering him inside.

The room was a palace of seduction. Decked out in hues of red and black, with lace hangings on the four poster silk sheeted bed, it's a dream come true. An adjoining room leads to a palace of depravity, where if the S&M scene is more your thing, we can take you there.

He sat on the edge of the bed, palming his wallet as if it was an extension of his body.

I sat next to him, and tucked my legs carefully, trying to look not only elegant, but a seductive goddess too.

"I'm Ravish."

"I know," he said, his voice thick with emotion.

I cocked my head. "I haven't seen you here before, have I?."

"I've just moved back to the area."

"Been anywhere nice?" I asked coyly.

He laughed; a short sharp laugh.

"Could say that."

I leant back on one arm, jutting my ample chest forward slightly. I watched him take a deep breath as his eyes flickered

173

over me.

"I didn't catch your name."

He ran a hand through his thick brown hair.

"Sean."

My throat went dry. My hunch was right after all.

"Are you the same Sean that asked for me at the bar?" I asked.

He nodded. "I heard you were the best."

I blushed through the heavy make-up. I wasn't the best by far, but who was I to turn down a compliment?

"And what may we do for you tonight, Sean?"

My fingers danced over to him, trailing my nails over the skin of his hand. He looked up, and our eyes caught. They were nearly pitch black, like the night's sky. He had a tiny scar underneath his left eye and I wondered how he'd got it.

"I want to have sex with you. And I want to be on top."

I nodded and licked my lips. It was in that instant that everything changed.

His lips crashed into mine so hard that I swear I felt teeth. His mouth covered mine, his tongue trying to probe my lips apart.

I shoved my hands into his shoulders, trying to prise him off me. I needed air, I was going light-headed. One of his arms wrapped around my waist and pressed our bodies together. The other he kept a firm grip on my skull. He was crushing me.

He sank us backwards onto the bed so I was on the bottom, like he wanted. He broke his excuse for a kiss, a twisted smile on his face.

"You whores are all the same."

I scrabbled backwards, sliding up the bed, striking my head on the headboard.

"Look you don't have to hurt me!"

"Don't you bitches get off on pain?" He grabbed for my ankle, and I kicked out. He caught my heel and started pulling

174

me back. My dress shot further up my thighs and the money from the top of my stocking spilled out. My legs flailed faster. My foot collided with his forearm and the heel scraped along his forearm.

"That's it bitch, hurt me!"

Oh God, he was a masochist.

"You really don't know what you're getting yourself into, do you Rachel?"

I stopped moving, as he tugged me forwards and pinned my shoulders with his hands. I winced and tried to move, but it was useless.

"You think I wouldn't recognise the girl who broke my heart all those years ago? Left me a complete and utter wreck. And now look at you, selling yourself like the cheap slut you fucking are!"

"How did… did I break… y-your heart?"

"You know what you did."

"I don't even know you!" I screamed into his face. His body was over mine, trapping me.

"Lindsey. Lindsey School! Year Eleven!"

And then it hit me like a bolt of lightning.

*

"Rachel! Rachel!"

Sean Barton hurried along the corridor, his backpack trailing along the floor. His face was flushed and he had to take a drag from his inhaler as he neared the classroom door.

The angel of his desire was right ahead of him now. Her dark hair was springing free of its French plait. Her friends were surrounding her, a gaggle of preening swans.

"Rachel, hi." He breathed, giving her a smile that he had practised too many times in the bathroom mirror.

"Sean." She pressed her lips together.

"Did you get my texts last night?"

"Yeah I got them. All fifteen of them," she giggled.

"Fifteen?" one of the girls cackled. "You do have an admirer."

"What do you want Sean? I've got dance to get to," Rachel sighed.

"I was wondering... whether you'd like to go to the prom with me?" Sean ventured.

Rachel laughed. A cold heartless laugh that left him stunned.

"Look you're nice and all that, but you're just not my type. Sorry." She spun on her heel, strutting off to the studios, the girls laughing with her.

"Rachel!" he shouted.

She threw her hand into the air, her middle finger raised as she walked through the double doors.

Sean was appalled. The rest of the school day passed in a blur. He deleted everything about her except... Except the photo he had taken – looking like the little slag she really was.

*

"Sean, please I was just a kid then, we both were! Please don't do this, I'm sorry!" He had unzipped my dress and was tugging it down. I pushed and scratched at him, but my attempts were failing badly. He grasped my wrists together and pinned me them above my head. The alarm cord was out of my reach. I felt like my bones were going to break at any minute.

"Sorry? You're *sorry*? Do you have any idea what you've done to me? I've spent most of my adult like stuck in a fucking nut house! All because of you! You knew what you were doing all those years ago! And believe me, I know what I'm doing now."

He reached into his coat, and my eyes popped out. I twisted and tried to heave myself of the bed with my feet. I heard a rip

176

as my heels pierced the sheets.

I whimpered underneath the bulk of his body and I felt the knife at the bottom of my ribcage.

"Shut the fuck up bitch! Don't even move a fucking muscle or I'll split you wide open!"

He trailed the tip of the knife up my body until he reached my cheek. He pressed down and I gasped. He drew it away, a malicious grin on his face.

"Now you're going to spread your legs for me, like a good little whore. And I'm going to fuck you. You'll enjoy it, won't you?"

He pressed the knife in again and I gave a cry of pain.

"Say 'yes master'."

"Y... Yes mast... master."

Master.

In a brief moment of inspiration, I spread my legs and pushed my pelvis upwards slightly. I instantly felt him go hard underneath me and the knife was gone. He slashed at my thong, and I felt blood raising to the surface. You're going to pay for that you bastard. It was obvious where his brain lay, as he made to unzip his trousers.

I moved.

The knife was in my hand and in his face before he knew what was happening.

"Move!" I hissed through my teeth.

Pure panic flooded his face. He moved back slowly, his hand still on the zip of his crotch. I waved the knife, as he moved further back.

My dress slipped from my body and the tattered sheets entangled in the heels fluttered like wings

"Don't you ever threaten me again, you ugly fucking bastard!"

I lunged, striking the knife down into his shoulder.

He hissed and moaned, as the knife sank further into him.

His blood spurted onto my face and my bare chest.

"Again."

Yielding, I struck. Once, twice, thrice, he was still going, crying that he felt close, so close to the edge. His blood patterned my skin, like a grotesque tattoo.

I slammed the knife down one last time, and hit his heart. His blood sprayed violently as he took his last breath. He shuddered, falling back onto the wall with a bang. I stepped back in silence as his lifeless body slumped to the floor.

My pulse raced like a stallion and yet… I felt strange. I gathered towels from the adjoining bathroom and spread them over the pool of blood as best as I could. I stuffed a towel into the gaping chest wound, while I disposed of the knife into the waste-bin.

I left his body on the floor, while I cleaned up in the bathroom with the sweetest smelling soap we had. I sluiced the blood from my dress and rubbed it dry, before zipping it back into place. The underwear I could do without.

Back in the bedroom, I unlocked the long window and heaved it open. The cold wind blew the tendrils of hair about my and for an instant I felt light-headed.

I heaved Sean's body towards the window. Using every ounce of strength, I hauled him upright and straight through the window.

The snap of his neck was quite satisfying.

I slammed down the window, drawing the curtains tightly behind me. Surveying the room once more, I smiled. Everything was back to normal.

Back in the waiting room, the customers were still waiting for me. There were more empty glasses, and high pitched giggling filled the air.

I struck a pose against the door jamb, knee up, head resting backwards.

"Who's next boys?"

THUNDER

HOLLY DAY

1

Johnny was a streak of black paint on a blood-red canvas surface, all angles and white bone and a smile that could melt butter and sear flesh. His hair flopped back in a greasy oil slick from his carrion bird face, his beak of a nose jutting out against the smooth of his pale skin like the warning fin of an albino shark surfacing and closing in for the kill. He was a bad boy. He was a good lay and he walked like he knew it.

The Dragon Lady was a beautiful green and gold flower blooming sickly amongst the other dying junkies in her shooting gallery-slash-parlor. She somehow managed to still have firm, full breasts and shapely thighs, despite having been a pretty solid heroin addict for nearly a year. Her sisters and brothers in bone and blood sprawled around her in various states of recline and decline, pale scarecrows and skeletons with bright, unhurried worried eyes. The pizza from the night before sat opened and uneaten on the coffee table in the middle of the room, cold, the cheese coagulated, a thick layer of red grease pooling on its surface. "Could someone please close the pizza box?" The Dragon Lady murmured, closing her eyes and turning away. "It's making me sick just looking at it."

The little bus boy was a streak of brown grease on an old wash cloth left up to dry without a decent rinsing. He loved The Dragon Lady with all his heart and head and soul, and told her so many, many times, although he wasn't sure he had actually ever spoken to her in English or out loud. He lay on the floor, far across the room from The Dragon Lady, and could just make out her green bathrobe-clad form from where he lay. "I'll get it," he whispered, his own body barely strong enough to shape the words, much less walk over to the pizza box and close it. He stretched his arms out, over his head, and rolled over onto his stomach. He slithered along the puke-stained carpet slowly, each movement a tremendous, soul-sucking effort.

Johnny's black stud-covered leather boot suddenly blocked off the little bus boy's vision of the elusive pizza box. The little bus boy looked up to see Johnny lean down from an impossible height and carefully fold the box lid down, tucking the flap closed tightly. "I got it," Johnny said, picking the pizza box up and leaving the room, heading towards the kitchen. The little bus boy collapsed when he lay, angry to the point of near tears. "I said I'd get it!" he shouted after the stronger man, not sure the words were leaving him loud enough to be heard.

The little bus boy started his new job the following Monday. He was to be the official guinea pig for the shipments of heroin that were coming through Mexico to The Dragon Lady and her friends. She had personally recommended him for the job, citing him as an excellent judge of quality to his face, citing him as not too much for her to lose behind his back. He showed up at the aluminum-sided phallic-shaped silo behind Farmer's ancient hacienda a full half-hour early.

Two other men were waiting in the shadows as the little busboy entered the dark silo, motes of ancient dust from maize and wheat no longer stored caught in the sudden flash of sunlight. "Hey," said the first one, a short, dark troll with faded black hair and skin.

"Hey," returned the little busboy, thrusting his chest out and swaggering into the room. "Is this the party?"

"Not yet," answered the second. He was a lean, tan Indian with corn-straight hair and black-blue eyes. "You the one replacing Hector?"

"I'm not sure," said the little busboy. "They gave me these shoes when they gave me the job. Were these Hector's?" He held his right foot out for inspection, pointing the toe tip of his new purple suede creepers directly at the Indian.

The Indian snorted and nodded his head. "Those're

Hector's shoes, all right. You'll only have to wear them the first couple of times, just until they know you by sight. Then you can retire the poor ugly things and wear your own shoes."

"I dunno," said the little busboy, pulling his foot back. "I kind of like them. I might just keep on wearing them."

"They're a dead man's shoes, boy," said the first man, the Negro. "I think you'd better start wearing your own as soon as you're allowed. Bad juju, soon-brother-in-blood."

"Don't listen to him," said the Indian, waving his hand in dismissal. "Paulson sees ghosts in everything."

The little busboy shrugged and sat down on the ground. He did not feel like talking to these two—he did not come here to talk. He leaned back against the hot aluminum lining that made up the silo wall and smiled affably, idiotically, at the two men, stilling whatever fresh conversations were forming in their minds. He closed his eyes and thought of The Dragon Lady, of her waist-length golden hair that she always wore loose and spread like a halo or a cape over her white shoulders, of her glazed blue eyes that glittered like ice whenever she was high, of the way her faded green bathrobe had fallen open the night before just before she passed out, revealing the sudden pink of one perfect nipple pasted onto a perfect ivory palm-sized breast. He thought about the way her slurred voice purred into his head like a subliminal drill bit, thought about how he would die happy if he could just cup one of those perfect breasts in his own palm someday.

Low voices outside the door of the silo rustled the little busboy out of his sweet dreams of she. Three men, all business-suit-clad Mexicans, pushed their way into the large, round room and poised no-nonsenselike in front of the three crash test junkies. They each carried briefcases the color and texture of sharkskin, each holding their briefcase in front of them as if it was some sort of shield against the common world, the commoners before them, and everything common and dirty and heart-wrenchingly depressing that they represented.

"You're new," said one of the men, glaring at the little busboy through the black panels of his sunglasses.

"I have Hector's shoes," answered the little busboy quickly, again lifting his leg and pointing the tip of his toe at the man to inspect. "I'm his replacement."

"Ah yes, Lisa's friend," the first man nodded. "Good. I am glad you are here."

The little busboy cringed at the sound of The Dragon Lady's name. He had never heard anyone actually call her by her Christian name before, not even Johnny, who got to fuck her on occasion. It was always The Dragon Lady, both out loud and in his head.

"We don't have a lot of time here," said the second man, his voice and inflection nearly identical to the first. He glanced at his watch and frowned. "Shall we get to business?"

The Indian and the Negro immediately began to strip, as if on cue. The little busboy watched them for a second, curiously, then began to take his own clothes off as well. He relaxed a bit when he saw the two other men stopped short of taking their underwear off, leaving their briefs and boxers on as they waited for the suited men to assemble their paraphernalia.

The little busboy winced a bit as the thick needle of the syringe entered his body, just behind his elbow., He really preferred to shoot himself up, preferred to know exactly when to expect the pinch and the ensuing rush rather than let someone else control him, surprise him. He felt his legs give out beneath him as wave upon wave of white light engulfed him, felt his hand reach out instinctively and catch him from falling flat on the ground, felt his hand push his body up into a sitting position from somewhere far, far away. His skull buzzed loudly, vibrating as though a little tiny man with a little tiny jackhammer was perched on top of his head, breaking up the bone and cartilage to make room for future shopping malls and public parks.

"How does it feel?" asked a disembodied voice the little busboy barely recognized as being that of the first businessman.

"What?" he shouted back, confused. "Feel? What do you mean?"

"It's a little too strong," said the Negro's voice from beyond the white mist. "I'd cut it down by about half. No one wants to rush this hard, 'specially vanilla junkies."

"I concur with the gentleman," said the Indian. The world was starting to come back into focus, black shadows reforming into the inside walls of the silo around the little busboy. He shook his head violently and stood up shakily, holding on to the wall behind him for support.

"Too strong, *si*," he said, finally. "Cut it way down."

"Are you okay, man?" the Negro asked the little busboy, concerned. "Can you pull out of it?"

"Yeah, I'm fine. I'm already out. Just wasn't expecting it to hit me so hard." The little busboy could stand up straight without any help from the back wall now. The Negro grunted and nodded his head, satisfied.

"Get rid of the shoes as soon as you can," he said. "They've got bad juju all over them."

"That's funny," gasped the little busboy. "I could've swore it was puke."

3

"So how was work, Honey?" slurred the Dragon Lady, barely looking up as the little busboy dragged his emaciated carcass over the threshold of Starbuck's, his nose spazzing at the smell of fresh coffee, his stomach carefully and quickly filling with phlegm to protect itself from the anticipated onslaught of acid and caffeine. He hadn't eaten in nearly a week—the only thing really keeping him alive was the spoonful of cream he dumped into the first cup of coffee of the day.

"There are no vitamins in junk," he declared as he lowered himself into a chair across from the Dragon Lady, too tired to worry about the impropriety of speaking to her on such familiar terms.

"You got that right." She actually smiled at him as she stubbed her cigarette out on the lip of the overflowing ashcan. "If there was, I'd be, uh, Jane-fucking-Fonda."

"And I'd be Richard-fucking-Simmons," finished the little busboy. It was starting to creep through the mud that he was actually having a conversation with the Dragon Lady, with Lisa—he hurriedly downed his coffee and concentrated instead on the blisters forming on his tongue. "So, uh, where's Johnny?" he finally ventured painfully.

"Who the hell knows?" Another cigarette fluttered and bloomed red and orange between her fingers. "He's a rat bastard, you know. You know that, don't you?"

"Um…"

"If I was your girlfriend, would you fuck someone else?" She leaned forward and spread her free hand out on the table in front of the little busboy, almost touching his hand. "I'm very good, you know. There wouldn't be any reason to."

"Um…."

"No reason at all." She pulled her hand back and turned it into a perch for her chin instead. "No reason at all."

The little busboy looked up and saw her eyes were unusually bright. The brightness faded a bit from the right eye as the first and only tear fell and ran down her rouged and powdered cheek. "Are you all right?" he asked, quietly. "Are you okay?"

"You ever wish you were dead?" she whispered. "Or that you were someone else?"

"Of course I have," he answered. "Why do you think I make all these little holes in my body?" He shook his head and bit his lip. "No, I guess I haven't. I like being alive."

"I wish I could go home and find a closet full of business suits and high heels, and Don Johnson watching TV in my living room," whispered the Dragon Lady. "Or it wouldn't even have to be Don Johnson. Just someone….clean." She raked her nails up and down her arms and winced as she actually broke skin. "Baby, I'm just so dirty. I wish I could wake up and not be so dirty."

"I think you're beautiful." The words slipped out before the little busboy could stop them. He dug himself in deeper: "I think you're beautiful just the way you are."

4

So the plan was, the little busboy would kill Johnny, and then he and the Dragon Lady would skip town and check themselves into rehab down in Tijuana. If they were fast enough, they could slip past the border guards and into Mexico before the cops found the junkie-boy's corpse. Once they were in Mexico, it was bye-bye IDs, bye-bye former shit lives, and hello to a little one-acre organic farm by the ocean, hundreds of miles down the coast where no one would look for them or even know they existed. Then the children would come pouring out of the Dragon Lady's womb, one after another, and they would all look as beautiful as her and she would be the perfect mother and she and the little busboy would be in love with each other until they died.

The Dragon Lady knew nothing about the children or the farm or even the love part, of course, but it was a natural progression in the fantasy, so far as the little busboy was concerned. He knew what their children would look like by the end of the first day, knew what the Dragon Lady smelled like in bed, imagined all the things they would say to each other the first time they kissed when they were finally free to do so. Because she, unlike Johnny, never cheated on her men, and if she kissed the little busboy before Johnny was dead, she'd be a nasty cheat, just like him.

The little busboy had managed to save several hundred

dollars over the past few weeks—free drugs meant one major bank account drain. He idly thought about hiring someone to knock off Johnny, but random queries at "work" brought the price tag for murder somewhere high above anything the little busboy could ever save up. He figured another couple of weeks at the barn and he would have just enough money to do everything he needed to, but not enough to pay someone else to kill Johnny.

Could he poison him? There was something poetic about poisoning a junkie, something nasty and gritty and poetic about slipping drain cleaner into the hypo meant for his former friend. The thought made him pause before slipping the dulling needle into his own receding veins, pause enough to make the Mexican dealers glare suspiciously at him.

"Wha's wrong, José?" asked the straight-looking man who only wore suits. "We don' got all day."

"Nothin's wrong, man," answered the little busboy, digging the spike in deep. The world went 2D for a moment, then slid back into place with different hues and light. His eyes felt heavy, too heavy, but he shook them back open and sat the rush out. "Cut it down some more," he called out to the men standing in shadow. "Too fuckin' strong."

"Yeah, okay. You don't have to shout already. We can hear you just fine." But the little busboy could barely hear them at all. His ears hurt with all the other noises, the ocean pounding in his head, and far away in his mind he realized that he couldn't do this anymore, that this was going to have to be the last ride and if he and the Dragon Lady were going to ever go away, it'd have to be now.

5

The little busboy was still walking with gigantic feet and no peripheral vision when he made it back to his loft. His heart was singing and the sun had never seemed brighter when he stumbled through the hallway to his door and found it hanging wide open. And not just unlocked and politely opened, either— someone had kicked it off its hinges and splintered the door frame up good.

"Thank God for bank accounts," he slurred aloud as he leaned against the wall outside his door. He couldn't hear anything inside, but that didn't mean shit. "Lisa?" he queried hopefully.

"Wrong answer, cocksuck," snarled Johnny's voice from far, far away. "Wrong, wrong, wrong."

The little busboy peeked around the corner into his apartment and Johnny was coming for him, walking across the long expanse of concrete and dirty laundry and unpaid utility bills on legs that grew and shrank with each wobbly step. Halfway across the room, Johnny just stopped, stopped and stood and wobbled back and forth, arms spread out for balance.

"Man, are you fucked," snorted the little busboy, just as unsteadily crossing the studio threshold. "Why don't you sit down before you puke all over my bed."

Johnny grinned weakly and fell face first onto the soiled mattress at his feet. The little busboy's heart jumped a happy little jump, thinking maybe Johnny was dead already and he wouldn't have to do anything at all, when Johnny's voice came again, muffled through the thick wad of stained foam rubber.

"'I thank my God for graciously granting me the opportunity of learning that death is the *key* which unlocks the door to our true happiness.'"

Johnny rolled over onto his back and looked up at the ceiling. "Fucking Mozart."

"What?" asked the little busboy, confused. "What the fuck are you talking about?"

"Mozart," said Johnny. "Mo-zart," he said again, dragging the words out. "That's what he said about death, that being dead was the way to finding true happiness. What do you think? You think when we're dead, we'll find true happiness?"

"Are you unhappy?" stammered the little busboy, his heart racing, pounding in his chest. Was Johnny asking him to kill him? And, if so, how? His eyes flew around the room, inventorying Things To Kill Johnny With. The loose brick in the corner. The dull, dented butter knife in the sink. The lumpy gray pillow on his bed that always smelled like ass, no matter how many times it was run through the shitty industrial washer at the laundromat. His bare hands.

"I'm fucking ecstatic," said Johnny, his voice barely audible over the roaring of blood in the little busboy's ears. "I'm in heaven already. My life is a dream come true. My girlfriend wants me to kill you, you know," he added, sitting up suddenly, dangerously fast. "My girlfriend was saying what a nice guy she thought you were, that you were her friend. That's code for 'kill the stupid fucking spic.'"

The little busboy lunged for the brick and the knife and the pillow, all at once. He reached the knife first, the brick second, ran out of hands. Johnny was up and lurching across the room towards the little busboy, his arms flailing like windmill blades, fingers curled like claws. Spit rolled out of the corner of his mouth and dribbled down his shirt. The little busboy swung out with the butter knife, once, twice, back, forth, in, out, in and out again.

"Ow!" screamed Johnny, holding his hands to his chest. Thin scratches, a tiny hole, from the dull butter knife trickled red. "You fuck!" He swung his fist at the little busboy, caught him on the side of the head. The little busboy fell to the ground. He closed his eye and saw the boot coming at him. He opened his eyes and saw the boot coming down.

Frozen in time, the little busboy saw the boot coming down at his face, stopped just short of impact. Was this, as Johnny/Wolfgang Amadeus said, the key to happiness? Was he about to find peace, comfort, Heaven, reincarnation, rebirth? Was he about to be an angel in Heaven, or a scum-sucking lamprey seeking enlightenment in the next life? Or would Johnny stop himself, not kill him, let him live?

"I promise…." the little busboy began. "I won't…"

Johnny's boot smashed through the little busboy's head, smashed his face into putty, his skull into wet fragments. He stomped again and again, his eyes closed tight, not wanting to look down and see what his boot had done. He stomped and stomped until the woman who lived in the shithole downstairs starting yelling at him through the floor to stop making so much fucking noise. He did not look down at the little busboy, backed away with his eyes closed and found the splintered door with blind, outreached hands. He did not look down at his boots as he walked away, nor at the wake of brain and blood and bone and flesh that marked his path. The puddles outside would wash away any detritus on the soles of his boots. He would be clean by the time he got home.

EYE FOR AN EYE

ALLEN JACOBY

Harrelson moaned as he opened his eyes, the cancerous bright light from a flickering fluorescent sending sharper pains through his already aching head. His eyes felt puffy, but at the very least, he could see out of both of them. His lips were chapped to the point of cracking, and he could taste blood on his dry tongue. And speaking of blood, it seemed to be everywhere, clotting through the front of his shirt and lining his socks, sticking to his shoes with sick squelching sounds. From the way he hurt all over, he knew the blood was his. All of it.

His arms and legs were bound, tightly. He was in a small concrete room, almost like a prison, except without a window. The door was some rusted over metal, but the lock and handle on it were fresh and new, stainless steel. There was no bed, no desk, no fixtures whatsoever, the only exception being the fluorescent lights overhead and a drain on the floor covered in blood so fresh and thick it reminded him of overripe pomegranate. Harrelson inched his way out of the center of the room toward a corner, opposite the door. He had expected more resistance from his aching body, but the pain hadn't been too extreme. Taking stock of his wounds, he was pretty certain that nothing was broken, at least not seriously, and that the blood had come from abrasions and minor cuts that had mostly clotted over. His wounds were mostly blunt force trauma, and as shitty as that made his head feel, he thought things could be worse, considering the circumstances.

He had been abducted last night, on his way home from

work. Harrelson worked as a museum security guard downtown, and had to take the subway home. They had jumped him just outside of the subway station, less than a block from his apartment. No one had come to his rescue, they probably hadn't even heard him scream as three men had slammed him up against a wall and beaten him merciless. The rest of the night was very hazy in his memory; suffice to say he thought that the men had only used their fists, though one might have had brass knuckles on. They had thrown him in the trunk of a car lined with plastic wrap, and he had woken up here, in this room. Harrelson was mildly surprised; he had not expected to survive. He had been prepared to die. He deserved to die.

Harrelson's introspection was interrupted as a noise scuffled from outside. There was a click, followed by a creak, and then the rusty door slowly opened to reveal not three burly thugs, but a small man in a dentist's scrubs, of all things. The man pushed a silver tray on wheels in with him, but its contents were hidden from Harrelson's vantage point on the floor. The dentist fidgeted with the contents of the tray for a moment, then removed a pair of lavender latex gloves, putting them on in a prissy little gesture that reminded Harrelson of Roger Moore as James Bond. Harrelson almost laughed, but the smile hurt, and the dentist saw him wince.

The dentist turned fully toward Harrelson on the floor, and smiled down at him. It was a pleasant smile, and it almost caught the beaten man off-guard. His whole demeanor was pleasant to a near Christmasy degree; he had ginger hair, a ruddy complexion, and watery blue eyes that seemed to catch the light as lazily as a shallow creek. His smile was that of a man who felt he was contributing to society as a whole, and happened to enjoy doing it.

"Mr. Harrelson," his voice matched his face with Shakespearean perfection, despite a lack of any accent. "I trust

195

you had a good night's sleep. You suffered quite the knock on your head."

Harrelson tried to look inquisitive but probably only managed to look tired. He flicked his tongue around his mouth. God he wanted a drink! He couldn't speak, his throat was like sandpaper. He barely spat out a louder groan before looking back up at the dentist, who simply smiled down at him and continued speaking as though nothing had happened.

"Yes, well, I suppose it was necessary. This is all happening rather fast, I'm afraid, and I'm sure you have a lot of questions —"

"I know why I'm here." Harrelson surprised himself and the dentist both by speaking. He blinked and shrugged off the pain, trying to look resolved. He felt resolved. After all, he deserved this.

"Do you now?" questioned the dentist. "I wonder. Either way, you may simply call me 'Doctor'...not that you'll need to say much to me at all. Shall we get started?"

Harrelson glared up at him, now mustering a small component of rage. He deserved this, yes, but he didn't deserve to be played with.

"I don't need to hear what you have to say," he spat. "Just kill me."

Doctor chuckled, and damn if it didn't sound more like Christmas than he looked. His smile broadened.

"Kill you? I'm afraid you are mistaken, Mr. Harrelson..."

The dentist turned back to the tray and removed not a knife, or a gun, as Harrelson had expected, but instead, two little silver objects that looked almost like women's eyelash curlers. Harrelson blinked, unsure of what was happening, as Doctor walked over to him, leaning down to his level. The bonds on his hands and feet felt tighter than ever. Harrelson tried to struggle as the dentist paced his index finger and thumb on either side of his black eye, his fidgets in vain as the latex glove pressed harder into the bruised flesh, and then metal bit into his skin just below his eye socket. The metal device was to keep him from blinking, he quickly realized, as Doctor fixed one to his other eye as well. Immediately he fought to close his eyes, and immediately he failed. His vision was filled with Doctor's smiling face, and he really realized what this was all about. It wasn't about retribution, how could he have been so naïve? It was never an eye for an eye. That was too easy, too simple. It was an eye for a tooth and an ear and maybe even a hand, because with time, some angers only got worse. And it had been so long since Harrelson had sinned so heinously, committed that grave act against that innocent girl.

It was payback, with interest. Would they show him pictures of her? Of her body? He didn't know if he could stomach it. He wasn't a sociopath. He felt guilty. He felt sick.

Doctor leaned back, stepping away from Harrelson and smiling. He walked back over to the little silver tray, but, despite Harrelson's fears, he removed neither an old photo album nor tools of torture. Instead, he stood there, smiling. For a minute, neither Doctor nor Harrelson made any movements, nor did they speak. Harrelson's eyes were watering, but not enough. They were drying out, and he wanted to blink. More than anything he wanted to blink. *Two minutes now,* he thought. *Two minutes at least.* Not that there was any real way to tell time in the room. Harrelson thought back to the longest staring contest he'd ever been in, and wished he could just surrender now like he must have then. Just blink, and poof! You lose. You lose, but at least that nagging itch and dryness goes away. He strained his forehead. How long had it been? Five minutes? Ten?

Doctor leaned over the silver tray and smiled more broadly. He reached into his pocket with one gloved hand and glanced down at something there. A watch.

"That was three minutes, Mr. Harrelson," he chuckled. "I

197

imagine you must be quite uncomfortable. A bit of psychological torture to start out with is always amusing, but, just that. Amusing. Nothing quite effective. I'll remove them now, of course."

Harrelson sat, incredulous, as Doctor moved swiftly towards him and, unbelievably, bent over and began removing the small metal braces. They bit slightly as Doctor removed them, but once they were out, Harrelson shut his eyes tighter than he had in his entire life. Any amount of physical pain was worth the end of that nagging itch that seemed to stretch time out *ad infinitum*. Of course, just as Harrelson drew himself out of the haze of relief, he felt a hand like a vice gripping at his neck. Doctor was strong, almost too strong for a man his size. Harrelson, numb from his bonds and weak from the beating the night before, was helpless as he tried to struggle, and could only watch numbly as Doctor removed, from God knew where, a sharp shiny scalpel. The dentist held it up to the fluorescent light, just for a moment, to admire it, and then he swiftly brought it downward and removed Harrelson's right eyelid.

The action was precise, smooth, and agonizing. Warm red flowed quickly into Harrelson's eye, and as his vision swam with crimson, Doctor shifted slightly and removed the left eyelid with equal ease. Harrelson was screaming now, his raw throat seeming to tear with the act. He tried to blink but that only increased the pain and bloodflow, tears mixing in to make a sickly pink that flowed pale from his eyes to his chest. Perhaps worst of all, Harrelson found that he could see fine through the scarlet haze, that everything was set out in perfect detail, just with a pink tinge. Doctor was clearly visible, smiling over him, the scalpel gleaming and dripping with blood.

Harrelson managed to stop screaming, and bit his lip through the pain, lying there, panting. He looked at Doctor, forcing himself not to try and close his eyes, because that would only

198

make the pain worse. The wound was slowing its flow, but every fresh drop brought new agony. He couldn't help but moan low, which only seemed to encourage Doctor. The dentist laughed now, all subtlety gone.

"You should revel in the blood now, Mr. Harrelson! Once it begins to clot, your eyes will be drier than ever, and you won't be closing them any time soon. Three minutes seemed so unbearable then, didn't it?"

He leaned in close to Harrelson's face, all twisted crimson by the blood in his eyes.

"I plan on keeping you alive much longer than three minutes."

After that, Doctor produced a hypodermic needle from the silver tray and filled Harrelson's veins full of a clear liquid that brought blessed sleep, eyelids or none. His eyes rolled back into his skull and the last thing he saw was the dentist's ruddy face, smiling away.

*

When he awoke there was no way to tell how much time had passed, for the lighting in the room remained unchanged, save for the occasionally flicker from the fluorescent. He was no longer seated against the wall; his bonds had been removed, only so he could be strapped into what appeared to be a gurney. His clothes were gone. Tight leather belts snaked around his body at waist, legs, and shoulders, making anything but simply neck movement impossible. There was no sign of Doctor himself, though the sadistic dentist may have been lurking quietly in some corner of the room.

His eyes were agony.

As Doctor had predicted, the blood had clotted, and thickly. His first flickers left and right caused red flakes to dance along his vision, and sent fresh tendrils of agony up through his skull.

199

His body, unaware that it was missing the vital appendages, continued to attempt to blink. This, of course, only aggravated the wounds and further alerted Harrelson to the increasing dryness of his corneas. Three minutes before? The torture of earlier seemed kind in comparison now, as his eyes begged for some lubrication, what few tears his ducts could produce now rolling helplessly over the sides of his face. To add to the pain, he was maddeningly thirsty, he felt the need to urinate, and his wounds from the beating last night (two nights ago?) still ached over his entire body. Trying to focus on one horror at a time, Harrelson lapped his dry tongue through his mouth, in a fruitless attempt to bring some sanctuary to his cracked desert of a throat. All he accomplished was a weak little cough, which of course raised hellfire up through his bloody larynx. Harrelson had just recovered from the torture of the cough, when Doctor chose to make his appearance.

"Good Morning, Mr. Harrelson," he cooed calmly. "I suppose you're wondering how long you were out."

Harrelson could only lie there on the gurney, gazing up at the dentist, who had moved from the left corner of his vision to stand right beside him. Doctor's outfit was exactly the same as before, though there was no blood on the lavender latex gloves, leading the trapped man to believe that at least enough time had passed that Doctor had thought to change them.

He smiled warmly.

"It's not important. Suffice to say, I hope you enjoyed it, for now we will begin. I've decided..." here he paused, moving over to some unseen corner of the room to retrieve the steel tray, wheeling it beside the gurney so that Harrelson was unable to see inside.

"I've decided I'm going to tell you exactly what I'm going to do with you. It's not my usual *modus operandi*, but I feel as though this is a special case."

He spoke as though Harrelson should honestly be quite

flattered, and there was flair of relish to his voice, as he rummaged within the silver tray. The bound man could hear a tiny thud, as well as the occasional clink of metal against metal. Doctor continued:

"I'm a businessman, Mr. Harrelson. The act of torture without financial gain is truly a sin in my eyes. Such a waste. So what I'm going to do is remove all of your vital organs, starting with your kidneys, then your liver, spleen, first lung, corneas, second lung, and finally, your heart. In all likelihood you'll die after the liver, that's where most seem to go..."

Doctor practically beamed as he made eye contact with his prisoner.

"But you seem like a reasonable, healthy man, without too much violence in you. I wouldn't be surprised if your cool head let you live all the way to the corneal biopsy, which I'm sure can't be too pleasant when you're awake for it."

The dentist busied himself for a moment, and Harrelson leaned his head back against the gurney, trying to ignore the many, almost trivial pains that racked him. So this was it, then. His karma. Perhaps karma was too new age, but it fit. After what he had done to the girl, the poor sweet innocent girl...but that was not something he wished to dwell on, if he was to endure the agony of literally having his heart ripped out. He managed to lift his head up, facing Doctor, who turned towards him.

The dentist's smile broadened to a macabre, Jack-O'-Lantern grin.

"Of course, that all comes a bit later. Right now, I get to have a little fun with the not so vital bits.

After all," noted Doctor as he reached down into the silver tray. "Nothing wrong with a man enjoying his work."

He produced a small plastic bag, filled with little gray rectangles. Moving closer to Harrelson, the dentist withdrew one of the gray rectangles and held it far enough away from

Harrelson's cracked eyes so that the bound man could see it clearly. A razor blade. Ever smiling, Doctor gripped his subject by the chin with one hand, and again Harrelson was surprised by the smaller man's strength.

"Don't fight," whispered Doctor. "This is to make sure you don't fight. See, I'm going to place them into the muscle tissues in your neck, so that every time you move it, the blades will burrow in deeper."

Doctor gripped tighter, and the hand holding the razor blade was removed from view.

"First one!"

There was a sudden and very demanding pain in Harrelson's throat, just to the left of his Adam's apple. The blade sunk in like a steak knife into a soft fillet, and Harrelson could feel each individual tear of sinew. It wasn't until he struggled, out of impulse, that the razor really took effect. No longer smoothly pushing, the blade raggedly tore at the muscles in Harrelson's neck, and he screamed freely as the razor sunk deeper, fresh blood running down his neck.

"Uh-Uh!" called Doctor, wagging his finger in front of his victim's face. The bound man longed to have his eyelids back. Just that one small gift, in place of the bloodied, burning lumps against his brow! But before he could begin praying for some small mercies, Doctor was already calling out:

"Second one!" and soon more metal bit at his skin, this time almost dangerously close to his spine. Harrelson's nerves cried out at the twinge of the invading razor, and it took all of his self-control not to whip his head back and cry out. Even if he deserved this, he didn't want Doctor to have the satisfaction of seeing him succumb to the pain.

"And here comes three and four!"

This time Harrelson felt two distinct pressures, on opposite sides of his throat an inch or two below his jaw. There was a spare moment, just before the blades pierced the skin, where he could feel his brain trying to prepare his body for what he knew would be the worst pain yet. Then there was simply the sensation of the shredding of flesh and the heartless burrowing of the razorblades as they embedded themselves into his muscle, and for a moment he wondered if this must be what a hooked fish felt, as the angler tugged hard on the line. He began to moan deeply.

Doctor made a clicking noise like an old schoolmarm.

"I'm trying to enjoy this, Mr. Harrelson. Are you determined to end the fun so quickly?"

The bound man realized with mounting horror that, in addition to the four razor blades snug within his neck, there was still one clean gray rectangle left in the plastic bag. The dentist (Harrelson could not help but think of the man that way) patted him almost fatherly on the cheek, then disappeared somewhere above him.

"But, if you've decided, I have one last game that I love to play."

Doctor had moved behind the gurney, and now he swiftly brought one last leather strap up over Harrelson's forehead, binding it tighter than the rest, which caused even more pain to run through his eyelid wounds, though they did not start bleeding again. Now Harrelson's vision was restricted to the region of space just underneath the fluorescent lights, which caught a slight corner of the silver tray and some of his own lower body. He could flex his neck slightly and look further, but each simple jerk caused pain to flair up in powerful pockets around each of the razor blades, one of which felt as though it was about to rip through into the inside of his throat.

The dentist spoke from Harrelson's right. "I've got one last razor blade left, and I certainly don't want to put it in your neck again. So what I'm going to do is place it somewhere in your body, and you have to guess where. Sounds like fun, yes?" Harrelson said nothing, but Doctor didn't appear to require consent to begin his game, as the dentist began to move in and out of view. Harrelson felt the cold tooth of the razor bite into the flesh just above his right nipple, and blood beaded up, but the blade didn't go very deep.

Doctor, back in Harrelson's vision, shook his head.

"No, too high. Not enough nerves."

He vanished, and even though he could see nothing but the fluorescent light, Harrelson wished more than anything that he could shut his eyes. More nicks along his chest at the same level, and then one bit deeper, directly at the top of his ribcage. Blood dribbled out, and with a chuckle, Doctor pressed slightly harder and began to pull the razor down. Through the heavy curtain of fresh pain, Harrelson realized that the razor was just deep enough to cut through all the layers of skin, and that the dentist was literally flaying him. He didn't have the strength to moan, and was quite prepared for Doctor to just rip him open then and there and start pulling out organs, but wasn't in the cards, for the tip of the blade tugged out of the bound man's skin just before his belly button, which Doctor began to tap lightly.

"Almost," he spoke so casually, he could've been putting on the back nine. "Almost, but not quite."

Doctor changed his style to little cuts that were barely scratches, all along Harrelson's waist and down his right thigh, skipping over the knee completely. The scratches alone were fairly weak, but coupled with the maddening itching of his eyes, the burrowing sting of the blades in his throat, and the sheer exhaustion of his position, Harrelson wanted to break down with each weak little sheer. His breathing quickened. His eyes darted in their sockets, heedless of the pain, trying in vain to see more, even though what they wanted most was to see nothing at all.

"There we are." Doctor said suddenly, and grabbed Harrelson's groin with sudden intensity. The fifth and final razorblade pierced his scrotum instantly, tearing through thin flesh with ease. Now Doctor was roaring, like a drunk at a prize-fight, as his own latex-gloved hand pressed the sharp metal of the razor into Harrelson's left testicle with a tearing pop.

Harrelson screamed.

It was such an inhuman sound that had he been capable of introspection, the bound man might not have believed he himself had made it. His throat ripped apart with the dryness and the intensity of the cry, and his hands clamped upon the edges of the gurney like vice-grips. The pain was unimaginable, and it soared through every fiber of his frame and made him feel weak and sick and full of bile, and although there was nothing in his stomach, warm acid flowed up into his mouth and worsened the cracking agony. Warm urine burst out of him shamelessly, seeping into the fresh wound, and still Doctor pressed harder, every infinitesimal change in pressure rocketing through Harrelson's nervous system. He did not go into shock. He did not go unconscious.

Instead, he screamed:

"For her! For her! OhgawdI'msosorry, I deserve this I'msosorry."

Doctor leaned back, quizzical. He wiped his gloved hands, dripping with blood and fluid, on his scrubs.

"What?" he inquired. He seemed to be genuinely interested, and totally unaware of the state of his victim.

Harrelson was panting madly now, like a dog, obscenities passing his lips along with blood and bile. He bit his teeth hard, and the pain slowly shifted from fresh searing agony to a series of throbs and aches that came in waves, starting in his groin and spiraling up through his whole body.

"I—" he choked back something acidic. "I know why I deserve this, and I do for what I did, and I am sorry. *Ohgawdwhycan'tyouseethatI'msorry!?*"

He was begging, blood dripping from his mouth and tears from his eyes.

Doctor just leaned down at him, watching, waiting for the man to continue.

"She was innocent. So innocent. I didn't even know her name, I don't know if that makes what I did better or worse, but I know it was wrong, I've known it was wrong, so can't you see that I'm sorry?"

His eyes were wide with pleading. He fought back another wave of cries and coughed. "I know she begged like I'm begging. I know there was no reason...no reason to...to..."

Doctor raised one hand to stop Harrelson, who obliged, roaring in his throat.

"This isn't about that, Mr. Harrelson."

Harrelson continued to pant and babble.

"YouhavetoknowhowsorryIamandthatIwishIcould—"

"Mr. Harrelson."

The bound man fell silent, and Doctor spoke again.

"I haven't the faintest idea what you're talking about."

There was a long, paused silence, broken only by soft sobs from Harrelson. For over a minute, Doctor simply stood over his victim not speaking, and Harrelson just breathed shaky breaths and gripped the gurney. He tried to speak but fell silent, grimacing. Finally, he girded himself and faced the dentist, his tone incredulous.

"Then why? Why all of this? Why me?"

Doctor blinked.

"Because you walked out of the subway station."

The true horror of it all washed over Harrelson like a high tide, easing his mind not into madness, but a terrible clarity of vision. The pain and discomfort sharpened him now, and he spoke with some semblance of sanity.

"And my name? How did you know who I was?"

Doctor chuckled and removed a chunk of leather from the

silver tray. Harrelson's wallet.

"Your driver's license."

Harrelson swallowed, and his throat clicked. The room felt heavy, as though all of the air had been switched with fog. Harrelson felt a drop of sweat roll lazily over his cheek and down to the edge of the gurney. He felt blood leaking out of his body. He felt the razor blades burrowing deeper into him with each breath, and he felt all of this with a new intense perception he had never before thought possible.

"Then what for? Why all of this?"

"I already told you," replied Doctor, raising his scalpel with a grin sharp enough to match. "I'm a man who enjoys his job."

There it was. He was no agent of karma, no force of revenge from the parents of a long dead girl. There was no hidden penance for the sins of Harrelson's past. It was a random act, a chaotic horror that was made all the more awful by its *ad hoc* victim. Harrelson was unable to laugh, or even to cry; he simply lay there, dumbstruck and bleeding, as Doctor moved about.

Finally, the dentist produced a large plastic cooler, and his victim could hear ice crashing about inside it. He moved around to the back of Harrelson's gurney and, without warning, undid the buckle upon the strap there, permitting movement once more. The victim's neck screamed from the razorblades.

"I though you might like to watch," Doctor explained, as he placed the plastic cooler on a cart next to the silver tray. He pursed his lips for a moment, then selected a new, clean scalpel from within the tray. He moved to Harrelson's side, and smiled greater. Harrelson felt every detail of the scalpel as it sliced effortlessly through his skin into the abdominal cavity.

Doctor chuckled as he went about his work.

"As I said, first your kidneys, then your liver, spleen, first lung..."

POTATO MAN

DALE ELDON

Chapter One

INTERVIEW, As told by Trevor DeBlase
INTERVIEWER, Geoff Ferguson

"There's nothing like waking up naked, paralyzed from the neck down, on a cold steel slab to make you think about your life." Trevor said with a cigarette pinched between his fingers. "Well usually people think about their life when they're about to lose it." A pause. "At that point, I was thinking how the hell am I gonna to get the fuck out of there?"

"So, how did you get out?" Geoff asked.

"I was unable to move anything below my chin. I tried to see around the room. It was barely lit, there weren't any windows, metal tables everywhere. There must have been at least a dozen people down there. I was in some kind of basement.

"I saw blood spray onto the walls... The sound of a chainsaw blade... I-I heard it slice into the others." Trevor inhaled hard on the cigarette, taking the cherry down by a third. "Bones cracked, and the only other sound that drowned out the buzzing... were the screams.

"The man with the chainsaw came for me.

"He came into my peripheral, the first thought that popped into my head, was that he looked like a walking baked potato. He had a plastic face mask, smothered in blood, with a silver apron. I don't know why I thought that, I think it was the apron. I wasn't exactly in right mind at that point.

"Anyways, he was only a few feet away from me when he switched the chainsaw off. He dropped it on a wood desk with a thud. He went upstairs to do God knows what. And each step thundered. The boots he wore sounded like led.

"The thunking sounds from his feet disappeared and then I could hear Kenzie. That's when I really got scared."

"Why did hearing her scare you more?"

"I love her, and I didn't know she was there until she woke up."

"So what next?"

"I thought, now's my chance, my only chance. All I could do, was lay there like a fucking lump on a log. I can say "fuck", right?"

"It's okay, I can bleep it out later."

"I couldn't move, I couldn't save Kenzie, just lay there in my birthday suit for the Potato Man to chop up."

"Potato Man? I like that."

"Right." Trevor pressed the butt into the ashtray, and lit up another one.

"Not really sure how much time passed before he started back down the stairs, the sound of police sirens in the distance gave me hope. He must have heard them a moment before me, because he stopped midway on the steps.

"Old Lead-Foot jogged back up and a few seconds later, gun shots. As it turned out, he was just a man. First couple of rounds sounded like .22 caliber. Then the barrage of nine-millimetre and shot gun rounds.

"SWAT charged down the stairs and checked to see if we were still alive.

"Only Kenzie and I survived that day. Potato Fuck got his. Ten innocent people died at the end of a chainsaw, and the police never did find the hands that the freak lopped off from the victims."

"Wow, this is Geoff Ferguson with Trevor DeBlase. After hearing his amazing story of survival, I think it's clear he is going to have a hard time coming back of that."

Chapter Two

After four months Trevor and Kenzie agreed it was time to return to Florence Illinois. They dropped out of school in their last semester when the chainsaw wielding maniac tried to kill them. It was time to pick up where they left off. Trevor's aunt Martha had a house she was willing to rent out to them for a low price, she set up a job at the quarry for Trevor, and even bought him a Dodge Charger. Martha rarely did anything for family, she was the richest member and hated it when the others would try to get money out of her. But this was an exception.

His first night back and there was no chance of sleep. From time to time he would slip into brief spurts of sleep, and the moment his eyes closed he was paralyzed again. But unlike before, he can feel the chainsaw cutting into his limbs.

He fought against drifting off. As soon as the room would go dark, the blaring sound of buzzing echoed in his ears. The last time he dozed off, Trevor forced himself awake with a loud moan. Seconds after he awoke he still felt paralyzed.

Trevor finally fell asleep without macabre themes captivating his mind when the alarm went off.

"Ah, c'mon."

His hand slammed the off button. He rolled over to hug Kenzie. *Gone?*

Water from the bathroom sink made Trevor feel better.

"GOD! I don't wanna get up." Trevor said.

"You have to, Sweetie. If I have to, so do you." Kenzie said from the bathroom.

"I think I'm sick."

"Right. I doubt that will fly on the first day at school. Get up you lazy sack."

"Gee honey, you say the sweetest things."

He closed his eyes and thought he won when she didn't respond. Dozing off, cold water trickled on his head.

"Hey!"

"Lookie who's up now." Kenzie stood over him with one hand on her hip, and a glass of water.

"Now UP, I'm not kidding."

"Okay... you win. Damn, I was just joking."

"No you weren't, I know you well enough to tell the difference when you're just joking around." She sat the glass on the night stand.

Trevor lunged and wrapped his arms around Kenzie as she let out a scream. "You're mine, little girl."

"Shit-head, I'll show you little." She grabbed his junk, and flipped him over on his back. "We don't have time for this. If you stop fucking around we can play when we get off from class." She stared into his dark blue eyes. "K?"

"Yes dear. There's no arguing with you."

"Get off your ass."

*

Briefly, Trevor forgot about everything. Just like his girlfriend. Or so she seemed. The sun was too bright, and Trevor left his sunglasses at home. But at least it was a beautiful day. Trevor and Kenzie stood in front of the Spoon Lake Community College entrance, oddly enough there were dozens of students finishing up cigarettes before class. Last time they were in town, Spoon Lake was a quiet school. The

Potato Man Murders probably drew the students. Get an education and site-see all in one. And now Trevor DeBlase, Florence's Mascot for the tourist.

Trevor didn't recognize most of the students, except for a hand full from last semester. And most of them he had wished moved away. But at least for the most part they got along. The bright side, if there was one, Geoff Ferguson was no where to be seen.

Geoff was the type who walked and talked like a white guy, but had no problems hanging out with uneducated thugs from his home city. Trevor started out his friend when Geoff first arrived to Florence. But Geoff was a strange fella. He knew everyone in town after a short time, and got a job fast with the local news station. But for some reason he always had a problem with Trevor. At first it came across as banter, but after the Potato Man incident, Geoff made it clear just how much he disliked Trevor.

The man acted like he was a people person, but never got close to anyone. Just friendly enough to get interviews for his column, and his thirty minute news show. The Potato Man murders made Geoff the local star. Before long he will probably move onto a bigger news agency, and his head will swell ten times the size it is now.

It was surprising that he would miss an opportunity to make Trevor suffer.

Almost to the door, and there's Nick Teslow. Scrawny little red-headed punk. His hair slicked up into a wanna-be mo-hawk. His face pierced, from nose, to lips, to eyebrows, and God knows what else. Not that how he presented himself was all that bad, it was his personality. He dressed like this to make himself seem like a bad-ass. Put this punk in the inner city, and he wouldn't last a day. It didn't help that he melted his brain with every kind of drug on the DEA's list. But for some reason, he liked Trevor. Nick didn't have too many friends despite his best efforts.

"Hey Trev, how you doing?" He slid off his small lens sunglasses, and held his trademark spaced-out look.

"Just peachy. Have you seen Geoff around?"

"Naw man, he hasn't been around much lately. It's strange, he was all ready for you to show up."

"I bet I can expect him to pop up."

"I didn't know you were coming back."

"Gotta go to school."

"I'm thinking about droppin'."

"Never a good idea, Nick." Trevor pushed passed his friend with Kenzie following close behind. "It was good seeing you. I'm late for class."

In the reflection of the glass door, Trevor saw Nick's eyes trained on Kenzie's ass.

Finally inside and the hall was packed with a slow moving herd of students. As they passed class room entrances, the crowd slowly dispersed. Their class room was at the very end of the hall. Now the only person between them and class was the asshole janitor. Gerald Caffy. Trevor forgot just how many people of this town he didn't like, but this one hated everybody.

Caffy slowly mopped the floor with his eyes glaring through his Coke-bottle glasses. Long mangy gray hair swung back and fourth in motion with the mop. His mustache hid his mouth. He was tall and hunched. He looked like what any of the students would call, a pedophile. Anyone that knew Caffy wouldn't think that for one fact, and that was that he didn't like anyone.

Trevor was forced to walked around him since Caffy refused to let him pass. Kenzie gripped Trevor's hand tight. He wasn't sure if she was creeped out, or if she was just trying not to slip on the wet floor.

Caffy whispered under his breath. "Stupid kids."

There were only two seats left. One in the back, and one in the front. Kenzie hated to sit in front, Trevor decided to be a gentlemen and let her have the one in the back. The teacher had his back to Trevor as he wrote out lecture notes on the Smart-Board.

He looked down as his chair fought to roll forward. After scooting it into place, he looked up just in time to see the teacher's eyes fixed on him.

"Well, well, well, class, we have a celebrity with us today." He appeared unamused. "Trevor DeBlase is kind enough to share his time."

The whole damn town seemed to be against him.

"I hope this semester you plan showing up for class."

"Um sir, I cut last semester because of what happened."

"And what exactly happened?"

"You didn't see it on the news?"

"Yes, I saw a slacker who got himself mixed up with a psychopath, and as result missed out on school. Maybe for now on you will pay more attention to your education, less to chainsaw wielding maniacs. Just a thought."

This gonna be a long school year.

*

"NO! Not here. Stop." Sophia Thomson said as she sat on top of a tombstone.

"C'mon babe, it's just a finger." Logan Barnet replied.

"I know I said I was up for it, but I just can't. I wanna wait until we get back to my apartment."

"Whatever. Your roommate will still be home. And she bitches every time we do anything."

"I'm sorry. But doing it in a cemetery isn't as hot as I thought it would be."

"Fine. If you don't wanna do it, then what do you wanna do?"

"I dunno. It's pretty boring. Creepy, but boring."

"Maybe we can dig up one of the graves." Logan said as he reached for an abandoned shovel.

"Logan, no. You'll get us into trouble."

"Trouble must be your new favorite word." She glared at him. "No." He continued in a mock tone. "No. No. No. Okay I won't touch you. Go play with your toys if you want it. I'm gonna have some fun without you."

"Dammit Logan. Just stop."

"Stop." The mock tone returned. "Seriously, I'm tired of, "No" and "Stop". I came out here to have a good time."

"Fine. You want to get yourself arrested, then go for it. I'm gone."

"Hate to see you go, but damn do I like to watch you leave."

Sophia didn't stop walking away as she flipped Logan off.

Logan headed towards the grave of the Potato Man.

"Okie doke, Pot Man, I'm digging your ass up."

He swung the shovel in pace with his steps as something moved in the nearby brush. Raccoons? *I wonder how they taste bar-bee-cued?*

Logan looked over the tombstones and saw Potato Man's. His stone just said John Doe, but it was the only one in the lot without a real name. Logan walked up to start digging, and he fell into a hole.

"What the hell? Where the fuck is the ground?"

He climbed out and didn't understand why the grave was dug up. A snapping of a tree branch cause his head to jerk, and by the time he confronted the sound, a huge man grabbed the shovel and sliced the blade into Logan's mouth.

*

Sophia was clearing the cemetery and about to step onto the main road when she heard a fast and imperceptible scream. Or at least that was what her imagination told her she heard. *It's*

215

just Logan fucking around.

She continued towards home. Sophia lived about forty-minutes away, and it was on the outskirts of town. The houses along the sides slowly dwindled, and wooded creek beds took their place. As creepy as the trees were at night, she kind of enjoyed them. A nice segue from the urban life.

The air was still, enough so that any sound from night animals in the woods made a huge impact. But the sounds that became very clear weren't form the woods. She stopped. They stopped. She turned and at first she thought her eyes were playing tricks on her. It looked like dozens of severed hands standing on their fingertips stood covering the entire street.

She stepped back, and they stepped forward. She stopped they stopped. The light of the night along with the occasional street lamp made a clear visual difficult, but it was obvious enough that what she was seeing was what it appeared.

She took off running and the skitter-scatter of fingers followed suit. She peeked over her shoulder and the hands were getting closer.

The road bowed up as it crossed a huge drainage ditch. She wondered if she could hop down into the wooded creek, but it was too far of a drop. She would definitely break something.

Sophia cleared the top of arc as the hands lunged and grabbed her. She grabbed back yanking them, but they had a dead-man's grip. The last hand to grasp her her throat, its fingers wrapped tightly, and they all pushed her over the small guardrail. She fell head first into the broken pieces of concrete.

*

It was suppose to be a day for Trevor to do absolutely nothing. Saturday was his day. At ten A.M. In the morning the phone stabbed through his perfect sleep. The first perfect rest he had in months. He reaches unsteady and in a raspy voice answers.

"Whoa, Kenzie, slow down. What? Logan's dead? Sophia too? How do you know they were murdered? That's what Geoff Ferguson says. Why the hell would you believe anything that— oh, the police told him. That's better. No, not because it's murder, because Geoff Ferguson is the last person to listen to regarding the facts. Exactly. What? Yeah, I gotta get dressed first. Yes, I will be there shortly, yes, I'm sure. Love you."

*

Trevor pulled up in the Dodge Charger. Kenzie was standing a few feet from the crime-scene tape by the drainage ditch.

"Trevor!" She didn't waste time squeezing him. "Her hands, her hands were chopped off."

Now it struck Trevor. The hands. The missing body parts from the murders. How could that man come back? He's dead. Someone must be picking up where he left off.

"Oh fuck." Geoff Ferguson walked towards Trevor in almost a sprint. "Here he comes."

"Trevor DeBlase, I've been meaning to talk to you." He was now close enough to speak in a normal range, though his heavy breathing made it hard. "I guess this a good of time as any. What do you think is going on here?"

"You're the man with the contacts, you tell me."

"I only know the crime-scene details, and only what the police will tell me. The only reason I know as much as I do is because the bodies were found before the police could hush up the part about the hands. But, you are the one who went through this before, so I figure you're the guy with the inside knowledge."

"After the shit you put me through with that fucking interview, you get nothing from me."

"C'mon man, I didn't mean for it to come out like that. And

who else knows as much about these murders?"

"The original killer is dead. The police shot him, DEAD. Whoever this is, it ain't the guy from before."

"Yeah I know. I'm thinking someone the killer knew before his death. Someone fucked up enough to pick up where he left off. Know anyone like that?"

"No Geoff, I don't."

"You sure?"

"What are you saying?"

"I'm just asking. It looks like someone is recreating themselves as The Potato Man."

"A name you coined."

"Are we gonna fight over that interview? Or are we gonna talk about this new killer?"

"WE, aren't talking. I'm done. Go stalk the Kardashians."

"We'll talk. After this next article, you will wanna talk."

Trevor flips Geoff his middle finger, and puts his other arm around Kenzie. He takes her to the car, and drives off immediately.

"If he approaches you, don't talk to him, okay?"

"Huh?" She looked up from her dazed state. "Oh, yeah, right. I'm sorry. Yeah I won't talk to him."

"The police will catch the guy who killed them. This isn't like last time."

"Yeah. I don't know. It's just so weird. You just don't see murders like this around this kind of town. With the Potato Man—" She caught herself. "I mean, the guy who tried to kill us, that was bizarre enough. Now there's another psycho running around doing basically the same thing? I think we need to leave Florence."

"As much as I would love to, we can't. We have to finish school."

"Right. So we can be next for Potato Man Jr. to chop up."

Trevor didn't say a word.

Followed with a sigh, "I'm sorry. I'm just, terrified. And I don't know how to handle this situation."

"This time, I will protect us. Okay?"

"Okay." She looked over at him, and stared into his eyes. She wanted to believe him.

Chapter Three

Last night was the one time in a long time that Trevor managed to sleep, tonight has been the worst. He didn't hide form his dreams. His brain wouldn't shut down. Three O'clock in the morning, and there wasn't a chance in hell he was going to rest.

Laying on his side as he stroked Kenzie's hair. She could always fall asleep so easy, no matter what was going on. A loud rap of pounds startled him out of his trance. Someone was at the door during this time of the night.

A voice said muffled: "OPEN UP, IT'S THE POLICE."

Trevor pulled on his boxers, and a T-shirt, and went to the door.

"Hey officer, can I—"

One cop stepped in before he could finish. "Trevor DeBlase, you are under arrest."

Trevor was instructed to put his hands on top of his head. "Why am I being arrested?"

"For the murders of Sophia Thomson, and Logan Barnet." The cop continued to read Trevor's rights to him as Trevor spaced-out.

He was scooted into the back seat of the squad car after having his pockets padded and poked. The lights from other units strobe across his face as the police instructed his girlfriend, and others questioned the neighbors. The arresting officer came back and slid into the driver's seat.

"Officer, I'm confused, how am I tied to the murders?"

"Dunno kid. Just know that a warrant for your arrest came up for the double-homicide. The "why" is not my area."

"Great."

"Look kid, I can't see you doing any of this, you don't seem the type. But you are being investigated for the murders, and apparently the lead detectives like you for this case. I'm sure it will work out, but until then, just keep your nose clean."

Trevor didn't bother to respond. He sat there working hard to figure out why he was in the squad car to begin with.

*

Kenzie couldn't stop crying. The one man who she depended on protecting her was now behind bars. She checked her bank account from her iPhone, and made sure there was enough to money to bail Trevor out. Though she had no idea what the amount was.

She grabbed her overnight bag, her purse, and headed out the door. She peeled out in the Dodge Charger and headed towards the station. It was about twenty minutes away, but felt more like twenty hours. She wasn't going to stay home without him. The Potato Man would kill her for sure.

She kept one hand on the wheel with the other wiping the tears from her eyes. She jerked the car over into the other lane when something touched her bare leg. She adjusted the car back into her lane and told herself that it was skirt brushing against her skin.

Something like a finger brushed against her private region. She fought to keep the car straight, and the finger continued to press against her underwear.

She reached down and felt a hand.

She slammed it against the window. *Nice going moron, it*

helps if you roll down the damn window.

She rolled it down and looked for the hand. It was gone.

Another hand covered her mouth, as another covered her eyes.

A third hand pushed down on her foot speeding the car up.

She straddled the wheel trying to keep the car centered.

The limited vision appeared between the fingers, the window front of Grindhouse-Video grew close.

The car smashed through the glass and crashed into the adult video room. The hands left the car as Kenzie's bloody forehead lay like a paperweight on the horn.

*

The next day the judge had set Trevor's bail at 1,500. He waited for Kenzie to show, but she didn't. Trevor couldn't get a hold of her, so he called Nick. The little prick was his only hope. His aunt had already helped him out enough, and Nick always has cash. Trevor never asked from where, and now he was glad.

Trevor came out with his stuff, and jumped into Nick's T-Bird.

"Where we going, man?"

"To the hospital to see your girlfriend."

"What's she doing in the hospital?"

"No one told you?"

"Tell me what?"

"She crashed the Charger, man."

"What?"

"Right into the video store."

"What the fuck? I leave for twenty-four hours and she gets herself in a car accident."

"Weird one too. The police still don't know why she crashed. She wasn't drinking, wasn't on drugs, hell she wasn't even texting. They found her cell in her purse."

"Is she alive?"

"Yeah, but she has been in and out since she arrived at the ICU."

"You sure she wasn't texting?"

*

"Damn kids." Gerald Caffy said in a rusty voice under his breath.

He begged to any god listening for his time to be up, either in death, or in some fluke space-time-continuum time warp to where he is sitting in a log a cabin, sipping Earl Grey tea, and watching the deer run across the wooded mountain slopes.

Oh hell, he would settle to live somewhere where children didn't exist. "Pedo-Caffy", that was his nickname. It didn't help that Gerald avoided people in general with few exceptions. Not only did he hide like a leper, but he displayed his hatred for the human race every chance he got. Some people could relate to his feelings, overbearing as they were. Though there were times his views were justified, he never gave most people a chance.

So here he was. Working at a college. As a janitor. Now he scrubs the floors, the windows and the toilets of those he despises most. Not only children who should act like adults, but the spawn of the very delinquents he abhorred as a youth. And thanks to one of those peers' son, he lost his job as a bus transit driver.

Gerald stroked the hard floor with the wet dirty mop, not even a care if all of the shit water from a toilet that was plugged up on purpose would be all cleaned up before the college opened. *Fuck `em.* Gerald was about done. Going home was his core thoughts, and putting his Stub Nose pistol to his temple, and doing the work he had been praying for.

Gerald leaned his mop against his cleaning cart, and grabbed a bottle of cheap Canadian Whiskey. He took the last long swallow, taking every drop, every trace amount, leaving it as dry as a baron desert. He dropped it into a recycle bin. If anyone found it, they would just assume one of the students snuck it in. The only benefit of working at a college.

He turned to grab the mop and was startled by a tall, ragged man a few feet away.

"Hey there... you can't be here." Gerald said in his normal baritone voice. "School's closed. Can't you read the damn sign?"

The man, like a motionless statue, stood shadowed in defiance. The one thing Gerald could finally make out was the shape of a chainsaw.

He held up his mop in both hands across his body. What the hell? There wasn't much else could do. Only hope that this freak slip on the shit-water that engulfed the floor.

"Listen here, you can't be here. Get out, or I'm calling the police."

The man jerked his arm and the chainsaw came to life.

He marched fast towards Gerald. The janitor tried to put a few extra feet between him and the lumberjack, but the building was locked up. In the time it would take to turn the right key, he would be chopped to scraps.

Gerald released a slight grin. The thought of fearing for his life tickled him. He was just thinking about ending it, and what the hell does he do? He gives-a-shit.

The man was close.

The chainsaw came down on top of Gerald as he blocked with the mop.

He fell back, his mop handle was now in half.

The deadly weapon fell from his grasp.

The chainsaw came forward.

Gerald kicked the cleaning cart and sent it slamming into the madman.

He struggled for a grip in the fecal water. The sound of tiny pounds smacking the wet floor caught his attention.

The light from the street lamps outside beamed through the windows and spotlighted several severed hands charging at Gerald like a pack of animals.

The strange man reached for his chainsaw. Gerald took the mop-head of the broken spear. He lifted it ready to impale when the man kicked him in the kneecap.

Gerald fell backwards too fast to catch his balance.

The jagged and splintered point of the other half of the mop-handle protruded from his crotch.

Something struggled beneath his back. Like a small animal trying to escape. Then whatever it was broke free and tapped across the fecal smothered floor.

Pain thrusted through his asshole and pulsated through his nether region.

Dozens of hands crawled over his body as life ebbed away.

*

After a long night without sleep by Kenzie's side at the hospital, Trevor returned home. He was greeted by Geoff Ferguson and a camera crew.

"Minster DeBlase," Geoff said with a microphone in Trevor's direction. "The college janitor was murdered last night after you were bailed out. What do you have to say about this?"

"Leave me alone."

"Hey man, I just wanna talk."

"Last time you just wanted to talk, you trashed my name, and Kenzie's. You made us sound crazy. Not to mention you insinuated that I had something to do with a double-murder."

"Look man, I wanna make it right. Help me out here. I promise to return the favor."

"What do you want?"

"Just your perspective on what's happening. You heard about your old pal, Gerald Caffy?"

"Of course, you are the reporter that plastered it all over the front page."

"Yup. Anyways, the details of his death—"

"The details that you leaked."

"ANYWAYS, the details of the death, sounds like the same kinda shit you went through."

"I didn't get a sharp stick shoved up my ass."

"No, no you didn't." Geoff managed to say through a huge fit of laughter.

"I don't know anything about the latest murders."

"You knew the Potato Man. You think he did this?"

"He's dead. How many times do I have to say that?"

"Well, that's the problem. I went to his grave just to have a look around, and it was dug out."

"What?"

"Ye-ah, Strange little footprints all over the lose dirt. They're small round holes, like several kids might have poked their fingers in the dirt. Weird I know. But maybe this Potato Man had followers. I don't understand why the best footprints I can find look like footfalls from fingers, but then again the psycho man wasn't exactly sane himself. So, maybe his followers are a bit nuts too."

"You're fucking with me."

"I wish I was. But he ain't in the grave anymore. Now I'm not saying he's alive, but someone wants everyone to think he is."

"Probably just a prank." Trevor said with a lack of patients.

"Nah, I think someone who went through a life-altering event has it in their head, that they are the Potato Man reincarnated."

"Sounds perfect for a tabloid."

"I just wondered, since the police arrested you and questioned you about the murders, what's your take on this? Could be a survivor from the Potato Man murders be doing this?"

"I am one of two survivors, Kenzie and I are it."

"So, you or Kenzie responsible? You know I gotta ask."

"I've something to say about that." Trevor stopped, looked Geoff in the eye, then slugged him. "You can file charges if it want, get the fuck away from my apartment, and get the fuck outta my face."

"I know it's you, Trevor. You're the copycat." Geoff held his eye with one hand as he stood back up.

"For all we know, it's you." Nick piped in. "Stupid-fuck. Where were you for a week?"

"I was visiting my dying grandmother."

"Sure you were." Nick said standing inches away from Geoff.

"She has cancer, meth-head."

"Good cover."

Geoff tackled Nick to the ground. They exchanged blows, and the police pulled up and jumped from their cars to interject. Geoff was on top of Nick pounding his face when three officers grabbed him.

"Good one, stupid." Trevor said as he gave a helping hand to Nick.

"I was just trying to stick up for you."

"Now you will end up in prison."

"Nope. Geoff attacked me, he's the dick that's getting locked up."

"If that's the case, then why isn't he in cuffs?"

Geoff talked to one of the officers and pointed at Trevor and Nick from time to time. Then one of the other cops walked over to Trevor and Nick.

"I understand that you three got yourselves in a little fight."

"Actually—" Trevor tried to say.

"Look, from what I see all three of you should be sitting in a cell somewhere. But we are in the middle of a manhunt. Everyone is a suspect in this case. The police department is spending its energy in finding this monster. Mr. Ferguson has agreed to stay away from you, if you do the same."

"If I stay away from him? He's the one who approached me. If—"

"Yeah I know. He said he's leaving you alone for now on. He wants the same in return."

"I will stay away from him. But if he doesn't live up to his promise, I will be calling you back here."

"Goodie. It seems we have an understanding."

*

Geoff Fergus grabbed a Keystone Light from his fridge and went back to work on his laptop. He held the ice cold can against his eye as he typed with one hand. Finally the temptation got the better of him, and he popped the tab and took a sip.

He took another sip as a footstep from the other room broke his concentration.

"Hello?" He said with a feeling of stupidity.

There's no one there. His doors are locked.

Another footstep.

Geoff grabbed his small baseball bat he kept by the couch.

"Hello?" He didn't feel so stupid this time.

Another step.

He carefully peeked around the corner into the kitchen. He felt like Trevor DeBlase. He had lost his mind, not in the figure of speech kind of way, but literally.

Dozens of severed hands ran like hyper-active spiders across the counter tops, the table, and the top of the fridge.

One hand grasped the handle to the fridge, in an attempt to open the door.

Geoff stepped back slowly, and backed his way to the front door. With one hand he felt for the knob. He unlocked it, then the knob turned on its own.

Geoff tightened his grip, but the knob slowly turned. He dropped the bat, and seized the knob with both hands. It stopped turning.

He locked it back up, and started to move quietly towards the window in his bedroom. The hands from the kitchen still seemed to be oblivious to his presence. Groceries smacked the floor as they ravaged the shelves.

Then the sound of the refrigerator door opened. The next sound was a beer tab.

The fuckers are opening the beer in the fridge. How the hell does a hand drink beer?

Before Geoff could get three feet to his bedroom, a loud buzzing sound emanated from the outside of his front door. A chainsaw blade began cutting through, and splintered the wood.

Enough with being quiet. He ran for the window.

The door broke open.

Geoff looked back and saw a huge man with tattered clothes, and human body parts sewn to his face. Lips, a nose, eye lids, and mismatched eyeballs. All in the proper places, but all not belonging to him. The Potato Man. Just like Trevor had described, only with a new face. *Fuck.*

Geoff dove for the window trying break it with his weight. Instead he manage to cracked the glass, and gave himself one hell of a headache.

The Potato Man came walking fast with the chainsaw buzzing.

He grabbed the cordless phone and chucked at the man. It bounced off his head. He didn't even notice.

Geoff looked around his room, but there was nothing to hold

228

off this kind of attack. He was anti-gun, and the only weapon he had was on the living room floor.

*

REPORTER FOUND DEAD, BODY CUT IN HALF BY CHAINSAW. By Charles Matthews.

That was the headline Trevor DeBlase awoke to. He grabbed the paper expecting to see Geoff's smear article. One look at Geoff's ugly mug from his Press Pass, and Trevor figured Geoff wanted to paste his face on his prize piece. But to Trevor's surprise, it was about his death. Not that Trevor was all that sad of his demise, but he didn't want the guy dead. Maybe jacked-up a bit, but not dead.

And who the hell was this Charles Matthews? Must be some newbie reporter. Trevor hoped he didn't harass him like Geoff did. It was ironic that the copycat Geoff was seeking out killed him. But the crazy part was that he thought Trevor was the killer. So the real killer had nothing to worry about. Unless Geoff discovered something after his run with Trevor, and got himself killed. Now that sounded about right.

Trevor forced himself to not think about Geoff. He threw on his gray and black jacket and headed out the door. Nick just pulled up.

"Hey buddy, wanna go check out that grave-site?"

"You're serious?"

"Hell-yeah. I dunno if the killer some junkie-copycat, or if the Pot Man really came back. I didn't use to believe in these things, but shit is happening, and there has to be a reason. I wanna see if what Geoff said was true."

The druggie had a point. Trevor had been thinking the same thing. He was on his way out to check the grave.

"What-the-hell? Lets do it."

229

*

Nick pulled the car around the curved drive-way of the cemetery, and parked it with the front-end facing out towards the road. They got out and Trevor scanned for the grave.

"I never did visit when they put him into the ground."

"Shit, I don't blame you Trev, I wouldn't have come if it was me who went through what you did."

"No, I was planning on coming out. I wanted to see his ass in that coffin, watch the lid shut, and watch the coffin lower down. I wanted to be guy who shoved the first scoop of dirt on his corpse. But when Geoff interviewed me, and the whole town looked at me like I was some kind of freak, I had to leave. Kenzie didn't want to stay here without me, and if I left her here, she would have received the same treatment. Now I'm back, so are the killings. I really hope this nut-job didn't rise from the dead."

"Lets get it on then."

They checked the rows until finally they ended up in the back of the lot. Trees were everywhere to the point of invading the burial spots. Trevor saw an empty grave, the only one in cemetery. Crime-scene tape wrapped around it.

"There it is. Along with the taped off spot where Logan died."

They approached the grave and saw what Geoff was talking about. There were strange finger-holes in the ground. Too many for two hands. It had to come from several people. *Could Potato Man have so many followers?*

"This is giving me the wiggins." Nick said as he rubbed arms. "C'mon man, we saw it, now we gotta go."

"This doesn't mean that he rose from the dead. Look at the holes, he was probably dug up by his supporters."

"You think this psycho had a following? Maybe a few, but not enough to make all of those finger marks."

"There's no way this guy came back. He must have been like Charles Manson."

Chapter Four

Later that night Nick locked all of his windows. Something he never did out of laziness. He locked his door, and slid his couch across it.

He felt better now. Nick went to restroom and squatted on the pot. He thumbed his phone screen texting to a girl he had been flirting with. His phone was like a limb to him.

Something brushed up against his ass. Nick jumped and placed his back against the wall with his pants around his ankles. Dirty, dead fingers gripped the toilet seat as it pulled itself up from the basin.

Nick grabbed the plunger and poked at it. The hand reached for the wood handle. Nick yanked back and switched his grip. He swung the plunger cup first at the hand, slamming it back inside of the toilet. He pushed the flush lever. The hand got suck and wiggled its fingers in desperate hope of rescue.

"What-the-fuck are you?"

He started to poke it at it again, trying to force the hand back down the drain. He hit lever for a second time. The hand took a hold of the wood handle and Nick dropped the plunger.

He ran out of the room and slammed the door shut.

There was a thunk on the other-side, followed by the scampering taps of fingers along the base of the door.

He leaned against the door with both hands pressed, and looked around for a weapon. Switching his palms with his back, dozens of hands stand inches from him.

Maybe I can get these little fucks locked up in the bathroom.

As the door opened, the hands lunged onto him. They shoved

him back tripping him backwards on top of the toilet.

His head hovered over the bowl. He grabs at the hands, but they continue to pile on him. Then the sound something scooting along the sink counter. A bottle of bleach appeared and tipped. The hands propped his mouth open as the liquid poured down his throat.

*

Trevor pulled up in the smashed up Charger in front of Nick's house. He honked three times to announce his arrival. He read over the latest newspaper reports about the murders. He compared them to the reports that led up to Potato Man's hand chopping prior to his death. There was nothing to indicate that this was a different killer. If it wasn't for the fact that Trevor was there when Potato Man was shot down, we would swear that this was the same person.

After ten minutes, Trevor honked his horn again. Four times.

He tossed the papers in the back seat and rubbed his eyes and text Nick.

Another ten minutes passed, Trevor got out of the Charger.

He walked up to the door and pounded. There was no rustling around inside. He tried the windows, but they were locked. There didn't seem to be anyone watching. Then he took his crowbar and shattered ta window.

He carefully stepped inside. Everything seemed okay. Except the couch was against the door. Checking the rooms one by one, he stopped once he made it to the bathroom. The door was part way open. Using the crowbar, Trevor pulled the door back. Nick's dead body lay on his back with his mouth wide open. White dried bleach circled his lips. The bottle from the act still sat on the edge of the sink counter, tipped on its side.

"The fucker got you too."

The only person Trevor could depend on, was now dead.
Kenzie!

It hit Trevor hard. If the Potato Man was killing off everyone that Trevor knew, then he would surely go after Kenzie.

*

Kenzie stared golf-ball size holes into the ceiling as she waited for the nurse to come back. She started to better, and was about to go insane if the IV wasn't removed.

Something fell over on the movable table next to her bed. She looked over her almost full water bottle had tipped.

Then something ran under her bed.

"Nurse?" She yelled.

Kenzie pushed the help button. Something ran on top of her leg under the sheet. The image of the hands form the wreck popped into her mind.

"Oh God, no."

She removed the IV, and jumped out of bed. One of the severed hands still gripped to her bare leg.

She smacked at it as she hopped over to the window.

*

Trevor arrived at the room just in time to see Kenzie half way out the window with the hands all over her. They tried shoving her out the window as she cling to the sill.

Trevor slammed the crowbar into the other hands that failed to stop him. Reaching for Kenzie she fell before her fingers could touch his.

They are three floors up.

He heard a crash.

Trevor looked out the window and saw Kenzie on top of a plastic table on a patio one floor down. She sluggishly scooted

233

off.

Trevor jumped into the bushes planted along the sides of the patio. He wrapped her arm around his neck and lead her towards a stairwell.

The hands chased them from outside as Trevor swung at them.

From the other end of the hall, the Potato Man.

The chainsaw revved, and the Potato Man charged towards him. The rest of the hands in suit.

Trevor pulled the fire-alarm. Security guards attempted to stop Potato Man. He sliced right through them.

Trevor took Kenzie though the fire-escape doors.

*

They barely made it to the Charger. The Potato Man along with his severed minions followed in the furthering distance. After several turns to make sure he lost them, Trevor headed for a place in the woods where he and Kenzie use to hang out as kids. It was ways out of town. In the middle of a forest that separated Florence from a major highway.

He pulled up on a shrouded shoulder, and helped Kenzie out of the car. He took her through the bumpy path. And after twenty minutes of walking, he placed her on top of a huge rock. This was their hideout back in the day. They never did find out how the rock got there.

"Okay Kenzie, you stay here. I'm gonna kill this fucker."

"How? He's unstoppable."

"No. I'm gonna to do this. He has to go. I can't do this if I have to worry about you."

"Oh but it's okay for me to worry about you?"

"Trust me. I can do this."

He gave her a long kiss, and left.

Trevor went to the one place he knew the Potato Man would

come for him.
  Trevor's house.

Chapter Five

  He pulled up across the street. No sight of the maniac, or his
minions. Trevor bolted out with crowbar in hand. Went to
straight to his closet. He pulled out the chest his aunt left him
for his job at the quarry, and grabbed a stick of dynamite, he
cut the fuse short, and ran back to the car.
  As soon as he slid into the driver's seat, he saw Potato Man
in the rear-view mirror. He was coming right for Trevor. He
contemplated backing into him, but as big as the goon was, and
with that chainsaw, the odds were good that the Charger would
be totaled, and Trevor next.
  He peeled out, and watched the Potato Man steal a modified
pick-up truck.
  The fucker can drive!
  It was a beast of a vehicle, looked like the owner used it for
anything from mudding, to monster truck rallies. And it moved
fast.
  The Charger wanted to crap-out. Trevor held the accelerator
down, and only let up when he approached curves. The town
slowly disappeared. The road twisted in bends, and blurred
trees became the walls of Trevor's tomb.
  Potato Man was catching up.
  If he remembered what his aunt told him, the quarry wasn't
far. The only problem he had never been there before. He had
no idea where the entrance was located.
  The truck was closing in.

Trevor lost speed at a tight, long curve. Potato Man was on top of him.

A slam to the back of the car made Trevor bounce around. He wouldn't be able to keep it on the road at this rate.

The curve started to straighten out but Potato Man was pulling up beside him. He slammed into the Charger, causing the car to drive off a huge embankment.

It went from a grassy slope, to a rocky wall. The Charger's wheels rolled along the rocky road and continued to go on its own as the ground became more sloped.

Trevor stopped it as he ran out of wall. He was now a few yards from the quarry. He made it to the parking area, and there was the entrance.

He drove the battered Charger to the door. When he turned the engine off, the car let out a dying sigh.

As he opened his door, he caught the image of Potato Man in the mirror. The truck was coming for him still. He found the way in.

Trevor smashed the lock with the crowbar after five or so swings. He hobbled down the darkening path as Potato Man forced the Charger out of the way. He jumped out of the truck, with chainsaw buzzing, and followed after Trevor.

The darkness made it impossible to see the path ahead. Even Potato Man had a hard time finding Trevor. He pressed his hands against the walls as he walked down the center of the corridor. Then his foot met something in the way. He fell hard on the ground, and the Potato Man picked up speed. It was a fucking coal-mining-cart.

Trevor groped at the ground and found the cart. He felt around the area for other weapons and his hand discovered a void.

He flicked his lighter, and he sat on the edge of a pit.

The Potato Man was almost close enough to cut him in half.

He lit the fuse on the dynamite.

The lighter went out and the chainsaw sliced through dirt, barely scraping Trevor's arm.

He kicked Potato Man off into the pit.

The chainsaw followed as the buzzing became more of an echo. A huge thump at the end notified Trevor that Potato Man didn't prematurely stop his decent. The sound of him staggering to his feet was enough to remind Trevor of what he needed to do.

The fuse was almost gone and he chucked the stick into the pit. An amber glow crackled its luminescence among the dark walls until it struck the Potato Man on the head. Before it could slide to the ground, it went off.

Trevor jumped back, taking cover as the blast shook the mine.

Chapter Six

The smell of powder burned Trevor's nose. He tried to move, but his legs were stuck under rocks. The light from the door he came through was gone. He dug in his pocket for his cell phone.

No Service

Not that it mattered. He used the background glow as a flashlight. He scanned over the rocks, and found the reason why he survived. He was behind the mine-cart. It blocked some of the debris. Now if he could just crawl through the rocks, or get someone to dig him out.

*

Trevor didn't dream of being paralyzed, or a chainsaw buzzing after him. Or Kenzie crying next to him. He didn't dream of being buried alive, or the burning powder, or a herd of severed hands chasing after him. The one thing he dreamed, Kenzie's hand against his cheek. This time she is there for him.

Pain ensued as the dream sliced in half by the daylight beaming through a window. It forced its way through his eyes, and the pain was from cut on the eyelid.

He couldn't see anything, but the warmth of Kenzie's hand was there on his cheek. Her scent intoxicated his senses. The room slowly superseded with Kenzie's lightly freckled face. Her green eyes that went with the adorable smile grounded Trevor to reality. The pain faded to a low murmur of what transpired.

"Hey handsome, you kept your promise." She kissed his forehead.

"Told ya I would." Trevor's voice was low and gravelly.

"You get some rest, I'll be back a little later."

"Where are you going? Hey they won't let you leave."

"I'm out, hun."

"Damn. I figured you still had some time left."

"Nope. After you left, I called the hospital. I'm good to go now."

"I-is, he dead?"

"Yes. I think so. I mean, you were the only one pulled out alive."

"That's good. I think I will sleep now." Kenzie tucked him in, and kissed him gently on the lips. "Wait. The hands, what about the hands?"

"I dunno. The police never found them."

"Just like last time."

"I'm sure they're gone. Get some rest."

*

Trevor woke up to the skitter-scatter taps along the floor. It was in the middle of the night. He laid still, and the sound was gone.

Must have been another stupid dream.

HOME INVASION

WESLEY SOUTHARD AND NIKKI MCKENZIE

"…and that was the third time I caught the Clap!" Cooter squealed and slapped his dusty knee.

For the fourth time that day, Fisher managed to swallow the tidal wave of vomit before it burst from his lips. His stomach *rolled* at the thought.

"Boy, I'll tell you what, you better pray you don't ever catch that *goner-ree-a*. Nasty stuff." Every *S*, hard or soft, whistled through the gap between the old man's two front teeth. "I had puss runnin' from the tip of my pecker like a leaky faucet fo' well over a month, and ma' balls went and swelled up bigger than a head of lettuce too! After the doctor – who was a nice feller by the way – fixed me up with that…whatchamacallit? Tetra-something? Anyway, once he done cured me of that stuff, I went back ta' that old whore Frieda and said, 'You old cooze! You done gave me the dick snots!' And she came back with, 'Well, whadja expect, Cooter? Didn't you learn the first two times?' Can you believe the balls on the old washboard? Mercy, mercy, mercy…"

Eight hours. That's how long Fisher had been enduring the non-stop ramblings of Cooter's "sexual prowess" in the old man's eighteen-wheeler on their route back from Ft. Wayne, and for eight hours – the last few rocketing down I-24 East through Nashville – Fisher wondered how much of it was complete bullshit. He had to have been damn near seventy, and it still tickled the old fart pink to brag about every conquest

240

from Albuquerque to Syracuse. For the first few hours Fisher smiled and nodded, but several hours in − and several upchuck close-calls later − he began to wonder how the old bastard wasn't a walking herpes sore. Fisher's grip tightened on the steering wheel. He was dog-tired. Enough was enough.

"Hot damn! I haven't told you about the time I covered myself in peanut butter—"

"Cooter," Fisher finally stopped him. "Seriously, I've had enough."

The old man glared at Fisher with a cocked, bushy brow. "Enough, eh? Really, boy, you really wanna go there? You know, the last I checked you were on probation with the company - skippin' out on work, wreckin' a truck, never makin' it on time ta' your scheduled stops. As far as Mr. Coscom is concerned - as far as Titan Foods is concerned - they've had enough of your malarkey. But bein' the sweetheart that I am, I stopped them from shit-canning your sorry behind, and instead I get ta' watch you for a few months on your trips until you get your head straight again. Hell, I did it 'cause I like you. You remind me of me at your age."

Wonderful, Fisher thought.

"And don't worry about what happened back there at the drop. I won't tell ol' Coscom about you forgettin' ta' turn the cooler back on after stopping in Indy, spoiling all that food and the like. I'll take the hit on that, don't you worry. Ain't no way that bag of hot air is gonna get rid of me. But you just remember you owe me big time."

Fisher threw his head back against the headrest and sighed. All he wanted was to get home, pet his stupid cat, hold his fiancée Missy and the future little Fisher blooming inside her, and assure them everything was going to be okay. *It* is *going to be ok*, he repeated. He knew he'd fucked up time and time again with Missy − the lying, ditching work and making side trips to Lexington for the horse track, blowing through the money her grandparents had gifted them for their wedding and their child in a matter of minutes – but he swore he was finished with all that. And he was. But Mr. Coscom felt the need to regularly remind him what a royal screw-up he really was, and his so called "gambling addiction" was a threat to the company's perfect record of timeliness. With Coscom's remarks and Cooter's rants, Fisher was damn near ready to drive the old man's rig right off the Tennessee mountainside. Lucky for him – and Cooter – he was careful at keeping cool.

The sign for the first downgrade before Monteagle passed by in a flash.

Not much longer, Missy. He glanced down at his cell phone in the cup holder. He wanted to call her. Bad.

But as much as he wanted to rush home, Fisher reluctantly pulled off the accelerator and rode the brake pedal as the interstate began to slope. His knuckles popped as he gripped the wheel tight, ass clenching against the seat. The big rig groaned as it pulled the empty cooler trailer behind it. He steered the truck into the far right lane, then clicked on his emergency lights, to let the rest of the smaller vehicles behind him pass. Their taillights bloomed in the darkness, lighting the granite mountain walls in bright cherry reds. Fisher kept his focus straight ahead and knew it was only a matter of time before the truck's buzzer would go off and they would have to stop for the night. *Goddamn federal time regulations!*

"Hot damn," the old redneck giggled, "I can't wait to get back home! Been living in Chattanooga for almost all my life, probably same as you. Love that city. So full of history and beauty…and long-legged women. I always love crossing that ol' Nickajack Lake, 'cause you know it ain't but a few more miles 'till we hit that Chattahoochee. You know, the way it sits in the bottom of that mountain bowl, so beautiful. It's like Atlantis…with Waffle Houses."

Something bright flashed overhead, momentarily blinding

Fisher. Before he could cover his eyes, the light narrowed, then zipped past the front of his rig and smashed into the adjacent rock wall. Fisher screamed as he slammed his brake pedal to the floor. The brakes squealed in protest, and the trailer's rear end swung toward the left lane. Soda bottles and half-empty Frito bags spilled across the floorboard. An SUV blared its horn from behind. Fisher panicked and jerked the wheel to the left, nearly colliding with the smaller vehicle. Cooter yelped as his head slammed against the window. The SUV screeched and spun until it faced the opposite direction. Fisher righted himself but knew he was getting too close to the edge. He aimed for the emergency truck ramp and pumped on the breaks. Gravel and sand exploded across the road as the big rig soared up the rocky path. Fisher ground his teeth, fought to keep the rig straight on the path and kept the brake jammed to the floor until the truck finally halted at the top of the incline.

"God damn, boy!" Cooter hollered, rubbing his head. "Did you see that?"

Fisher, arms locked against the wheel, finally exhaled. "Yes, Cooter, I obviously saw that!"

"Holy mother and Mary, that was brighter than shit! By the way, you better hope you didn't damage my rig, otherwise someone's gonna owe me twice!"

Cooter dug under the passenger seat until he found his Maglite, then leapt out of the truck and carefully crept along the rock wall. "Come on, boy! Get out here and let's see what you almost killed us over."

Knees shaking, Fisher reluctantly snatched his own flashlight and lowered himself out of the truck while leaving his cell phone behind. He jogged to catch up with Cooter.

Something glowed on the ground up ahead.

From behind, the truck's buzzer sounded off.

*

Several miles away on the outskirts of Chattanooga, Missy struggled with her own upchuck reflex. "Ewe, Sondra. Don't say that."

Sondra peeked over the colossal coffee mug she held with both hands, steam rising over her face. "Say what?"

"You know what," Missy shuddered. "Ugh."

Sondra placed her mug on the little diner-style table in the corner of the soon-to-be Fisher family kitchen and smirked at her friend. "What? All I said was, 'Don't get your panties in a twist!'"

Missy shifted before the oven, back to her friend − a nervous, disjointed, twitchy sort of dance. The metal tongs in her hand waved through the air as if to swat some unseen fly. "*That*, Sondra! Don't say…*panties*."

She said the word with child-like embarrassment, spoke so softly the sizzling of the pork in the pan was almost louder. Her cheeks flushed, which had nothing to do with the heat of the stove-top, and she could not keep the grin off her face.

"Don't say that. Say *underwear* or something."

"Are you kidding, Missy? Panties? You can't handle the word *panties*?" Sondra said the word loud and hard, and Missy jerked every time. "How did Justin ever get *into* those panties?"

"Hey!" Missy turned from the oven, wielding the tongs at her Bestie like a Catholic school teacher would a ruler at an errant child. "He got into them by being a *gentleman*, by being sweet and gracious and well-mannered. He could teach you a thing or two."

Missy caressed her growing belly, something she did instinctively at the thought of her future husband. Even if Justin was away, as was often the case, she could still feel him, in her, in their little one. She glanced down and smiled.

"You miss him."

Missy looked up to find her friend's big, green eyes probing, a soft smile on her face.

"Of course I do. I love him."

"Oh, I know," Sondra said, nodding. "I can see it all over your face. And in that belly, there."

Both women giggled.

"When will you find out the sex?"

Missy put up a finger as if to say *wait*, moved the bacon in the skillet about − grease popping and splattering over the electric flat-top sending the scent of smoke and spices throughout the room − and placed it on the back burner to join her friend at the table.

"I'm not sure we want to," Missy replied as she lifted Sondra's giant mug from the table, cupping it in her own delicate hands. "Well…we want to, but I think we'd like the surprise more. I mean, how often in life do you get to be *genuinely* surprised? I think it would make for such a beautiful moment. This smells *so* good."

She didn't drink Sondra's coffee as much as took in the aroma. Mocha. Her favorite. Caffeine was *no bueno* for the Fisher Guppy − Justin's coinage. As torturous as it was for Missy, she knew it was best for the health of the baby.

"You have such a good heart, Missy. You're going to make a wonderful mother."

Missy slid the cup across the table and fanned her face. "*Stoooooop.* You're going to make me cry! You know I'm hormonal."

Sondra reclaimed her coffee with one hand and patted Missy's arm with the other. "Honey, I hate to break it to you, but you're a sap *all the time*."

She winked, and Missy had to choke back the tears. "You hush. I am not."

Total lie, of course.

Missy's mother Ines, Brazilian and stunningly beautiful (as was Missy), was wise to her daughter's sensitivity early on. In fact, she was convinced the only reason Missy cried upon delivery was because she somehow knew childbirth hurt, and felt bad for inflicting pain on her mother. Ines also attributed Missy's vegetarianism to this predisposed want to only aid and comfort. She seemed to know the proteins in front of her had come at something else's expense, something that could think and feel pain, and she wanted nothing to do with it. The bacon was for Justin.

She smiled again.

"You never did answer my question," Sondra said, gently slapping the table top to snap Missy from her stupor.

"What question?"

"What it is you two plan on doing about all this."

Missy's smile slipped some but never quite fashioned into a frown. Only on the rarest of occasions could she find something to make her miserable enough to do so. But she did sigh. "Honestly? I don't know. We're not *totally* broke − Justin did use some discretion − but I want to keep what we have left of Grands' money stashed away, just in case. With this economy…"

Missy trailed off on purpose. What she said wasn't a lie, but it also wasn't the whole truth. It was nice to have a cushion, but it was better to have a safety net - particularly if your fiancé was prone to falling.

"You know you can always come to me, right? If you need help?"

"I know. And I'm grateful. But really…we're going to be okay. It won't be easy, and it won't be quick, but Justin wants to change; he means to be better, and he's working hard to prove it. Whatever the solution, we'll find it. Together."

"Honey, I just hope you're not setting yourself up for disappointment - and I mean that in the nicest possible way.

246

You know I love Justin as much as I love you, but addiction is a savage beast and difficult to slay. I would hate for you to get anything less than everything you hope for. That's all."

"I'm not afraid."

Missy sat back in the aluminum folding chair and clasped her hands over her budding belly. She spoke to the child in utero as much as to Sondra.

"I know Justin − I *know* him. He means to change, and he will. Nothing short of some cosmic event could stop things from working out for the better. I'm not afraid."

But Missy *was* afraid of one thing, and when she looked into her lap and saw it, there wasn't enough positive thinking or good will in the world to keep her from losing her cool. She jumped from her chair, simultaneously knocking it over and launching Sondra's coffee mug into the air. The vessel slammed back down splashing dark liquid over the black and white checkerboard pattern and onto her friend's blue jeans. Sondra herself pushed back in a hurry, tipping her own chair as well.

"What! What happened?"

Sondra used both hands to shoo the excess java from her jeans, but her eyes remained fixed on Missy who, by now, was in full-blown seize mode. Her legs shuffled as if she were running in place, her hands swatting and slapping at her body − thighs, hips, stomach (she was more careful there but still spastic), chest, neck, and finally her hair. She bent over and batted at her head like a schizo shaking the senseless out.

"Missy, *what*?"

Missy heard Sondra holler but wasn't quite ready to relax yet. She hopped away toward the center of the room and continued to rake her hands through her hair, though she had little of it, a pixie cut style of her choice.

"*Mesalina*!"

That did it. Missy's eyes shot up at the shout of her given

name – sort of a Pavlov's dogs thing. The only person who called her Mesalina anymore was her father when he had his 'I-am-Daddy' pants on. "Huh?"

The stillness, however, was not to be. It took only seconds for the shimmying – and a string of *ewewew's*! – to resume.

Eventually, Missy mellowed. Meanwhile, Sondra grabbed a dish towel and cleaned the coffee from the table, shaking her head. "Was that some sort of pregnancy-induced demon possession? Do we need a priest?"

Missy gave herself one last rub-down, stuck her tongue out in a gagging gesture and said, "It was a creepy crawler."

Sondra raised an eyebrow. "A creepy crawler?"

"A creepy crawler. One of those *unholy* things that has nine thousand legs and moves faster than…poop…through a goose. It was on me."

"A bug, you're saying? That was about a bug."

"They're gross! I can't relax when I see those things. One appears, vanishes a split second later, and I wait for it to turn up *on* me. Blech."

"They're a good thing, you know," Sondra reasoned. "When those are around, you won't find any ants or roaches or any other pests. They're basically nature's little exterminators. A good thing."

"If those things *cured cancer* they wouldn't be a good thing."

Missy took a plate from the cupboard, lined it with paper towels, and scooped the bacon on top. At one point, a mound of meat dangling in the air between the tongs, she turned back to Sondra.

"That was mean. I shouldn't have said that. I'm a terrible person."

Sondra chuckled as she pulled her black hooded sweatshirt over her pale blond hair, and straightened her short bangs once everything was in place. She took the bacon out of Missy's hand and hugged her tight. "You're not a terrible person. I don't think you could be if you tried. I love you. I'll see you tomorrow, 'kay?"

"I love *you*," Missy said, hugging her friend tighter. "And yes, I'll see you tomorrow. Thank you for not making fun of me."

"I would never…to your face!"

Then she cried *HUGS!* and hurried out, her face disappearing from the crack in the screen door. Cool Tennessee springtime air fanned in behind her.

"Very funny," Missy shouted, knowing Sondra would hear. "You're evil!"

She went back to the bacon and mumbled to herself. "*I'm* evil, too, for cooking this bacon. Poor little piggy. If the animal gods demand restitution, take it from Justin's karmic stock."

And then…*CRASH!*

*

Fisher's stomach growled.

They should have been at least ten miles closer to home by now with Cooter warning him to slow down, you're goin' too darn fast! Not here, stuck with the old bastard, creeping up on God-knows-what on the side of the Interstate. His stomach churned. Hunger or nerves, something was not sitting well. Missy had said something on the phone earlier about bacon. Four years in and he still did not have the heart to tell her he preferred sausage.

With his head kept low and his senses on high, he followed the old man among the rocky outcroppings of the mountainside wall, stepping over shredded tires and heaps of garbage thrown from windows. "Damnit, Cooter, the buzzer's going off! We've only got 15 minutes before the rig shuts down, and

249

we're stuck for the night!"

Cooter shushed him as they drew closer to the glowing red object. Somewhere close, water dripped and pooled into a roadside trench. The cool night air brushed past their faces, bringing to them the odor of scorched metal and…something else. Something peppery and sharp. *Like an unwashed arm pit*, Fisher thought, wincing.

Guided by the weak glow of flashlights, they approached.

Surrounded by thick, curled sheets of smoking metal at the bottom of the mountain floor lay a small, cylindrical tube no bigger than a can of tennis balls. Even after the crash, it remained smooth and unmarked. A crimson glow seemed to luminate the tube itself; the red metal blushed with heat. The few twigs that had sunk into the blackened earth of the crater had turned to ash.

Fisher drew in a deep breath, keeping his distance.

"Well, I'll be damned," Cooter mumbled, shuffling closer. "I think that's one of them illegal aliens!"

Fisher exhaled loudly. "It's not a Mexican, Cooter. It's…" *What the hell* is *that thing?*

Without a word, Cooter snatched a long stick from the roadside and knelt down before the crater.

Fisher grabbed his shoulder. "What are you doing?"

"Gonna give it a poke, boy, to see what the funky hell this thing is."

"Do you think that's such a good idea?"

Cooter laughed dryly. "Boy, you don't get to be my age by being stupid. Back in the old days we used to poke road patties – you know, road kill – with sticks just for fun. But we also did it to make damn sure that whatever lay there was doornail-dead, so it didn't get back up and run into the road. I want to make sure whatever the hell this thing is has bit the dust, that way we can figure out what to do about it."

I just want to go home! Fisher wanted to scream.

Tongue jutting between his lips, Cooter leaned forward and, without hesitation, jabbed the tube with the stick three times.

Something shrieked.

The two jumped back, Cooter falling on his rear end, the end of his stick singed and smoking.

"What the hell was that!" Fisher yelled.

Cooter slapped a wet cough from his chest. "Damned if I know." His eyes grew wide in the red light. He pointed forward. "Look."

Slowly, Fisher shuffled forward to the crater.

A thin, white line of light appeared down the middle of the tube, and after several seconds of *pops* and *clicks* the tube cracked and split open, the two halves falling apart. Steam hissed from the opening and released more of that hot, peppery stink. The red glow dulled. Once it completely died, they both aimed their flashlights at the contents within.

Something long and green wriggled between the separate halves. Two small arms reached up, and two tiny, clawed hands gripped the sides.

Fisher dropped his flashlight when a small pair of eyes blinked back at him.

"Holy shit!" He jumped backwards, nearly tripping over his own feet. "Come on, Cooter! Let's go! I don't want to see anymore of this."

But the old man's focus was on their find. "Say what? We can't just leave!"

"Screw it!" Fisher tapped at his pants pockets and silently cursed himself. "You stay here, and I'll go back to the rig and grab my cell, okay?"

Cooter didn't blink. "Sure…"

Without his flashlight, Fisher darted up the rocky incline and hopped into the cab. The buzzer demanded his attention, but all it received was a quick middle finger. He located his cell phone, jabbed the HOME button to wake it from sleep mode, and sighed. No bars. "Figures."

At the bottom of the hill, Cooter screamed.

Heart racing, Fisher leapt from the cab and hurried down the hill, gravel scattering with every step. In the darkness ahead, Cooter's outline flailed about, the beam of his flashlight swirling against the granite walls. Just as Fisher approached, the old man gurgled and collapsed. Fisher then grabbed his own flashlight, knelt down and grabbed the back of Cooter's head. The old man's eyes rolled into the back of his skull, showing only the whites. "Cooter! Cooter! Wake up, man! What happened?"

Something made Fisher turn. He aimed the flashlight into the crater.

The tube was empty.

Panicked, Fisher jabbed the flashlight in all directions finding nothing but an empty interstate. "Cooter, man, come on, wake up," he said, not sure why he was suddenly whispering. When he only responded with another wet gurgle Fisher pulled Cooter to his feet and held him up under his arms. Thankfully, the old pervert didn't weight much.

Fisher struggled, but managed to drag the two of them up the hill and situated Cooter back into the passenger seat. Fisher buckled him in and got back behind the wheel. The rig started up easily, but the trip back down would be anything but. Carefully, he dropped the truck into reverse and slowly − *very* slowly − backed it down the hill. He was terrified a smaller vehicle would come around the bend and crash into the trailer, but no one did.

Once they pulled back onto the Interstate, Fisher guided the truck into the far right lane, finally letting himself breathe. But he was far from calm. Something was seriously wrong with Cooter, and the rig, no matter how fast he drove, only had five more minutes before it would shut off and remain inoperable for the next eight hours. He had to get the old man to a hospital quick, but he wasn't sure Monteagle even had one. His thoughts kept going back to the red metal tube…and the green worm-like *thing* squirming within. It was gone when he came back, so where did it…

Fisher turned toward Cooter.

Cooter's wide eyes were locked onto his as something large ballooned in his throat.

*

Missy hauled butt into the living room, from which the commotion seemed to come.

Easily startled and already on pins and needles, she jogged through the narrow hall and into the gloom of their living room, bacon-greased tongs still in hand. With only one window and little to go off but moonlight, Missy focused hard, not only on finding the source of the noise but remembering what it was in the first place.

Did books fall off the shelf? Did glass break?

She used her free hand to feel along the wall for the light switch behind her, but her eyes continued to search the room. She could make out more of the rectangular recesses in the wall serving as her book shelves - Justin wasn't much of a reader - but nothing appeared out of place. The glass of the window remained intact, so that wasn't it. Missy eventually found the switch, flipped it, and the floor lamp in the back corner, opposite the books, filled the space with soft amber light.

The search was over.

On the floor behind the futon was Missy's aloe plant, overturned. A few of the thick, fleshy leaves had snapped and oozed their soothing fluid onto her no longer spotless carpet. Dirt spilled over the decorative clay pot and spread out like filthy tendrils. Little brown paw-print shaped smudges led away from the plant and out the way she'd come.

"Ugh! Flippin' cat! Puss, where are you?"

She did a quick search of the room, but there weren't too many places for the pain in the rump to hide.

"Pussface!"

She didn't expect the cat to respond but bent down on all fours to check beneath the sofa, careful not to grind *more* soil into the carpet. She thought she heard something, a rustling, but assumed it was her weight on the futon as she went down. Missy put her face in the space between the couch and the floor and...

Nothing.

Stupid cat was stupid *and* M.I.A.

Missy sighed, sat on her legs and set to scooping up her spilt potted plant.

She turned it upright, pouting as she fingered the broken leaves, then set the tongs on the table from which it had fallen - she'd need both hands to scoop up the excess dirt. The soil cooled her hands and warmed her heart, one of Missy's favorite sensations. It reminded her of her mother and the times they'd spent in her backyard garden.

The first handful, aerated and silky, she fiddled with a bit before returning it to the pot, more lost in thought than anything. But when she did actually *look* at the second handful...she wanted to be sick all over it.

Squirming throughout the soil were at least two of the same horrid bugs she'd earlier found nesting in her lap.

Their eighteen-thousand legs wriggled as the creatures tunneled in and out of sight, above the dirt and below it. Long antennae stuck straight up off their heads - *two, like devil horns, because they're evil* - and whirled through the air as if to draw in and feed off Missy's discomfort. Not wanting to but forcing herself to do so, Missy looked down at the mess on the floor.

More bugs.

Two, three…ten? It didn't matter. And there were more still in the plant itself, a couple slinking out over the edge and scurrying out of sight.

All this happened in a matter of seconds, but, after what felt like an eon, she flung the contents of her hands as far from herself as possible and dashed, still on hands and knees, for the doorway.

She'd almost made it through before Puss barreled into the room, zipping right under and straight through her arms and legs like she'd never been there at all.

"What the—?"

Missy put her head down and watched between her knees and upside down as the cat wigged out on the other side of the room. He darted from one spot to the next, shook his head and kicked his legs out, sometimes lying down and rolling over, grinding his head into the carpet before doing it all over again.

"Pudder…"

She forgot all about the bugs. The cat was upset, which made *her* upset. Missy pulled herself up and approached the tabby.

"Pussface…Pudder…what's up, buddy? What's got you spooked?"

The poor, stupid beast was still tweaked but he calmed a bit when he saw Missy coming. He sat down but wouldn't stop jerking his head to the side, pawing at his ear.

"Come here, fat boy. Let me see."

Missy scratched Puss's opposite ear to soothe him while she checked the one giving him grief. She folded his dark ear back and, at first, thought there was a wad of hair stuck in there, which would explain his irritation. It must have itched like crazy. But then she watched the wad unfold…unfurl…and crawl out of the animals ear drum and down his white fur throat.

Missy hollered and jumped back. Pussface shook himself and ran out into the hall.

"That's it!" she cried, waving her hands as if she'd burned them. "I've had it! Where's my phone?"

She knew Justin couldn't do anything about it at the moment, but she was starting to get a complex, and she could at least whine to someone other than the cat. Missy hopped the stairs two at a time to retrieve her phone from the bedroom.

She found her trusty old clam-shell phone on the night stand and dialed Justin's number as she continued to dry-heave and shoo imaginary bugs from her body. "Come on, boy, answer the phone." Missy bounced impatiently and counted the rings - two, three, four. Justin answered on the fifth ring, but he barely got through *Missy!* before she shrieked.

"You need to come home! And take me to a hotel! No way I'm staying here...*ugh!*"

There was a lot of interference on Justin's end. She had a hard time making out what he said.

"Justin? Can you hear me? Are you almost home? I'm bugging out!"

Missy smacked herself in the forehead for the ridiculous pun.

"They were on me, Justin," she whined. "They had legs and intentions."

She thought she heard someone cry out in the background, heard Justin yell, but again, the interference. "Justin!"

Call dropped.

She dialed his number again, but it went straight to voicemail.

"Perfect! Lovely! Just me and the stupid cat in a house full of scuttling parasites."

The words resonated, echoed off the walls of her mind. *A house full of scuttling parasites...*

"A house full?"

256

Missy caught her reflection in the mirror atop the dresser.
It moved.
Or rather, things moved *over* it.
"Justin," she whispered. "Please come home."

*

The truck shut off as they rolled into the parking lot of the
crowded rest area. Fisher carefully glided the rig into the last
free spot in the back of the lot and shifted it into park. The
engine sighed, but Fisher found he could not do the same.
He quickly unbuckled and crawled over to Cooter. He
reached out to touch him, but something stopped him. The
massive bulge in the old man's throat had − thankfully −
receded and disappeared, but Fisher still felt uneasy, helpless.
The old man lay motionless in his seat other than his eyes
rolling in his head like bowling balls down a greased lane.
"Cooter! Come on, you old fuck, say something!" Now that
he was this close, he noticed something was very off. Cooter's
skin appeared splotchy and gray, and speckled with flakes of
black. And was that smoke drifting out between his teeth?
The black spots grew larger.
Fisher panicked.
The nearest hospital could be miles away, and the rig − the
Goddamn rig! − was dead for the next eight hours. "Seriously,
Cooter, say something − anything!"
Cooter's body jerked and tensed up. His fingers curled over
the edge of the arm rests. Smoke seeped from his fingertips.
The overhead light snapped on as the passenger door clicked
and swung open. An obese woman wearing little more than a
tube top and fishnets stepped up into the cab and grinned a
jagged smile. Her massive breasts jiggled beneath the
painfully thin material. "Heya, boys! Either of you two manly
men lookin' fo a little slap 'n tickle?"

Lot lizard.

"Get lost," Fisher growled.

The woman turned toward Cooter. "Coota! Ya old fart! I haven't seen ya in a dog's age. Why haven't ya been visiting with dear ol' Mama Gracie?"

Cooter hitched and coughed, exhaling a thick cloud of noxious smoke.

She bent forward, eyes narrowed. "What's wrong with him?" She slapped Fisher's shoulder.

"Nothing, he's just a little sick right now - bad gas station hot dog. Look, just leave us—"

Another lot lizard appeared behind Mama Gracie, this one more petite but no less sordid. "Cooter! Well, I'll be damned!"

Fisher tried to reason. "Ladies, listen, Cooter is very sick right now. I need to get him to a hospital."

Mama Gracie unbuckled Cooter and lifted him from his seat like an infant. "I'll tell ya what, string bean. I'll take care of sweet ol' Coota here. I'm all this ol' man needs."

"No, no, no!" Fisher exited the cab and met her on the other side. "Please, just put him back. I need to find—"

The smaller lizard stepped up to him and jabbed the business end of a switch blade to his neck, stopping Fisher dead.

"Ya best jus' let Mama do her magic, string bean. If you're good, maybe I'll letcha have a crack at *this* crack later!" The girl licked her lips and smiled, revealing a mouth absent of teeth. She lowered the knife, blew him a kiss and took off after Mama and Cooter.

"Jesus…" Fisher sighed. "Could this night get any worse?"

Fisher reluctantly followed the two hookers and his work mate into the brightly lit welcome center, past the pamphlet stands, then into the Men's restroom. An old security guard slept soundlessly at his desk in a small room across the hall. The two women giggled and cooed, whispering charming obscenities to Cooter as they carried him into the handicap stall against the far wall and closed the door behind them.

Drained, Fisher collapsed onto the tiled bathroom floor − *It looks clean enough*, he thought − and closed his eyes. In his mind's eye he could still see the bright flash, the near collision, the tube…the thing inside. Fisher curled into himself and shivered violently. It wasn't that he was cold; he had finally snapped. His body couldn't handle anymore. The day was done. He was supposed to be back home by now, hugging his fiancée, petting his cat, eating his stupid bacon. Instead, he was sitting on the floor of a rest area bathroom while two hookers gave Cooter a full service check under his hood.

Fisher nearly screamed when his phone vibrated. He pulled his cell from his pocket and stared at it for a minute before finally snapping it open.

"Missy!"

"*Shhhhhhhhhh*…need…*shhhhhhh*…hotel! And… *shhhhhhhhh*…staying here…"

The static and interference was so thick he could only make out every other word.

"Missy? Missy, can you hear me?"

"*Shhhhhhhhhhh...* they were on me!"

From inside the stall, the two hookers screamed. Fisher dropped his cell phone. The back cover snapped, sending the battery skipping across the floor.

The hookers continued to shriek, long and hard, as they threw themselves against the thin metal walls of the stall. Smoke plumed and filled the corner of the room. Fisher leaned over and peered under the door.

An explosion rocked the small restroom throwing Fisher clear to the other side. His back hit the far wall near the door before he crumpled like a wet blanket. Fisher sat up, groaned at the throbbing in his side and tried to stand. The billows of smoke lifted and expired as quickly as they'd come.

The hookers had stopped screaming.

"Cooter?" he coughed.

Fisher took a step forward, but stopped when the door to the stall swung open.

The remnants of smoke separated as Cooter – or what he had become – *slithered* through the doorway.

*

I've had it up to my tits with this.

Missy heard Sondra say it a million times, and while she herself couldn't form the words, she could appreciate them now, particularly since, if things continued on this way then there would be enough of the disgusting beasts to do so.

There were almost more bugs on the mirror than glass, and dozens of others coming out of the woodwork. Literally. They crept out of holes in the baseboards she didn't even know were there, through windowsills, from under the closet door. But the final straw came when Missy found some scurrying out the corner of her underwear drawer. The thought of those things going anywhere *near* her unmentionables, whether on her body at the time or not, made her tingle in a most unwanted way.

"You are *totally* uninvited here," she said before running out the door.

Missy stood in the hall and ruffled her hair out of sheer blankness. She was confused, freaked out, agitated and concerned about her fiancé and didn't know which issue to tackle first. But, as was often the case in stressful situations, biology took over…and told her she had to pee.

Missy skipped a few feet down the hall and into the tiny bathroom, not bothering to hit the switch before sitting on the toilet - the faux candle in the window provided enough illumination for her to do what she needed to do.

Not a moment passed after she heard the first tinkle before

she saw the first creeper.

It had come from beneath the shelves not three feet from her. Pants around her ankles and heart in her throat, Missy did the first thing that came to her, which was to grab a bottle of bathroom cleaner beneath the sink. She was still…*going*…and therefore unable to run, so this seemed like the next best solution. Missy twisted her legs as far away from the bug — the *big* bug — as they would go and fired.

The beast was at least as thick as her thumb and too angry to die because no matter how many times she'd sprayed, it kept coming. And the closer it came, the louder Missy cried out. "*Gitgitgit*!"

The room reeked of noxious fumes and made Missy's eyes tear — at least, that's what she told herself. The bug had become a walking chemical cloud, a trail of white foam left in its wake. Its progress slowed, but not enough for her liking, so she put the nozzle as close to the insect as possible and pumped…and did not stop pumping until she blew the thing back into the corner, watching it like a hawk to make sure it moved no more.

When it didn't, Missy slipped her bottoms back on and went for the hand sanitizer — and found more bugs. The sanitizer, the faucet, the whole basin was crawling with them, all slinking up through the drain. Missy jumped back and almost fell into the tub but managed to grab the shower curtain in time, ripping it away from a few of the hooks to reveal a swarm within. Body wash, soap dish, the shower caddy with her toothbrush and toothpaste on it…not one surface went untouched by their filthy little legs. She could actually *hear* their rigid, wretched bodies rubbing against one another, an obscene whispering.

Missy gagged and made a break for the stairs but stopped at the landing.

So far she'd seen the crawlers in every room of the house, but there was still one space she hadn't checked. Missy put one hand on her belly and another over her mouth, palm out, nauseated by something other than the pregnancy. She *really* didn't want to check this room because part of her knew what she would find, and knew how upset, how *angry* she was going to be if the room had been violated by these revolting creatures. She sighed.

"Just open the door, Missy."

So she did.

And found her baby's nursery teeming with creeping life.

The soft green walls were crisscrossed with trails of them, not quite as organized as an ant march but following something reminiscent of a route. The white furniture was spotted with their wicked little bodies, light from the baby zoo animal lamp muted by the sheer amount of bugs amassed on the shade. And the crib… The *crib*. The green and purple pastel quilt Missy had loved so much was wholly concealed under the cover of the multi-legged cockroaches. The doe-eyed lion and the happy hippo she found so endearing were erased, her baby's haven, erased, and with it, Missy's patience.

She stomped her feet in the doorway and snarled.

"Soil our Guppy's room, will you? God help you, beasties, 'cause I sure won't."

Missy took one step into the hall and was body-checked.

*

The restroom door swung open and the old security guard from the lobby ran in, halting when he eyed the monstrosity slinking through the handicap stall door.

"What in tarnation!"

Fisher quickly shuffled backwards, away from the bloated, gray membrane Cooter had become, and stood behind the old man. The creature groaned and jiggled as two humanlike arms and legs stretched from its jellylike body and lifted its bulk

262

upright, though its torso remained a shapeless blob that trailed behind it like a coattail. Its face altered and rearranged until it formed something resembling the old man with which he had once shared his work duties.

Of all the things Fisher could have thought at that particular moment, the only thing to hit him was, *Mr. Coscom is going to be so pissed…*

The security guard looked beyond Cooter to the smoking piles of lot lizard gore staining the handicapped stall. "My God…"

In the time it took to blink, Cooter's bloated arm shot out and stretched across the room, attaching itself to the old security guard's face. Smoke billowed from the man's head, filling the room with the stink of cooked meat and burnt hair. He barely had time to scream before his entire body inflated and burst, showering Fisher in a chunky, liquid red nightmare. The creature retracted its arm and hissed.

Fisher threw open the door and broke into a sprint through the empty lobby, shouldering open the front doors.

He collided with several truckers standing at the entrance.

The one in front, who sported a jean jacket and golden, waistline mullet, grabbed Fisher by his shirt to stop him. "Whoa there, young buck!"

"Let me go!" Fisher struggled against his grip.

"Hold on a second. What the shit was that explosion a minute ago?"

Another trucker with a large gut spit a wad of tobacco on the sidewalk. "Yeah? You wasn't droppin' M-80's in the john, now was ya? Kids come through here all the time to do stupid shit like that and blame it on us."

The remaining truckers nodded. "Yeah!"

Mullet glanced over Fisher's shoulder, his eyes wide. "What the shit!"

The lobby exploded into a mess of glass and metal as Cooter

streamed through the front of the building as if it were not there. It appeared bigger now, its massive bulk swaying back and forth like Jell-O shaking on a plate. Mullet loosened his grip, and Fisher rolled out of the way before Cooter got any closer. After making it to the edge of parking lot, curiosity got the better of him. He stopped to look over his shoulder.

The truckers screamed and turned to run, but Cooter shot several more long, gray appendages their way, attaching themselves to the men and freezing them in place. Instantly, they became pillars of smoke and soon after steaming heaps of their former selves. Blood and various body parts showered the front lawn. Fisher gazed on in a sick fascination as Cooter grew larger becoming nearly as tall as the building itself.

Fisher kept low and weaved between the rows of trucks, doing his best to lose the creature following him. He ducked under the truck trailers near the back of the lot, checking every door handle as they came along. But he struggled with keeping quiet — his clothes were blood soaked, and his breath was nowhere to be found, each one more of a struggle than the last. Every cell in his body told him to scream, to rid his mind of the impossibilities he had witnessed, but he knew he couldn't. He had too much to live for. He had only just started to regain Missy's trust (but with someone as overly nice as her, it was not that difficult), and with their little guppy on the way… There was no chance he was going to watch its first steps from the afterlife.

Fisher jerked stiff when he heard something slide across the driveway. He slapped a hand over his mouth and slowly knelt down to peak under the rigs. Nothing. He checked a few more cabs before finally finding one unlocked. He quietly opened the door and slipped inside, ignoring the stale reek of marijuana and sweat. From that high up he could see over the hoods of several other cabs to the front of the building, where the remains of the truckers cooled in the night air. But no sign of Cooter.

Fisher searched the cab for a set of keys, silently hoping they weren't in someone's current possession. He popped open the glove compartment and was surprised to find a very shiny, very large Magnum revolver. He had heard of truckers carrying guns before, but had yet to encounter anyone who cared, for obvious reasons, to admit to it. Fisher snatched the gun, finding it fully loaded, and closed the compartment.

He looked down and sighed, feeling a bit stupid. The keys were still in the ignition. Hands sweating, he gripped the key and turned, praying the truck wasn't dead for the night. The rig purred to life, and the alarm remained mercifully silent. *There are some miracles still left in this world.* He caught his breath and shifted the cab into drive letting the truck and its attached trailer slowly roll out of its space. Then he thought, *Screw it,* and jammed down the accelerator. *I've got the truck now, and I've got the gun!*

But his thoughts changed immediately when he turned right toward the exit. Cooter towered over the last row of trucks, its girth nearly covering the entire exit ramp. It held several more unfortunate truckers in place while it proceeded to turn them inside-out. His fear gone, and gun in hand, Fisher floored the accelerator and drove straight toward it.

Cooter's massive bulk turned to face Fisher as he closed in.

The truck smashed directly into it which threw Fisher against the steering wheel. His face hit the dashboard, and his mouth filled with blood as his two front teeth flew from his mouth. He was frightened the monstrosity would stop the truck, and, for the moment, it did. Cooter's gray, distorted face filled the windshield and moved closer until its arm-sized lips pressed against the glass.

"*Fiiiiiisssshhhheeeeeeer.*"

Fisher lifted the gun and pulled the trigger three times.

Cooter squealed and toppled backwards onto the pavement.

Black blood splashed over the hood and into the open windshield. Fisher retched as it sprayed across his face and into his mouth, the foul taste rolling over his tongue and down his throat. He coughed up a puff of smoke. But there was no time to waste. He took his free moment and kicked the accelerator, pinning the creature to the ground as he drove right over it. The truck jostled and shook violently before hitting ground and continuing onto the mostly clear interstate.

He kept his eyes on the road, focusing with every inch of his being to make it home without crashing.

Fifteen miles, baby, and I'll be there!

Smoke poured out from the bottom of the cab.

*

Missy screamed and brought her hands up to protect her face, though she had already been knocked across the hall.

"It's just me, Missy! It's Sondra! Are you okay?"

Missy gritted her teeth and scowled at her friend. "Are you *bonkers?* You almost gave me a heart attack!"

"I'm sorry! I called you from the kitchen, but I guess you didn't hear. I didn't see you come out of there until it was too late. *Are you okay?* Tell me I didn't hit your stomach."

Missy grabbed her tiny hips and leaned against the wall, shaking her head. "No, hon, I'm fine. You just scared me, is all. What are you doing here, anyway?"

"Stupid me. I was on my way to the gallery when I realized I'd left my camera. I think I had it in the living room last?"

Missy nodded and tried to manage her harried nerves. "It should still be there."

"'Kay. I hate to hit and run but I have Neal waiting in the car. You sure you're all right? You looked razzed."

"*That* is an understatement."

"What's wrong?"

266

Missy told Sondra what had happened since she left - the cat, the bugs, and worst of all, not being able to reach Justin, not knowing if or when he would come home. She almost started to cry when she heard the rumble of a rig out front, followed by Justin's tell-tale honk.

It started as a joke at Missy's expense. He'd caught her watching *The Little Mermaid* videos online one morning, and thought it'd be funny to beep — as best he could — the tune to one of the songs when he got home that night. He'd never intended it to stick, he told her, but she'd taken such enjoyment from it he couldn't bring himself to stop.

Missy breathed a big sigh of relief. "Thank God."

Sondra started to say something but was cut off by a ruckus outside. "What was *that?*"

Missy shook her head in confusion and listened. Metal. Grinding. *A car accident?* Some kind of…*hissing…*like air escaping. *Did a hose on the truck blow?* And a man. Shouting. She couldn't make out what. "Neal?"

Sondra shrugged.

Concerned, both women made for the stairs when a tremendous crash rocked the house. *An earthquake!* The walls rumbled and the floor shook, knocking both Missy and Sondra on their keesters. Sondra recovered quick and got onto her hands and knees, while Missy stared at the ceiling to make sure it wasn't crumbling over their heads.

Moments went by before the din dissipated, the splintering wood and shattering glass thinning out, quieting, like the last few kernels of corn popping in the bag.

"Was that a *bomb?*" Sondra whispered.

"Who would want to bomb Chattanooga?"

"Someone who missed Nashville?" Sondra shook and rose to her feet. "I'll go find out. Stay here."

"No, Sondra! I'll come with you."

Before Missy could move, Sondra shot out a finger and

pointed at her belly. *You're pregnant, idiot,* her stern face said. *Stay.* She nodded and sat cross-legged in the center of the hall, watching her friend disappear down the stairwell, amazed she hadn't started to cry.

There was a clatter in the front yard.

Sondra screamed.

Missy shot upright. *"Sondra!"*

"Missy!" her friend cried. "Stay. Up. Stairs!"

Sondra appeared on the landing, her face void of all color, tears streaming. She grabbed Missy's hand and bawled. "We have to go! Is there a fire escape? A landing we could jump from a window down onto? I know it's dangerous for you, honey, but we don't have a choice."

Now! Missy cried. "I don't understand! Where's Justin?"

"Right here, baby girl!"

He's hurt, Missy thought. But he was coming up the stairs, which she assumed a good sign, so she went for him. "Justin!"

"NO!"

Sondra snatched her up, almost pulling Missy's arm from her shoulder. "Ow! Sondra…"

"Something's wrong with him, Missy! He's not—"

"What's wrong with him?" *Oh, God*, she begged. *Please don't take him from me. Not him. I couldn't bear it.* "Sondra, let me go!"

"Let her go, Sondra. Gonna getchas, anyway."

Missy stopped wrestling and stiffened, Sondra's warning sinking in. *Something's wrong with him.* She heard it in his voice and mistook it for injury, but hearing him now, listening to what he said, *how* he said it, he wasn't just hurt. He was… altered. His speech made her woozy. But before she could think of falling down, Justin bumbled into the crowded hall.

Or at least, something resembling Justin did.

Missy could hardly *begin* to process the nature of the creature swaying before her.

She *could* understand why he had trouble balancing, ambling – he had no feet to speak of. A tan boot was still on the end of one leg but something oozed through the eyelets, out over the top and down the laces. The other 'foot' was just a long… *tentacle?*…poking out of the pant-leg and dragging behind him.

His abdomen was distended, more of the gelatinous substance pushed through his flannel shirt, the buttons set to snap. His throat was swollen, and his head appeared misshapen, though it was hard to tell with the giant Native American headdress hanging over it.

The headdress was one of the more surreal but certainly not the *worst* part of Justin's appearance.

Missy put a hand over her belly.

Sondra put hers over Missy's, gently shooing Missy behind her.

Missy meant to run, *wanted* to run, but all she could do was press herself against the hallway wall, never taking her eyes off what she hoped, even now, could still be her fiancé. Sondra stayed close.

"Cooter blood," Justin gurgled. "Tube funk. WOO!"

Sondra wept as Justin lifted the amorphous mass of what could no longer pass as a human arm into the air, her little brother's head dangling from it.

"For Guppy!" Justin squealed. "A mobile. Spinny!"

He batted it with a semi-humanoid hand, and Neal's head made a few dizzying rotations before his hair tightened up, forcing it to spin in the opposite direction. Sondra sobbed louder.

"What have you done?" Missy whimpered.

"Gonna getchas, babies," Justin tittered, forming a grisly smile. "Gonna getchas. But first…"

Justin held the head high and raised his booted foot, taking a most flamboyant step. When he did so with the other gooey

269

appendage, the slopping made Missy teeter on the edge of sanity.

She didn't understand what he was doing at first, why he walked that way, but once he seemed more used to the movement and could keep himself from wobbling, she figured it out.

It was an awful masquerade, a shameful, alien imitation of an Indian marching.

He looked like something you'd find in a tasteless cartoon, bumbling down the hall, chanting, feathers on the headdress swaying – an embarrassing stereotype.

But in his current state, he was nothing short of terrifying.

His eyes were absolutely wild, rolling about in his head like nothing kept them in place. And Missy was almost certain he was…changing…before her very eyes. He seemed to take up more and more space in the hall as he progressed. And the smell, the *reek* of corruption…

Missy covered her mouth with both hands, tears pouring down over her fingers. Sondra, back also to the wall, still kept an arm stretched over Missy's belly. Both women's eyes were *wide* open, fixed on the perversion of this friend, this lover, as it did its macabre dance.

When it reached the end of the hall and could go no further, it stopped, shook and more of Justin disappeared with each passing second.

Missy looked away, almost unable to take anymore, when something screeched on the stairs. The light from the downstairs hall was swallowed by a *second* glutinous mass, this one taking up every inch of space in the stairwell. Smoke and slickened tendrils crept up over the landing.

"Cooter," Justin garbled, his human voice almost non-existent.

Missy grabbed Sondra's hand, held it tight, when something tickled her foot.

For an agonizing moment, she thought for sure one of the blob's slimy appendages had wrapped itself around her ankle and was about to suck her into itself. But when she looked down…

Bugs. Everywhere.

She'd forgotten all about them.

Missy breathed hard and watched as they poured through every doorway, grazed her and Sondra's feet, clearly in a hurry to get where they were going…and they appeared to be going for her fiancé and his former co-worker.

Missy watched in horror as hundreds, *thousands* of insects swarmed out of the rooms and into her living nightmare. She couldn't believe this many of the animals existed *anywhere* on earth, let alone in her home, as she watched them envelop both Justin and Cooter in seconds.

She could hear them cry out beneath − the creatures, *blobs*; she could hear them snarl in what she assumed was protest − but just barely. The swishing and scraping of the throng of pests - the ones she had cursed not thirty minutes ago now seemed to be saving her, her friend, and her infant's lives − was too great to ignore.

But she had to try.

Missy covered her ears, curled in on herself, and stayed that way − *Minutes? Hours?* − until she felt a hand brush through her hair. "It's done, sweetie."

Missy sniffed some of the snot she knew ran from her nose and looked up at Sondra.

"It's done."

Her first thought was often her only thought.

Justin.

She twisted around Sondra and found what she had expected: nothing but tattered garments.

Missy's mind diverted around this sad, miserable truth and steered her elsewhere, forced her to say something that would have been funny under difference circumstances.

Anaesthetized, staring at the back wall, she said, "He had a headdress."

"Neal was wearing it." Her friend sounded just as numb. "We were taking it back to the gallery."

"Hmmm."

Missy crawled across the hall and sat against the wall, facing Sondra.

They appeared to be the only life-forms left.

"See?" Sondra said, wiping a tear from her cheek. "What'd I say? You have these bugs...but no pests."

Missy leaned over and upchucked.

WWW.CROWDEDQUARANTINE.CO.UK